"I love him," she whispered aloud in the darkness of the night. "He is the best looking man I have ever seen, yet I believe I would still love him if he were maimed and ugly. I love him because I cannot help it; whether he wants me or not, I belong to him."

The Marquis had been in her dreams and her imagination ever since she could remember, but then he had been an idolized god. Now it was the man she loved, even when he was bitter or cynical, enraged or sarcastic. She loved him so overwhelmingly that she felt her whole body throb with the agony of it.

And she had nothing to offer him—save a heart which did not interest him!

Pyramid Books

by

BARBARA CARTLAND

A HALO
FOR THE DEVIL

Barbara Cartland

PYRAMID BOOKS ▲ NEW YORK

A HALO FOR THE DEVIL

A PYRAMID BOOK

Pyramid edition published September 1973
Fifth printing, October 1976

Printed in the United States of America

PYRAMID PUBLICATIONS
(Harcourt Brace Jovanovich, Inc.)
757 Third Avenue, New York. N.Y. 10017

1

A Gentleman put his head round the door of the room where the members of White's Club were sitting over their port.

"The Devils are at it again," he announced.

There was a burst of laughter, a buzz of chatter from the Bucks and Dandies reclining in the leather armchairs, and the majority of them rose to their feet.

"What has occurred?" a hard-riding Squire from Northumberland enquired of his host, Lord Hornblotton.

His Lordship, an elderly man with a twinkle in his eye, replied:

"Have you never heard of the Old and the Young Devil? They are the *'on dit'* of London at the present moment. Perhaps the gossip about them has not yet reached the north."

"No indeed," the Squire declared. "Tell me about them."

"It is quite an intriguing tale," Lord Hornblotton replied, pouring himself another glass of port. "The Old Devil is His Grace of Accrington, a nobleman for whom I must admit I have never had a partiality."

"Is he really wicked?" the Squire asked with a note of amusement in his voice.

"If I answer you truthfully," Lord Hornblotton replied, "and in one syllable, the answer is—yes! Accrington is a strange man, whom I have known for a great number of years. I have never known him do a kind deed, but I have known him do very many actions, none of which in my opinion were becoming to a man of noble blood."

"Well, what does he do?" the Squire asked in the tone of voice of one who fancies that the ill behaviour of the person criticised is being exaggerated.

"The story I am going to relate to you," Lord Hornblotton said, "concerns the Marquis of Thane—not the Young Devil with whom the Duke is at the present moment engaged at cards, but his father, a personage beloved by all who knew him, and with a charm which men, women and even children found irresistible."

"I see the good and the bad are clearly defined," the Squire said with a mocking smile.

"In this case, yes," Lord Hornblotton agreed. "The Duke of Accrington, who inherited when he was quite a young man, became engaged to an exceedingly lovely Lady. She was indeed one of the most beautiful females ever to be described as an 'Incomparable'—for once the expression was apt."

"I would like to have seen her," the Squire said. "I find the much vaunted wenches of today sadly unenticing."

Lord Hornblotton's response was a deep throaty chuckle which seemed to shake his vast frame.

"That is because you are getting old, my friend," he said. "When you are young every female is a fascinating enigma. As you get old, if you find them less attractive you blame them rather than yourself."

The Squire threw back his head and laughed.

6

"Perhaps you are right," he said. "Anyhow, continue."

"Just before the wedding date was announced," Lord Hornblotton went on, "this lovely creature, who had the hearts of almost the whole of the *Beau Ton* at her feet, ran away with the Marquis of Thane."

"That must have been somewhat irritating for the Duke," the Squire said drily.

"He was enraged," Lord Hornblotton said, "but at the same time few people blamed her. The Duke had an unsavoury reputation even in his youth, and, in fact, it was well-known that the Incomparable had been more or less coerced into marriage with him by her parents, who, quite naturally, wanted a brilliant match for their daughter."

"And the Marquis was not such a good catch?" the Squire suggested.

"On the contrary, save that his title was of lower rank in the hierarchy of nobility, he was of equal import and as rich, if not richer than the Duke. He was also, as I have already said, a most charming person. I imagine any woman would have found it hard to refuse his suit, if he loved her, as he undoubtedly loved the Lady Harriet."

"So they lived happily ever after," the Squire said sarcastically.

"They were, in fact, blissfully happy," Lord Hornblotton agreed. "And only two years after he had been jilted the Duke married an Irish beauty, a Miss O'Keary. I think it was she who persuaded the two men to make up their differences, because having attended a Young Ladies' Seminary with the new Marchioness of Thane, she felt it ridiculous that at every party to which she went the Duke should go out of his way either to ignore or to insult the Marquis."

7

"And then what happened?" the Squire prompted.

Lord Hornblotton sipped his port.

"I suppose that those of us who knew both of them well," Lord Hornblotton said, "must have been blind to the hate and resentment which still lingered in the Duke's heart. Outwardly the two men appeared friends, save that the Marquis of Thane seldom came to London, being content to occupy himself hunting and shooting on his vast Estates in the country, and being highly delighted when his wife presented him with a son and heir."

"And the Duke?" the Squire asked, feeling that here was perhaps the point of the story.

"The Duke and his Irish Duchess produced seven daughters in succession," Lord Hornblotton said. "Then, when it appeared almost too late to hope, the much longed for son arrived."

"So they both had their heirs," the Squire said. "Now what could go wrong?"

"The Marquis had several falls when hunting," Lord Hornblotton said, "and one in particular was almost fatal. It was obvious to those who loved him that he had not long to live, and there was, I assure you, a feeling of deep distress among his friends like myself, because we knew we were watching the passing of a great man."

After a momentary pause Lord Hornblotton said slowly:

"It was then the Duke struck!"

"What did he do?" the Squire demanded.

"His hatred for the Marquis must have always festered in his heart," Lord Hornblotton said. "Anyway, when he realised his old enemy was dying, he went to see him at Thane Castle and asked a favour."

He paused then continued:

8

"I should have told you that their Estates marched with each other. It appeared that the Duke was anxious to build a school for a small isolated village which lay just inside his boundary, and the most convenient piece of land adjoining it actually belonged to the Marquis."

Lord Hornblotton made a gesture with his hands.

"It seemed a very trifling matter," he said. "The Marquis agreed immediately, and the Duke produced a legal document together with his Attorney, who had waited in the Hall until he heard that the Duke's request had been granted."

"I have a suspicion that there is an unpleasant ending to this story," the Squire remarked.

"There is indeed," Lord Hornblotton agreed. "The Marquis's sight was bad. The Duke placed the document in front of him and asked His Lordship to sign his name. When the Marquis hesitated, the Duke said:

" 'Let me read you what is written, my dear fellow, for I can see you have a most sensible reluctance to sign any paper unless you know what it contains.'

" 'I apologise for being a nuisance,' the Marquis replied. 'Alas, my eyes are failing. Let me ask for my wife. She reads to me every day.'

" 'I would not wish to trouble Her Ladyship,' the Duke replied. 'Let me read out to you what is written on this unimportant bit of paper.' "

"He read the document aloud and then set it down once again in front of the Marquis.

" 'You read well, my friend,' the Marquis remarked. 'I wish I had your eyesight and indeed your strength.' "

"The Duke did not answer, but watched the

signature being afixed to the document. Then he said:

" 'Would you also sign a duplicate which must be sent to the School Commissioners in London? It is always wise to keep one copy for ourselves—you know full well how careless the authorities can be.'

" 'I do indeed,' the Marquis smiled, and signed his name again."

The Squire drew a deep breath, for already he could see where the story was leading.

"No one, of course, realised what had happened," Lord Hornblotton went on, "until the Marquis died three months later. It was then discovered that the second paper was a will cancelling his former behests and leaving the whole of his vast Estates, with the exception of Thane Castle, to the Duke of Accrington."

"My God, what a diabolical plot!" the Squire exclaimed.

"It was indeed," Lord Hornblotton said. "It was, in fact, a revenge thought out and planned since the Marquis stole his bride."

"What happened?" the Squire asked.

"The new Marquis, a delightful young man, found himself ruined. He still possessed the Castle, it was true, and the few acres surrounding it, but the whole of his father's Great wealth, derived from the rents of the London Estate and from the rich farmlands in the country, were no longer his.

He took legal advice, but as the Duke had taken the precaution of having his own Attorney present when the late Marquis signed, he was told that nothing could be gained by taking the matter to the Courts."

"Wretched youth, it seems an intolerable position!" the Squire ejaculated.

"It was indeed," Lord Hornblotton said, "so in-tolerable that I saw a decent, clean-living, upright young man changed overnight into one who is rightly named the Young Devil."

"Why? What did he do?" the Squire enquired curiously.

"Hate is a very strange emotion," Lord Hornblotton said. "It was hatred which made the Duke plan his revenge upon his friend and nurture the venom in his breast for thirty years . . ."

"And none of you had any idea of it?" the Squire interrupted. "That is what seems so extraordinary!"

"As I have already said, we had no liking for Accrington," Lord Hornblotton replied. "Perhaps if we had known him more intimately, perhaps if he had made a confidant of even one of us, we might have guessed what was afoot. As it was, he kept his own counsel. But with the young Marquis it was different."

"How?" the Squire enquired.

"He made it quite clear from the very beginning that it would be his life's work to revenge the treachery practised upon his father and to win back the lands that were rightfully his."

"And how could he do that?" the Squire asked.

"I forgot to mention that the old Duke is a game-ster," Lord Hornblotton said with a smile, "a very experienced, extremely shrewd, fantastically lucky one."

"If that is how the young Marquis meant to recover his lands, it does not seem that he had much hope," the Squire remarked.

"That was what we all thought when we first learnt what young Thane was planning," Lord Hornblotton said. "But for nearly a year after his father's funeral he disappeared. I made enquiries and

11

learnt that he was spending his time in the company of card-sharpers, cut-throats, charlatans and twisters of all types, in fact, the very dregs of humanity which feed on the lowest and most depraved night-life of London."

He sighed.

"At first I thought Thane was drowning his sorrows in an orgy of dissipation. Then on making further enquiries I conjectured that he had a very valid reason for associating with such riff-raff."

"He was learning the trade, I suppose," the Squire said shrewdly.

"Exactly," Lord Hornblotton agreed. "Not that Thane would stoop to cheating, but I suppose that with the exception of the Duke, there is no man in the whole kingdom today who knows more about cards. The Marquis lived with cards, thought of cards, dreamt of cards, played cards until they meant as much to him as food and drink."

"I can see the point of such an education," the Squire ruminated.

"So can I," Lord Hornblotton agreed. "When he came back amongst his fellows he seemed a changed man."

"In what way?" the Squire asked.

"He seemed immeasurably older, cynical, aloof, reserved. He offered no one kindliness or friendship, and he appeared to have no interest in anything or anybody except for one person."

"The Duke!" the Squire ejaculated.

"Exactly," Lord Hornblotton replied.

He bent forward to fill up his friend's glass.

"I think I omitted to tell you one thing," he said. "When the old Marquis died his son was betrothed. It seemed an eminently suitable match. She had been the belle of several seasons and was the most sought after young woman in society. He had been without doubt one of the greatest matrimonial catches in the land, besides being courageous, handsome and well liked by all who knew him."

"I can guess what happened," the Squire said.

"It was, I suppose, not surprising, human nature being what it is," Lord Hornblotton replied. "At the same time, I would have thought better of her had she stood by him."

"She jilted him?" the Squire enquired.

"Yes, as soon as she learnt that he had nothing to offer her save himself and a Castle without the means for its upkeep."

"Women have a lot to answer for," the Squire sighed.

"In this case you never spoke a truer word," Lord Hornblotton said. "I think it was perhaps this more than anything else which soured young Thane and sent him into a blue-devilled mood from which he appears never to have recovered.

"Sometimes when I talk to him I wonder if he is indeed the same laughing child that I dandled on my knees, the enthusiastic boy with whom I used to go shooting over the fields at Thane, or the young man spoken of by his Commanding officers in the Army as being a natural leader of men, the type of officer who is valued in every regiment."

"I must really see these two people for myself," the Squire said. "You tell me they are known as the Devils."

"The Old and the Young Devil," Lord Hornblotton replied.

"And the Marquis is still impoverished?" the Squire enquired.

"No indeed," Lord Hornblotton replied, "he is now extremely warm in the pocket. His education in cards stood him in good stead. He won several fortunes from unfledged nitwits who came to London wanting to cut a dash, and returned to their country estates wiser but considerably poorer for the experience. He could, if he wished, now retire to Thane and live there in comfort, but he is driven by this demon within him to revenge himself upon the Duke. He has no other interest in life."

"What about women?" the Squire asked.

Lord Hornblotton shrugged his shoulders.

"Women!" he exclaimed. "Have you ever known a Rake who is not surrounded by pretty and optimistic creatures, confident that the love of a good woman will reform him? And perhaps 'good' is not the most appropriate word!"

He smiled with no humour in his smile.

"Sylvanus is a young man and, as far as the opposite sex is concerned, obviously irresistibly attractive. There are innumerable husbands who swear the day will come when they will blow a piece of lead through him as he saunters down their stairway, having availed himself of their wife's favour. Nevertheless, Thane survives, and merely adds year by year, or rather month by month, to his reputation for devilry."

"And apparently he still plays cards with the Duke?" the Squire smiled.

"The Duke is not in London as often as he used to be," Lord Hornblotton replied. "But at least once a week he comes here to White's or the other places he frequents. Thane, who has his spies, is immediately informed of His Grace's arrival. No sooner does the Duke sit down at the card-table than the Marquis is opposite him."

"And who wins?" the Squire enquired.

"They do not play for money," Lord Hornblotton

14

said, "they play for land. At one time the Marquis had won quite a number of residential estates, comprising whole squares and streets in Mayfair, Belgravia and Chelsea. But now I understand the Duke is gradually winning them back again one by one."

"It is the most intriguing story I have ever heard," the Squire said. "Come, take me upstairs, let me see the Devils for myself. When I tell my friends in the north this tale it is doubtful that they will believe me."

"I assure you that what I have related to you is true in every particular," Lord Hornblotton declared.

He raised his large bulk from his chair somewhat reluctantly as though he found it an effort to walk upstairs to the card room.

Nevertheless he led the way, and crossing the landing at the top of the curved staircase they entered the card room to find the two Devils seated at a card-table facing each other, while round them stood a large silent audience, watching with fascinated eyes every movement they made.

Lord Hornblotton stopped in the doorway because it was impossible to go in further, while his friend squeezed in beside him and stood on tiptoe to watch the two men who played their cards apparently unconscious of everything else.

The old Duke was thin and tallow-faced, with deep dark lines running from nose to mouth. There was something almost repulsive about his sneering, thin-lipped mouth and the supercilious disdain of his high arched nose.

He had almost a cadaverous look, and his wrinkled skin and blue-veined hands acclaimed his age. His eyes, however, were still bright and shrewd, and they watched with the irrepressible glitter of a compulsive gamester every turn of the card.

15

The Marquis facing him was in actual years not more than twenty-eight, but he looked immeasurably older. He lounged back in his chair with a languid indifference which in itself was somehow insulting. He would have been outstandingly handsome, had it not been for an expression of contemptuous cynicism and the marks of dissipation on his face.

It was difficult to believe that he could smile, or indeed that he could find anything in life of interest. Only those who knew him well would have guessed that beneath his half-closed eyelids he was alert to every move his opponent might make.

They played in silence until finally as the Marquis turned up an ace, a sigh seemed to come simultaneously from the lips of those watching. The old Duke made no sign to show that he had lost, but merely sat still until a waiter, as if at some pre-arranged signal, brought him a glass of wine.

He sipped it as another servant carried a pile of documents to the Marquis, from which he selected one.

He placed it on the table, and instantly a flunkey brought an ink-pot with a long quill pen. The Marquis pushed the document towards the Duke, who scrawled his signature on it and flung the pen on the table, a blob of ink being left as he did so on the green baize cloth.

The Marquis picked up the document, still without speaking, and walked from the room. The gentlemen who had been watching parted silently to let him pass through their ranks towards the door.

"Good evening, Sylvanus," Lord Hornblotton said as the Marquis reached his side.

"Good evening, My Lord."

The Young Devil's voice was low and deep; it was also cold and distant, without any warmth or

16

friendliness in it. Then before Lord Hornblotton could speak again the Marquis had disappeared down the stairs.

"What has happened? Why has he left?" the Squire asked in a low voice.

"I should have told you," Lord Hornblotton answered, "that the Marquis plays for exactly two hours and no longer. Whether he is winning or losing, he leaves when the hand is finished. They may meet again this evening, they will certainly meet tomorrow as the Duke is in London. One session lasts two hours and then Thane rises from the table."

"And the Marquis won?" the Squire asked.

"He has won this time," Lord Hornblotton replied.

The Marquis had gone down the stairs and was being helped into his riding-coat in the Hall when through the door from St. James's Street came a tall, broad-shouldered man wearing the uniform of the Queen's Dragoon Guards. When he saw the Marquis his good-humoured face lightened.

"Any luck, Sylvanus?" he enquired.

"I won back Chelsea—for the third time," the Marquis replied, "and I also won Lambeth, which I have not gained previously."

"That is a triumph," the newcomer exclaimed. "The Old Devil has had the luck of his namesake lately. I wish I could have reached here earlier, it gives me intense pleasure to see my uncle lose. It is the one thing which can make him suffer like a human being, even if he seems impassive."

"We will talk about it later on," the Marquis said in a bored voice. "I am going home to change. You will be in the Club this evening?"

"I cannot afford to go anywhere else," Colonel Merrill replied.

"We will drink to the damnation of His Grace,"

17

the Marquis promised, but his voice was utterly indifferent.

He turned towards the door.

"There is a note for you, Your Lordship," one of the Club servants said, holding out a silver salver.

The Marquis glanced down at the envelope inscribed quite obviously in a feminine hand and smelling faintly of an exotic scent. With a gesture of his hand he waved it away.

"I will collect it later."

Colonel Merrill laughed.

"Doing it a bit brown, Sylvanus?" he asked. "What palpitating heart is awaiting an answer?"

The Marquis did not answer, but merely passed through the outer door to descend the steps outside. He stood for a moment waiting while his High Perch Phaeton was brought to him.

Drawn by two superbly matched chestnuts, the Phaeton in black and yellow was recognised in the streets of London as easily as one of the Royal carriages.

Although the Phaeton was standing outside White's Club for only a few seconds, a small crowd of passers-by stopped to watch the Marquis pick up the reins and turn his horses' heads towards Piccadilly.

There was no doubt that he made a dashing picture with his tall hat set at a rakish angle, his many-tiered riding-coat, his whip lash caught in the fingers of his right hand. The horses, as if they knew they were tooled by a Corinthian, arched their necks and tossed their long manes as if proud to be driven by him.

" 'e be a regular top-notcher!" one of the onlookers exclaimed as the Phaeton started to move.

The groom sprang up beside the Marquis, who

cracked his whip, and the horses swung off at a speed which left those who watched fascinated by their progress.

"There is nobody else as can drive like that," an old Gentleman who was walking down St. James's Street remarked. "Most of the young bloods today couldn't tool a pair of mules with elegance, let alone fine horse-flesh like those. What do you think, my dear?"

"I was thinking that he looked magnificent!" the Lady he addressed replied with a sigh.

There were a lot of women who watched the Marquis as he drove down Berkeley Street. There was something about him which captured the imagination, and perhaps when he was driving or riding the customary look of cynicism and boredom in his face was not so obvious as at other times.

There was little traffic about. The shops were closing and most of the *Beau Ton* were changing their fashionable day garments for even more fashionable ones in which to attend the dinners, Masques, Routs, or Assemblies where they intended to pass the evening.

The Marquis's horses were moving at a fine speed as they turned from Berkeley Street into Berkeley Square. Then as they rounded the corner by Charles Street, suddenly without any warning a woman ran from the pavement into the roadway.

It all seemed to happen in the flash of a second. The horses were almost upon her before she realised her danger. She turned, but as she did so her feet slipped on the road, which was muddy from a recent fall of rain, and she fell.

It was only by a superb, almost incredible piece of driving that the Marquis managed to prevent the

19

wheels of the Phaeton passing over her. He pulled in his horses sharply and flung the reins to his groom.

By the time he reached the woman who had fallen, he found she was being helped to her feet by a gentleman.

The Marquis recognised Sir Roger Crowley, a social hanger-on for whom he had a personal dislike. He looked down at the woman and saw she was little more than a girl. She was obviously not hurt, but appeared for the moment slightly dazed.

She was unfashionably dressed with a woollen shawl over her plain muslin gown, which was now bespattered with mud from the road. Her cheap straw bonnet, gaily trimmed with blue ribbons, was disarranged, and she pulled it into place with tiny mittened hands which were trembling a little with the shock of her fall.

"Are you hurt, Madam?" the Marquis enquired.

"She is only shaken," Sir Roger answered for her. "Do not perturb yourself, My Lord, I will attend this young lady."

"Thank you, but there is no need for . . . anyone to trouble about . . . me," the girl said in a low, curiously sweet voice.

"A glass of wine will do you good," Sir Roger said. "Take my arm."

The Marquis turned away, but he heard the girl say in a frightened voice:

"Please . . . please leave me alone. It was indeed your fault, Sir, that I was so . . . foolish as to run into . . . the roadway."

"We will talk about it somewhere more comfortable," Sir Roger said reassuringly.

He put his hand on the girl's arm, but she wrenched herself free.

"I will not go with you!" she said defiantly. "All I wish is to find Thane House."

The Marquis glanced at her.

"Did I hear you say Thane House?" he drawled.

"Yes, if you please," she answered eagerly. "Will you tell me the way? That is what I asked of this Gentleman, but I do not think he understood."

"Perhaps he did not wish to understand," the Marquis said, and his tone was insulting.

"Allow me to know what is best for this young woman," Sir Roger said angrily.

He was nearly middle-aged and red-faced. His vast wealth came from his mills in Yorkshire, which he never visited.

"The Lady has expressed herself quite clearly," the Marquis replied. "She wishes to be shown the way to Thane House. I am, I suggest, the obvious person to direct her there."

The eyes of the two men met. Then in a fury which seemed somehow out of proportion to the incident, Sir Roger said angrily:

"This is the second time you have interferred in my affairs, My Lord. Let me say I consider you aptly named."

The Marquis bowed ironically, then offered his arm to the girl who was standing between them looking bewildered.

"If you will permit me, Madam," he said, "I will escort you to Thane House. It is but a few doors from here on this side of the Square."

"Thank you . . . thank you very much," the girl said in a breathless voice, "but indeed there is no need for you to accompany me, I can find . . . my own way."

She ignored his arm and started walking switfly down the pavement. The Marquis, without a backward glance at the discomfited Sir Roger, moved beside her. She was so small that, while she appeared to be hurrying, he, on the other hand, appeared to be moving slowly.

"All . . . I want is to find . . . Thane House," she said nervously, as if his presence was somehow overwhelming.

"You desire to call on someone within? the Marquis asked.

"Yes indeed . . . I seek the Marquis of Thane," she replied.

The Marquis raised his eyebrows. By this time they had reached the door of his house, and the Phaeton having arrived before him, the red carpet had been rolled across the pavement, the door was open, and there was the usual array of powdered flunkeys in their claret and gold livery awaiting his return.

The girl hesitated for a moment, then with a courageous little lift of her chin she went forward.

"Will you inform the Marquis of Thane that I have a message for His Lordship," she said to the footman standing in the doorway.

The man looked surprised seeing his master was standing behind her. But before he could speak the Marquis said:

"I am the Marquis of Thane."

The girl turned round to look at him. He saw for the first time that she had a small heart-shaped face and very large eyes. Then she exclaimed:

"You are the Marquis! I might have guessed that you would run me over!"

The Marquis stared at her. For a moment his impassive expression of boredom seemed to crack. Then he said:

"Will you not enter? I am sure that what you may

22

have to import to me would be best said more privately."

"Yes . . . yes . . . of course," she agreed, as if suddenly conscious of the grandeur of the house, the listening servants, her mud-spattered gown.

The Marquis permitted a flunkey to take his hat and coat. Then he led the way down the marble Hall to the Library at the far end which extended the whole length of the house. Its windows opened onto a courtyard in which a stone fountain was throwing its water, iridescent in the evening sunshine, into an ornamental pool containing goldfish.

"Bring refreshments," he said to the butler.

"Very good, M'Lord."

The door closed behind them and the girl faced the Marquis, her eyes wide and excited.

"Oh, I am so glad to find you, My Lord!" she cried. "I was so afraid you would not be here. And when I asked that Gentleman the way, he said the strangest and most extraordinary things to me. I think he must be crazed! Still, I should not have run away from him. It was cowardly, and Gilly would have been ashamed of me.'"

"Gilly?" the Marquis questioned, a frown between his eyes.

"Miss Gillingham," the girl answered. "You remember her? She sent me to you."

"Miss Gillingham—Gilly! Of course I recall her," the Marquis exclaimed. "But I have not heard from her for years."

"She did not wish to trouble you," the girl answered. "She thought that in your gay social life you would find it tiresome to receive letters from your old governess. But she loved you—she loved you deeply up to the very moment she died."

The girl's voice broke on the words.

"And when did that happen?" the Marquis enquired.

"Last week."

There was something suspiciously like tears in the eyes looking up at him, and hastily the Marquis remembered his manners.

"Will you not be seated?" he asked. "I am afraid I have been remiss where Miss Gillingham is concerned. I should have enquired as to her whereabouts a long time ago."

"She was quite happy and not impoverished in any way," the girl answered.

She seated herself on the edge of a huge brocade armchair at the side of the hearth, while the Marquis availed himself of one opposite.

He lay back, his eyelids drooping, but he was watching her. He thought how small she looked, how unfashionable, and yet at the same time unusual—but he was not quite sure how. There was something about the little face under the plain bonnet, the large eyes and the tiny pointed chin which stirred some vague memory within him, but he could not think what it was.

"Your father gave Gilly the house in which she lived, and she also had an annuity. I think your father gave her that too. Anyway, we never wanted for any necessity."

"We?" the Marquis asked.

"I lived with her," the girl answered, "in fact she brought me up. That is why I have come to see you."

"Perhaps you had best start at the beginning," the Marquis suggested.

"Would Your Lordship permit me to take off my bonnet?" the girl asked. "It is uncomfortable . . . since I fell down."

"Of course!" the Marquis answered. "Would you like to retire? I will send for my housekeeper."

"No, thank you," she answered, "it is just that I hate bonnets. I am afraid I am not at all fashionable, and I do not wear them in the country."

She pulled the bonnet from her head as she spoke, and the Marquis looked at her with an undisguised astonishment.

Her hair was extraordinary. It was almost white, and yet there were faint strands of gold in it which made it not the white of old age but the very, very pale colour of the dawn when the first fingers of the sun rise over the horizon.

It was not only her hair which was so unusual, it was her eyes also, now that he could see them clearly. Somehow he had expected them to be blue, but instead they were grey—grey within their depths a touch of green—and set in naturally dark eyelashes against a skin as transparently clear as water rippling in a gravel stream, where every stone glistens clear beneath its flow.

"She is lovely," the Marquis thought in astonishment, "and quite unlike anyone I have ever seen before."

He stopped. That was not true, she was like someone. Again there was a faint stirring in his memory. Who was it? Who could it be?

She put her bonnet and shawl on a stool not far from the chair in which she was sitting. Then she smiled at him as she said:

"That is better, now we can talk. I am so glad that it was you who rescued me."

"What is your name?" the Marquis asked.

"Fortuna," she replied, "Fortuna Grimwood."

"Grimwood?" the Marquis repeated.

She wrinkled her straight little nose.

25

"It is not a very attractive name, is it?"

"And why Fortuna?" he enquired.

Two dimples appeared in her cheeks.

"That is what people always ask," she answered. "But when I arrived at Gilly's house she was translating the Second Olynthiac of Demosthenes. You remember how she loved Greek! When the knock came on the door she had just written 'Fortune has granted our wishes', and she made a mark at the place. Afterwards it seemed obvious that I must be called Fortuna."

"I still think you should start at the beginning," the Marquis said.

"No, what I ought to do," Fortuna contradicted, "is give Your Lordship Gilly's letter. I have it here with me."

There was a reticule hanging from her small waist, which she opened and drew out a letter. The envelope was rather creased because of the manner in which it had travelled, but nevertheless when the Marquis opened it he found it contained a letter of some six or seven closely written sheets.

"Do you know what is in this letter?" he asked.

"I wrote it," Fortuna replied.

"You wrote it?" he enquired.

"Gilly could not write for the last six months of her illness," Fortuna explained. "She could not use her hand. The Doctor said it was a stroke. So she told me what I was to say and I wrote it down. It took rather a long time because she became so tired. When it was finished she said:

" 'As soon as I am buried you are to go at once to London to the Marquis of Thane. Take him this letter, His Lordship will know what to do.' So here I am."

The Marquis looked down at the closely written sheets he held in his hand.

"Perhaps it would be easier," he said slowly, "if you told me what is in this letter, and later I can read it when there is more time."

"There is something else," Fortuna said, "something I have not seen, which Gilly addressed to you several years ago, and which she kept in a locked drawer. It is here."

She took from her reticule another envelope, small and yellowing with age, and so thin that it obviously contained little reading material. She passed it to the Marquis, who put it unopened on the table at his side.

"Now," he said, "tell me in your own words what Gilly wished to impart to me."

"I will, as Your Lordship suggests, begin at the beginning," Fortuna said in her soft voice.

She clasped her hands together, and sitting on the edge of the chair she looked like a small child reciting a lesson.

"It was one evening on the 30th August, 1801 . . ." she began.

"How old are you?" the Marquis interrupted.

"I shall be eighteen in four months time—on the 27th August," she answered.

"Very well," he said, "go on."

"Gilly was, as I have told you, at her desk when there came a knock at the door. She went to open it and a woman stood there holding a baby in her arms. She recognised her as a Mrs. Grimwood from a farm which was about two miles away from Little Waterless where we lived.

" 'Good evening, Mrs. Grimwood,' she said, 'what can I do for you?'

" ' 'Tis the baby, Miss,' Mrs. Grimwood replied. 'We be aleaving tonight and I canna take it with me, it's not agoing to live. And anyway, I dinna want it.'

27

" 'You do not want it!' Gilly exclaimed. 'Why? Surely it has only just been born.'

" 'Three days ago,' the woman said dully.

" 'Then you should not have walked all this way,' Gilly said sternly, 'it is not good for your health. Go back to bed.'

" 'We be aleaving, I tells you,' Mrs. Grimwood said, 'the baby won't survive the sea nor the cold. 'Tis sickly and 'twill doubtless be dead in the morning.'

"She thrust the baby into Gilly's arms and then ran—literally ran away. Gilly looked after her in surprise. She could hardly run after the woman, and she thought that she must be deranged with childbrith.

"The only thing to do was to keep the baby for the night, then drive to the farm in the morning and take the baby back to her.

"When she undid the shawl in which I was wrapped she was astonished to see how small and frail I was, not the sort of child she would have expected the Grimwoods to produce, and in a way she could understand why the mother felt apprehensive."

Fortuna paused and then went on slowly as if she were choosing her words:

"All the other Grimwood children—and Gilly knew them well because they came to school in the village— were strong, sturdy and dark. But I was tiny, and though I was new-born my skin was very white and the few hairs I had on my head were also white. In fact, Gilly always said that she thought at first I was an albino."

The Marquis gave a sudden start.

"An albino?" he murmured almost beneath his breath.

"That is what Gilly told me," Fortuna said. "Luckily, as you can see, I do not possess pink eyes. But I have always been teased about my hair."

28

"Continue," the Marquis commanded her.

He gave little sign of it, but he was in fact deeply interested in what she was saying.

"The next day Gilly asked the Doctor to drive her out to the Grimwood's farm. She carried me in her arms, but when they arrived the Grimwoods had gone. The woman had spoken truthfully when she said they were leaving that night. There was no one there, the farm was empty."

"Where had they gone?" the Marquis enquired.

"Nobody seemed to know. And when Gilly spoke to the Duke's Agent . . ."

"The Duke!" The Marquis's voice was unnaturally loud. "What Duke?"

"The Duke of Accrington," Fortuna replied. "The Grimwood's farm was on his land, although in those days Little Waterless belonged to Your Lordship's father. Later after the . . . trouble . . . His Grace owned the village also."

Fortuna paused, then she said quietly:

"When Gilly heard what had . . . occurred, she was very upset. I have never known her so angry."

The Marquis did not speak and Fortuna added with some hesitation:

"It was . . . then . . . she told me about the . . . envelope in the . . . locked drawer."

The Marquis looked down at the thin letter lying beside him, but he made no attempt to open it. It seemed to Fortuna that the expression in his eyes was ominous. Hastily, as if she feared she had said something wrong, she continued:

"The Duke's house, Merrill Park, was five miles away, but the Agent to the Estate lived in the next village. Gilly went to see him, but he knew nothing about the Grimwoods. He just said he thought they must have been offered a better farm somewhere else.

29

"Anyway, Gilly kept me and brought me up, and taught me my lessons as she used to teach you yours. I was very, very happy with her until she . . . died."

Again there was the hint of tears in the sweet voice, and the Marquis turned his head with relief as the door opened and the butler and two footmen entered with trays piled with food.

"I thought perhaps the young lady would fancy chocolate, M'lord," the butler said tentatively.

"Thank you very much," Fortuna said. "I would indeed prefer it to anything else."

A table was set down beside her and she looked a little bewildered at the number of dishes there were for her to choose from. The butler poured out the chocolate, put a decanter of wine and a glass on a table next to the Marquis and left the room.

Fortuna looked across at her host to find that he was staring at her with a strange expression on his face.

"How old did you say you were?" he asked.

"I am seventeen, nine months and three days," she smiled.

"And you were born in 1801 on the 27th August," the Marquis said.

Fortuna's eyes were apprehensive.

"Does it matter very much?" she said. "I thought when I was journeying here in the mail-coach that perhaps you would find me some . . . employment; but I hope I am not too young."

"For what employment have you any capability?" the Marquis asked.

She made a little gesture with her hands.

"I am well educated," she said, "I had exactly the same tuition as Your Lordship had. I thought perhaps I could be a governess—but there is one thing which may make it rather difficult if I am to teach—girls."

"What is that?" the Marquis asked.

"You see, Gilly has always been a governess to boys, and so she gave me a boy's education. I am proficient in Greek and Latin, mathematics, even geometry. I can speak French and Italian. But I cannot play the piano, I cannot paint, and I am not very good at embroidery. Do you think that will matter?"

"Matter?" the Marquis asked absent-mindedly as though he were thinking of something else.

"I am afraid that girls would require lessons in many things of which I have no knowledge," Fortuna explained.

The Marquis rose to his feet.

"Albino!" he said under his breath as though he were speaking to himself.

Fortuna looked at him with a worried expression on her face.

"Have you . . . a dislike . . . of my hair?" she asked shyly.

"A dislike? No, of course not," the Marquis replied indifferently.

"Oh, I am glad!" Fortuna exclaimed. "For I do want you to like me. I have thought of you so much, I have imagined what you would be like. And then when you came driving round the corner, when you nearly ran over me, it was just what I might have expected."

"And what do you mean by that?" the Marquis enquired sharply.

It was seldom that his proficiency with the reins was questioned. Fortuna looked up at him with a light in her eyes.

"You see," she said softly, "Gilly had talked of you

31

so much and described you so often that I always thought of you as Apollo—the Sun God driving across the sky in his chariot. In fact, to myself I have always called you Apollo. It may seem very impertinent of me, but that is how I have thought of Your Lordship."

She smiled.

"Then when you do appear it is in a chariot—well, an up-to-date version of one—and it does seem that all I imagined was right and that you are the Apollo I have dreamt about ever since I was a tiny girl."

Her voice died away and the Marquis did not seem to be listening. Suddenly he gave an exclamation.

"My God, I have it!" he said. "I know whom you resemble!"

He walked to the fireplace and tugged at the bell-pull. The door opened almost immediately.

"Send a carriage to White's Club," he said, "and ask Colonel Alistair Merrill to oblige me by returning in it as swiftly as possible."

"Very good, M'Lord."

The door shut behind the butler.

"I know now of whom you remind me," the Marquis repeated unnecessarily.

"Who is it?" Fortuna asked in a very small voice.

He did not seem to hear her. He was staring at her hair and it seemed as if for the first time since she had come into the room he was no longer bored or indifferent—rather there was a strange excitement about him.

2

"Colonel Alistair Merrill, M'Lord," the butler announced in the doorway.

The tall figure in military uniform entered the Library hurriedly, but the Marquis held up his hand.

"Wait," he said—it was a command.

As the Colonel, somewhat nonplussed, stood just inside the door, the Marquis turned to Fortuna.

"Would you oblige me by walking in the courtyard for a little while?" he asked. "I have someone to see on business of considerable import."

Fortuna, who had been sitting on a stool in front of the fireplace, rose quickly to her feet. She smiled at the Marquis, dropped him a little curtsy and then, with an almost imperceptible glance at the man watching her from the other side of the room, she opened the French windows and went out into the courtyard.

The evening sunshine was on her hair, giving it a faint gleam of gold which made her appear almost ethereal, a halo of light around her tiny pointed face. The Marquis crossed the room after her and closed the window. Then he turned towards the Colonel with a question in his eyes.

"Good God, Sylvanus!" Alistair Merrill exclaimed moving forward. "What the blazes is one of my cousins doing here in your house—and apparently alone?"

"One of your cousins?" the Marquis asked quietly.

33

"What mischief is afoot?" Colonel Merrill remarked, and then stopped. "No—now I come to think of it, none of my cousins have hair that colour. It is only my Aunt who . . ."

He stopped again to stare at the Marquis.

"Who the hell is she?"

"That is what I hoped you would tell me," the Marquis replied.

"I do not understand," Alistair Merrill said.

He walked towards the window to look to where Fortuna was standing by the fountain. As both men watched her one of the Marquis's dogs came bounding into the courtyard. It was a large black and white Dalmatian which habitually followed the Marquis when he rode in the Park.

It was the fashion amongst the Corinthians to be accompanied by Dalmatians, but those the Marquis owned were better bred, finer looking and capable of longer endurance than those sported by his contemporaries.

Fortuna bent to pat the dog, and delighted with her attention he frisked around her. She laughed at his antics, looking so entrancingly pretty as she did so that Alistair Merrill drew in his breath.

"Who is she, Sylvanus?" he repeated. "And where can you have found anyone with hair that particular colour?"

In answer the Marquis handed him the six-page letter from Miss Gillingham which had been written down so painstakingly by Fortuna.

"Read this," he said briefly, and obediently, but with his eyes continually straying to Fortuna in the courtyard, the Colonel read through the closely written sheets carefully, his face darkening as he reached the end.

34

Then with an oath which seemed to vibrate round the room, he sprang to his feet.

"My God! If it is what I think—I swear I will throttle the Old Devil to death with my bare hands."

"And let his secret die with him?" the Marquis asked.

"What this letter infers is that this girl was changed at birth," Alistair Merrill said more quietly. "The farmer—Grimwood—lived on the Duke's estate about five miles from Merrill Park."

"And you suspicion that the real Grimwood child was a son?" the Marquis asked. "While the girl in the courtyard . . ."

". . . Is my Aunt's daughter," Colonel Merrill finished. "I am convinced of it."

"I will convince you still further," the Marquis said.

He held in his hand a thin sheet of paper which he drew from a small envelope. It was the note which Fortuna told him she had not seen.

"This," he said, "is a page from my old governess's diary. Her name was Gillingham, and she brought up Fortuna after the farmer's wife, Mrs. Grimwood, who, as you have just read, left the baby behind when the family moved from your uncle's farm."

"It says here," Alistair Merrill said, looking at the letter he had been reading, "that Fortuna was born on the 27th August, 1801. You realise whose birthday that is?"

"I realise only too well," the Marquis said. "But before you make further comment let me read you this."

He held the paper in front of him and raised his quizzing-glass.

"The date on the page is the 20th September, 1801, and Miss Gillingham writes:

" '*The Baby is Thriving well on Goat's milk. I thought at first it would be Impossible for Her to Survive, but now I am convinced that She will do so. Her hair is growing, still strangely White; and Her eyes, dark grey like an Irish mist, are already fringed with dark Lashes. I have seen only one Person in my whole Life who has this particular Colouring'.*"

The Marquis glanced up at the Colonel, who he saw was listening with frowning concentration.

"My old governess continues," he went on:

" '*I went to see the Vicar today to ask that the Baby should be Christened. I shall call her Fortuna. I suggested that the Christening should be on Saturday, but the Vicar informed me this would be impossible as there are to be Celebrations at Merrill Park when the new Son and Heir to His Grace the Duke of Accrington is to be shown to the Tenants and all the local Notabilities.*

" '*On what date was the Baby born?' I enquired.*

" '*On August 27th,' he replied.*

" '*While we were Talking a Woman who was obviously in the last stages of Pregnancy enquired the whereabouts of Mrs. Tims the Midwife.*

" '*I regret to inform you that Mrs. Tims has left the Village,' the Vicar told Her.*

" '*Then who can I turn to for Help?' the Woman enquired. 'It will not be long now before I am in Labour.'*

" '*You can surely ask a Neighbour to assist You,' the Vicar said vaguely.*

" '*What has happened to Mrs. Tims?' I enquired. 'She was an Excellent Woman, and everyone about here relied on her.'*

" '*I know,' the Vicar agreed, 'She is indeed a*

grievous Loss. But she left the Village suddenly and without any Explanation. I should have thought She would have Confided in Me.'

" 'When did She leave?' I asked. 'I had not heard that She had gone.'

" 'It was on the 28th,' he replied. 'I remember it Particularly because I had promised to drive Her over the ford to visit Farmer Buller's wife. But when I called at her Cottage it was empty. The Woman who lived next Door told me she had departed in a great Hurry.' "

"The Duke thought of everything," Alistair Merrill said grimly. "The Grimwoods gone, the Midwife spirited away. It is just unfortunate as far as he was concerned that Mrs. Grimwood was afraid of the baby dying in her arms."

"There are two or three more lines of the diary," the Marquis said.

"Then read them," Alistair Merrill begged.

"The ink is very faint," the Marquis explained, "you must remember that this was written nearly eighteen years ago, but Gilly says:

" 'What Farmer—and Grimwood was a good Farmer—would leave his Farm in the middle of Harvest with the Hay only half gathered? Why did Mrs. Grimwood speak of the Baby as "It", and why had She a dislike of "It"? It is strange for a Mother to turn from her own Child, and Mrs. Grimwood was, I know, an excellent Mother.' "

The Marquis folded the paper and placed it in the envelope. Then he said:

"Miss Gillingham tore this page from her diary when she learnt of the treacherous manner in which the Duke had tricked my father. She sealed the envelope and placed it in a locked drawer."

"Why did she not come to you then," Alistair Merrill asked, "and show you Fortuna?"

"I have been thinking of that," the Marquis replied, "and the explanation which seems to me most probable is that by then Fortuna was twelve. Miss Gillingham, while she taught a number of children, had never had one of her own. She must have grown to love very deeply the child who was ostensibly her adopted daughter.

"I believe that she could not bear to part with Fortuna. But she knew she would not live for many years. She did not retire until she was really too aged to seek other employment. So she made her preparations to send Fortuna to me when there would be no one else to look after her."

Alistair Merrill rose to his feet.

"I will confront my uncle with the girl. He will be unable to deny she is, in fact, his child."

"Do you really credit that?" the Marquis said. "If you do you must have some remaining faith in the Duke's integrity. I have none. He will deny it utterly."

"But it will be impossible for him to do so," the Colonel expostulated. "There is no other family in the world which bears that peculiar combination of almost white hair and dark eyelashes."

"Tell me the story of how the O'Kearys came by it," the Marquis said. "I must have heard it in the past, but I would like to be sure of the details."

"It was when the Spanish Armada was defeated by the Elizabethan ships," Alistair Merrill began. "At the end of the battle a great storm arose and several of the Spanish galleons were swept away in the tempestuous seas to founder off the southern coast of Ireland.

One of these was wrecked on the land owned for generations by the O'Kearys."

"They were a clan?" the Marquis asked.

"They called themselves Kings," Alistair Merrill corrected, "but they were, in fact, equivalent to the Scottish clans. Legend has it that amongst the few survivors of this particular Spanish ship was a young nobleman who was carried ashore on the point of death and was nursed back to health by the King's youngest daughter.

"She was, in fact, the only unmarried child he had left; for no one had sought her hand because she was an albino."

"An albino!" the Marquis repeated almost beneath his breath. "That was what I was remembering at the back of my mind."

"They were married," Alistair Merrill went on, "and down through the centuries, every fifty or hundred years or so, those of the O'Kearys who are in the direct line of the King's family produce a child with that strange, almost white hair, but with Spanish eyes to make it not a deformity but a creature of strange and extraordinary beauty."

Alistair Merrill smiled.

"My father, who used to tell me the story, always said that the white-haired O'Kearys were like the white unicorn. A man was always hoping he would see one, but was continually disappointed. But yet here are two: my Aunt Erina, who I believe dazzled London when she was first presented at the Court of St. James, and now her daughter."

"You are really sure of that?" the Marquis asked.

"Her Grace is now nearly sixty," Colonel Merrill answered, "but that girl out there is the living image of what she was like when she was young. There are

39

half a dozen pictures at Merrill Park painted by famous artists to show you I am not lying."

"The Duke will deny it," the Marquis said quietly.

"Blast him, may his soul rot in hell!" Alistair Merrill shouted in a sudden fury. "Do you not realise what this means to me? An heir presumptive to the title of Accrington has always received an allowance from the trustees so that he could live in a decent and proper manner which befitted his expectations.

"Three thousand a year was what I enjoyed until seventeen years ago when I was informed that I no longer had any pretension to the title or estates.

"When I think of how I have had to skimp and save, how I have been afraid of facing my debtors, how at times I have had to hide from the Duns, then I only wish I could torture that Old Devil until he screams for mercy."

"He shall scream for mercy," the Marquis said. The way he spoke was almost in the nature of a vow.

"But how?" his friend asked. "Just answer me that, how can you make him? You say yourself he will deny it, he will say the girl is a bastard or that she must have come from some other source, a different branch of the family—though God knows there are none others left."

"I have a plan," the Marquis said, and his voice was hard.

"What is it?" Alistair Merrill enquired. "Quite frankly, Sylvanus, I am afraid. I am afraid of my uncle's diabolical cleverness, his capacity for riding triumphant over his opponents, however formidable they may be. Somehow, if we are not clever, he will wriggle out of this situation as he has wriggled out of so many. He will defeat us, he will laugh in our faces!"

The Colonel's voice rose almost to a shout. Then he

walked across the room to stare once more out into the courtyard at Fortuna.

"I would stake my hope of Heaven that that girl is my aunt's daughter," he said more calmly. "I am sure of it, convinced of it, even without the overwhelming evidence of this letter and the page from the diary."

"What sort of woman is your aunt?" the Marquis asked. "It is at least seven years since I last saw her, but I seem to remember her as being rather a nice person, kind and gentle—or am I mistaken?"

"You are not mistaken," Alistair Merrill replied. "I have always been fond of my Aunt Erina, even though I loathed and detested my uncle. She is completely under his thumb, of course, but even so I can hardly credit that she permitted him to give away her own flesh and blood and substitute a low-born farmer's brat in its place."

"I imagine she had little choice in the matter," the Marquis said. "The Duke would have arranged everything well in advance. There may have been various babies on the estate due at the time that Fortuna was actually born. The Duchess would have not realised what was happening until after the midwives had actually changed over the children."

"It is absolutely incredible!" Alistar Merrill murmured.

"And afterwards," the Marquis went on, "if she protested, what good would it have done? As far as the Duke knew, the Grimwoods were far away. You—my dear Alistair—must now find them."

"But how? Where? Where indeed do I start?" the Colonel asked.

"We shall get to that," the Marquis replied. "But first I have my plan to put into execution. From what you have told me of your aunt and what I remember of

41

her, I cannot believe she is very different from any other mother. And what mother would not be distressed if she knew that her daughter was—shall we say—"under the protection" of a notorious roué?"

For a moment Alistair Merrill stared at the Marquis in what appeared to be a stupefied silence. Then he ejaculated:

"You mean . . ."

"Fortuna will stay here with me," the Marquis said.

The Colonel moved his lips as if he would protest, then closed them again.

"Do you think . . ." he began almost feebly.

"I know this is the only way," the Marquis said positively. "And it will be your task, Alistair, to talk, talk and talk of this beautiful and strange creature who reminds you so vividly of your aunt. You will also contrive to call at Merrill Park and see the family. Your horse has dropped a shoe, you have a message from a friend—anything you like.

"But when you are there you will speak of a girl called Grimwood who is dazzling London, with O'Keary hair and O'Keary eyes. You will chatter, Alistair, and I am convinced that Her Grace the Duchess of Accrington will listen because she will not be able to prevent herself."

The Colonel got to his feet and walked up and down the long Library.

"I see what you are trying to do," he said, "but I wonder if it is feasible, if anything will come of it."

"It is, I am convinced, our only chance," the Marquis said. "Everyone has an Achilles heel, and where the Old Devil is concerned it is Erina O'Keary—the Duchess of Accrington."

"And how are you going to make that simple, unsophisticated girl, who has been brought up in the country, the talk of London?" Alistair Merrill asked.

"I have my ideas on that count too," the Marquis replied. "All I ask of you, Alistair, is that you will play your part well. You have as much at stake as I have."

"More," the Colonel corrected. "If this fails, Sylvanus, I shall end up in a debtors' prison. It is doubtful that I can remain in my Regiment by the end of the year."

"Then let us hope our plan will be successful," the Marquis said. "Now to business. First the girl must be well gowned, secondly I shall give a party."

"You do not suppose that anyone decent would come to this house and meet what they will think to be your 'bit of muslin'!" the Colonel ejaculated.

"I am not a fool," the Marquis answered. "And that is exactly what they are intended to think. Stop talking as though we were launching the girl as a debutante on the social scene. That is what she would have been had she been permitted by her father to take her rightful place in society. But he— not I—has decreed otherwise. The masculine members of the *Beau Ton* will accept my invitation."

The Colonel looked worried.

"She is so young," he said.

He was watching Fortuna as she threw a stick to the Dalmatian, her arm raised in a movement of exquisite grace, her hair blown by the evening wind across her cheeks.

"Miss Grimwood hoping for employment as a governess," the Marquis said scornfully. "What life do you imagine she would have in that capacity with those looks, and while there are men in the world like Crowley?"

"Crowley!" Alistair Merrill exclaimed in surprise.

"He frightened her in Berkeley Square into running away from him, so that I nearly drove her down as I was returning home," the Marquis said.

43

"Thank God she ran away!" the Colonel ejaculated. "Crowley is a lecher of the worst type. He specialises, I am told, in finding young and innocent girls on the streets or having them procured for him by the Abbess of some stew."

"I repeat, what chance has Fortuna in a world which holds such men?" the Marquis asked.

"You are right," Alistair Merrill agreed. "At the same time it seems a pity."

The Marquis did not listen to him, but was walking across the room to open the door of the window.

"Will you not come in, Fortuna?" he asked.

She turned to him with a light in her eyes.

"I was hoping you would call me," she said. "It is getting a little chilly, although the fun I have had playing with your dog has kept me warm."

"I want you to meet Colonel Merrill," the Marquis said as she entered the Library and he closed the window behind her. "Alistair, this is Fortuna Grimwood, about whom we have been speaking."

Fortuna put her little hand into his and dropped a curtsy. It seemed as if the Colonel was unable to speak, and she said to the Marquis:

"I would not wish to be a nuisance, My Lord, but it is growing late and I left my luggage—there is not much of it—at the Inn in Piccadilly where the coaches from the south set down their passengers. I think I should collect it and find somewhere to stay the night."

"I will send for it," the Marquis said, "and you will be staying here."

The anxiety on Fortuna's face vanished.

"I can stay here!" she exclaimed in tones of delight. "Oh, how wonderful! I did so hope that you would invite me, but I dared not presume to think it possible. It will be above all things marvellous to be in this house, to be your guest and to be with . . . you."

44

She said the last words shyly, but there was no disguising the joy in her eyes, the smile on her lips. Alistair Merrill stared at her in surprise.

"I hope you will enjoy being my guest," the Marquis said formally. "And now, we must make plans to have you dressed in a fashionable manner. I am sure Gilly would have wished that."

"I am sure she would have been pleased that you had thought of it," Fortuna said. "She often used to regret that there was no one in the village to tell us what was the latest vogue . . ."

She stopped, then said anxiously in a low voice: "You are sure you can afford it?"

The Marquis realised that she must be thinking he was as impoverished as he had been when the Duke had first tricked him out of his inheritance.

"I can assure you," he said in his deep voice, "that anything you require will not prove an extravagance as far as my bank balance is concerned."

"Then I shall not feel guilty of overspending," Fortuna cried. "And I would not wish you to be ashamed of me. I could not meet your friends as I am dressed now, could I?"

"You look very charming," Alistair Merrill interposed before the Marquis could speak.

She smiled at him and he saw that she had a dimple in each cheek.

"Thank you," she said, "but I know how sadly outdated this gown must be. Besides, the mud which splashed it when I fell in the roadway has not improved its appearance."

Fortuna obviously needs dresses, pelisses, ball gowns, bonnets and all the fippery which goes with them," the Marquis said. "Now where would we best procure them, Alistair?"

"Madame Bertin is where all the fashionable world buy their furbelows, but . . ."

The Colonel did not continue the sentence, and the eyes of the two men met. They knew Madame Bertin all too well. She would ferret the truth out of Fortuna however much they might tell her not to talk.

Madame Bertin knew everything; half the scandal and gossip in London was relayed in her fitting-rooms from one client to another.

Even if she did not open her mouth, Fortuna's innocence and lack of sophistication would be obvious the moment she crossed the threshold of the shop.

"I know who you need," Alistair Merrill exclaimed. "Do you remember Yvette?"

"Yvette?" the Marquis repeated.

"She was a very pretty ballet dancer five or six years ago," Colonel Merrill prompted.

"Of course," the Marquis exclaimed. "But I lost sight of her."

"So did everyone else," Alistair Merrill explained. "She married some Squire from the north and retired. But he has died, and she has returned to open a shop. Not in Bond Street, she is not yet fashionable enough for that, but just off Hanover Square."

"If I remember rightly Yvette had exquisite taste," the Marquis said reflectively.

"I swear she will not disappoint you," Alistair Merrill said, "and you can trust her. I am, in fact, meeting her later this evening. May I bring her here to see you?"

"Of course," the Marquis said, "I shall be glad to renew her acquaintance. And while you are about it, Alistair, ask Yvette for some clothes which Fortuna can wear tomorrow. She will be sadly bored if she cannot leave the house—besides I am impatient to show her—London."

"I will bring Yvette to you," the Colonel promised. "If I am not mistaken, her fitters will be working all night."

He looked down at Fortuna, and then taking her hand raised it to his lips.

"I cannot begin to tell you how glad I am to have met you," he said, and his voice was impassively sincere. "Perhaps one day you will understand why."

He went from the room without saying any more, and when the door shut behind him Fortuna turned to look at the Marquis with a puzzled look on her face.

"What did he mean by that?" she asked.

"I will explain another time," the Marquis said. "He is a man who has been extremely ill treated, Fortuna, and I think he imagines somehow you can help him to right what is a grievous wrong."

"I would rather help you," Fortuna replied. "Gilly told me that you had been despicably served and I used to pretend to myself that I would rescue you and perhaps restore your fortunes or save your life. Then I would think how foolish I was to imagine such a situation, because, after all, you are Apollo and nobody could really hurt the sun."

"If I remember right, Apollo disappears into the darkness of the night," the Marquis said.

"Not really," Fortuna corrected, "he merely vanishes from our sight. But he is still driving his chariot round on the other side of the world."

"Yet as far as we are concerned there is only darkness," the Marquis replied.

"And you have found it dark . . . very dark?" Fortuna said, her voice soft with sympathy. "Oh, I do hope I can help you! Perhaps my dreams were true, after all. I shall be able to save you and bring you your heart's desire, whatever that may be."

47

"If you could do that it would be a miracle," the Marquis said, and his tone was cynical.

"I shall do it! I will do it!" Fortuna cried. "I believe that if something is right and we want it badly enough, it comes true. I want whatever will make you happy . . . I want it with all my heart."

She spoke with an almost passionate sincerity.

"I believe you mean that," the Marquis said with a note of surprise in his voice.

"Of course I mean it," Fortuna declared.

He looked in her eyes as if he thought she could not be speaking the truth. She looked up at him and it seemed as if he held her captive. The Marquis's expression did not change but the colour rose in Fortuna's cheeks.

Almost roughly he turned away and pulled violently at the bell. The door was opened almost instantly.

"Miss Grimwood's luggage is to be collected immediately from the Posting Inn in Piccadilly," he said. "It is the White Bear if I am not mistaken."

"That is right," Fortuna said. "How clever of you to know; for I am sure you have never been there."

"It is well-known," the Marquis said briefly. "And then, Chambers, ask Mrs. Denvers to attend me immediately."

"Very good, M'Lord."

The door was closed and Fortuna said in a rather anxious voice:

"Who is Mrs. Denvers?"

"My housekeeper," the Marquis replied.

Her eyes lit up.

"Oh, I am glad," she said. "I thought it was perhaps some lady who lived in your house."

"I have no ladies living in my house," the Marquis said. "Does that perturb you?"

"No indeed," she answered. "I would so much rather

be alone with you. I think I am rather frightened of women. They always seem to disapprove of me. They stare at my hair almost as though I have deliberately chosen this colour."

"And men—what do you feel about men?" the Marquis asked, and there was a disagreeable twist to his lips.

"I have not known many gentlemen," Fortuna replied, "only the Squire who used to let me use his Library—he is nearly eighty—the Vicar and, of course, the Doctor. He was a very kind old man."

"And what about beaux?" the Marquis enquired. "Do you expect me to believe that there were no young bloods prepared to extol your charms?"

He spoke in such an unpleasant tone that Fortuna looked at him in surprise. Then she said hesitatingly:

"There was one young farmer who kept calling at the house. He was always asking me to go driving with him, but Gilly spoke to him, rather sharply I think, and then he did not come any more."

"And did you not wish to accompany him?" the Marquis enquired.

"No indeed, I do not think he was a very nice person, and he drove badly and rode worse."

"You are a judge of both, I presume," the Marquis said sarcastically.

"I can ride," Fortuna answered simply, "and I know how a man who drives well should tool his horses. Even people who live in the country are not entirely ignorant."

A little note of defiance in her voice and a sparkle in her eyes brought a faint twist to the Marquis's lips as he replied suavely:

"I stand corrected!"

"Was that rude?" Fortuna asked quickly. "I did not mean it to be, except that I feel it is somewhat aggravating when people assume that because one lives in the country one is an ignorant bumpkin."

"I never assumed anything of the sort," the Marquis assured her, "not of any pupil of Gilly's."

"It would have pleased her so much to hear you say that!" Fortuna was smiling again. She looked round the room. "How excited Gilly would be if she knew I was here in this lovely house. She used to tell me about all the treasures in your Castle."

"Do you not think that Gilly would find it strange that you should stay here alone with me?" the Marquis asked, choosing his words carefully.

Fortuna turned round and looked at him wide-eyed.

"Why should she? She sent me to you. I think she always planned that you would look after me when she was no longer there. She used to tell me what a wonderful person you were, how kind, how considerate, and how nobody ever appealed to you for help without your giving it to them. Gilly knew that you would not fail her or . . . me."

The Marquis was frowning. Just for a moment it seemed as if he was going to speak, to say something of import, and then before he could do so the door opened and Mrs. Denvers came in.

She was a small, thin, grey-haired woman wearing the conventional black silk dress and black apron of a housekeeper. At her waist hung a *châtelaine* of keys that clinked musically together as she walked. She curtsied respectfully.

"Good evening, Mrs. Denvers," the Marquis said. "Miss Fortuna Grimwood will be staying here. Please look after her for tonight and tomorrow engage for her a personal maid."

"Staying—here, M'Lord?"

50

Mrs. Denvers seemed to stiffen and her tone of voice indicated that such a course was impossible.

"Those are my instructions, Mrs. Denvers," the Marquis said. "I imagine our bedrooms are not overcrowded."

"No, M'Lord."

"Then show Miss Grimwood upstairs," the Marquis said. "But unless we delay dinner her luggage will not arrive in time for her to change her gown. However I assume, Mrs. Denvers, you can help her to feel more comfortable."

"I will carry out your wishes, M'Lord."

Mrs. Denvers' tone of voice was frigid. The straightness of her back was eloquent of her disapproval.

"Will you come this way—Miss."

The coldness in her tone made Fortuna glance at the Marquis as if for support, but he seemed to be staring at his snuffbox, apparently no longer interested in her. She curtsied and walked across the room to Mrs. Denvers.

"Shall I lead the way, Miss?" the Housekeeper enquired as they stepped into the Hall.

"Yes, please do," Fortuna answered. "How magnificent it all is! I never knew a house could be so impressive."

Mrs. Denvers did not answer, and they climbed the broad, soft-carpeted double staircase in silence. When they reached the first floor Fortuna saw through a half open door a room hung with fine tapestries and gilt furniture covered in blue damask.

"Is that the Salon?" she asked. "Oh, can I look at it? I have heard how elegant it is."

"If you are staying here, Miss, you will doubtless be shown it by His Lordship," Mrs. Denvers said, starting to climb the next flight.

The oppressiveness in her tone made Fortuna feel that she must follow without looking into the Salon. On the next landing Mrs. Denvers seemed to hesitate a moment as though debating which room she should give Fortuna.

Then with pursed lips she went towards the small, single bedroom which looked out over the back of the house. As she opened the door Fortuna said:

"Do tell me, is the wonderful bed shaped like a silver shell still here? Gilly used to tell me how exquisite it was and how beautiful the Marchioness looked in it."

Mrs. Denvers, with her hand on the handle, stopped suddenly.

"Gilly—did you say Gilly, Miss?"

"Yes, I was speaking of Miss Gillingham," Fortuna explained. "Perhaps you will remember her. It is a long time ago since she was here, but she was governess to His Lordship."

"Of course I recall Miss Gillingham," Mrs. Denvers said. "I've often wondered how she was and what happened to her."

"She died last week," Fortuna said, and her voice was forlorn. "That is why I am here. She sent me to His Lordship."

"She is dead?" Mrs. Denvers exclaimed. "I had no idea of it. And you lived with Miss Gillingham? Well, I'm surprised, Miss, but we're glad to welcome you here—and that's a fact. Come, you'll not be sleeping in that room. One on the front which gets the sun will suit you well. A comfortable room it is too. And tomorrow, when you're rested, I will show you Her Ladyship's bedchamber. It has been shut up ever since she died."

The change in Mrs. Denvers' attitude was astonishing. Now she was all smiles, her voice kind and respectful.

"They all loved Gilly," Fortuna thought to herself, and believed it to be the only explanation for the change.

There was so much to talk about, so much to tell to somebody who had known the woman who had been father and mother to her for her whole life, that when finally she came downstairs to dinner the Marquis was looking for the third time at his gold watch.

He was extremely elegant in a coat of blue satin with revers of a darker blue, his cravat was a triumph and his sapphire and diamond waistcoat buttons glittered in the light from the tapers in the candelabra.

As Fortuna entered the small Salon which led directly into the Dining-room, she was conscious of the inadequacy of her own attire. Her gown had been sponged, but even so it was still limp and creased from the long journey.

Mrs. Denvers had however found her a fresh muslin fichu to drape round her shoulders, and her hair had been brushed and arranged in a more fashionable manner. But it was not her clothes but her eyes dancing with excitement, the smile on her lips and the dimples in her cheeks that the Marquis noticed as she came running into the room.

"Am I late?" she asked unnecessarily. "Oh, please forgive me! I was afraid you would not have waited. But I have had such an exciting time. There were so many people to meet, so many people who wanted to talk to me; and I just could not contrive to be any quicker."

"People to meet?" the Marquis asked in amazement.

53

"Yes, all the people who knew Gilly," Fortuna explained. "Mrs. Denvers remembered her well, in fact they were friends. Then there were your first and second housemaids and Chambers the butler. He wanted to tell me how Gilly had once cured the rheumatism in his leg with a herbal tisane she made him.

"I have helped her make them, so I can go on mixing them for Chambers as he says his rheumatism is bad again.

"I was just coming to you when Mrs. Denvers said Chef, who has been with you for thirty-five years, would be very hurt if I did not slip down and meet him as I had met all the others. There was so much they wanted to tell me and I wanted to tell them. But Chambers said:

" 'His Lordship'll be mad as fire, that he'll be.'

"So I tore myself away!"

"That was most considerate of you," the Marquis said, but his tone was not as sarcastic as it might have been.

"You are not angry?" Fortuna pleaded.

"I shall be incensed only if your chattering has spoilt my dinner," the Marquis said, and Fortuna dimpled at him as she replied:

"I will keep my fingers crossed. Perhaps if I told you some very interesting things, maybe you would not notice so particularly."

The Marquis had no chance to reply. The doors into the Dining-room were flung open and Chambers announced in stentorian tones:

"Dinner is served, M'Lord."

"There," Fortuna exclaimed, "only five and a half minutes late. It might have been much worse, might it not?"

Without waiting for the Marquis's reply she preceded him towards the Dining-room. She seemed to float rather than walk, and there was such grace in the carriage of her head that the Marquis found himself following her without remembering that he was, in fact, extremely irritated at being kept waiting by a country chit.

Fortuna was shown to her place. There were four footmen, and the table, which was lit by two huge candelabra, was covered in gold ornaments and decorated with purple and white orchids. Fortuna looked awestruck.

"It is terribly grand," she said at length in a small voice. "Do you always dine like this?"

"When I am home," the Marquis replied in his habitual voice of boredom, "which I assure you is not very often."

"Then I am honoured," Fortuna said, "because I have kept you home tonight. I have . . . have I not?"

"You have," the Marquis replied briefly.

"And that means it is very exciting for me but not so exciting for you," Fortuna ruminated, "unless I can amuse you. Oh dear, I wonder if I can contrive to do that? You see, I am very ignorant of all the things which interest you."

She looked at him anxiously, and then suddenly she clapped her hands together.

"Of course, how stupid I am," she said. "Gilly always told me that gentlemen like to talk about themselves.

" 'That is something in which they are invariably interested,' she used to say, 'a subject which never fails.'

"So now I know the answer. All I have to do is to ask you to tell me about yourself and you will enjoy your dinner with me."

55

There was a moment's almost poignant silence.

Then Chambers was surprised into almost dropping a silver dish because for the first time in years he heard his master laugh.

3

The Marquis tooled his High Perch Phaeton with its magnificent pair of chestnuts through Stanhope Gate and into the Park.

There was no doubt that he was looking extremely elegant with his high hat at a rakish angle and his cravat tied in a new and intricate fashion which was to send the young Bucks cursing their valets before the day was out.

But the eyes of the Beau Ton and those of lesser importance driving, riding or perambulating in the Park, looked not at the Marquis and his superb horseflesh, which they had seen often enough before, but at his companion.

Alistair Merrill had been right in saying that Madame Yvette's fitters would sit up all night. Fortuna's gown had arrived only a few minutes before she was due to leave her bedchamber.

Although she had little enough time to look at herself in the mirror, she was well aware that Yvette's Parisian flair had not disappointed the Marquis as she came slowly down the stairs towards him.

Only a Frenchwoman would have thought of anything so clever as a strawberry pink satin bonnet which threw into prominence the paleness of her hair, and at the same time gave an impression of youth and the first budding of a damask rose.

57

There were indeed tiny rosebuds to trim the bonnet, and the rose motif was echoed again in the pink pelisse which covered a gown of the same colour. The coat was high waisted, and there was a touch of lace at the neck which was repeated on the cuffs; her kid gloves were dyed to match the dress.

There was something so lovely about Fortuna as she stood waiting for the Marquis's approval, her face turned up to his, her grey eyes searching his, that the lackeys waiting in the Hall broke years of training to glance appreciatively at her.

"You are pleased?" Fortuna asked anxiously.

"Yvette has obeyed my instructions," the Marquis said briefly.

They stepped into the Phaeton, and only when they were clear of the house and driving down the Square did Fortuna ask:

"What instructions did you give Madame?"

"What woman is not interested in anything that concerns her appearance?" the Marquis asked. "However as you are curious, I told Yvette to make you look sensational, but—very young."

"It will cost you a lot of money," Fortuna said in a low voice.

"I have already said that is of no significance," the Marquis replied.

There was a moment's pause and then Fortuna asked:

"Did you win last night?"

The Marquis glanced at her sharply.

"How did you know I played cards after you had retired to bed?" he enquired. "Who has been talking?"

Fortuna gave a little gurgle of laughter.

"Do you really believe that you can keep anything a secret from your household?" she enquired. "Naturally they know everything. Gilly always said nothing can be hidden from one's personal staff, and I am sure she was right. When the maid called me this morning, as she drew back the curtains she said:

" ' 'Tis a lovely morning, Miss, and His Lordship gained at cards yestereve.' "

The Marquis looked astonished.

"I had no idea that my servants were so well informed," he said, "or indeed that they were so interested."

"Of course they are interested," Fortuna said. "Do you not realise that they love you? Indeed that is not surprising; for I have always heard how kind your father and mother were to those they employed at the Castle and how they had all served your family for generations. And Mrs. Denvers tells me it is just the same here in London."

"Mrs. Denvers has indeed been with me for years," the Marquis answered. "In fact, I cannot remember when she was not in the house."

"Then how can you expect her not to care what happens to you or not be interested in what you do?" Fortuna asked. "Of course they are all concerned.

"Why, Mrs. Denvers told me this morning that when the trouble came and your father was so cruelly treated by the Duke, they were all, from the top servants to the lowest pantryboys, in the depths of despair. Not because they were afraid for their jobs, but because they could not bear such a tragedy to happen to you personally."

The Marquis seemed to have difficulty in controlling his horses. He did not answer, and Fortuna went on:

"As I have already said, they love you, and that

59

is why they are so delighted that you should have won last night."

"And yet you asked me knowing already the answer," the Marquis said.

It was almost as though he was glad to find something with which he could find fault.

"I thought you would like to tell me yourself," Fortuna replied. "It is so disappointing when you have a lovely surprise for someone and they already know what it is."

"And for you it is a lovely surprise?" the Marquis enquired.

"Of course," Fortuna answered. "Like Mrs. Denvers, Chambers and the rest of your household, I am praying that you will win everything back. And I am sure, absolutely sure that our prayers will be answered."

"I wish I had your confidence," the Marquis said drily.

By now they had reached the fashionable part of the Park, and the Ladies and Gentlemen walking elegantly in the Row or seated in their open landaus talking to their friends turned to look at them. The Gentlemen took off their hats, but when the Ladies would have bowed the Marquis passed them with averted eyes, making no gesture.

"Good Lord, who can Thane have with him?" not one but several of his friends exclaimed. "She must be a fair Cyprian, but I have never seen her before."

The Ladies said nothing, but their eyes, which had lit up at the Marquis's approach, narrowed, and there was a look of sulky resentment on several beautiful faces.

"Who can she be?" one Dandy asked another. "I could have sworn there is not a 'bit o' muslin' in the whole of London that I would not recognise if she has ever been seen anywhere before now."

"May be imported," someone suggested. "There are a lot of French ladybirds coming over here. They say that Motts sounds like the Rue de la Paix of an evening."

"Well, this Phryne has certainly not come from Motts," his friend said positively.

The Marquis drew up his Phaeton with a flourish halfway down the Row, and within a few seconds several of his friends came hurrying to engage him in conversation.

Well aware of their curiosity, the Marquis kept them talking for some time before he said:

"Fortuna, may I present Sir Guy Sherrington, Lord Worcester, Lord Boughton and Sir George Freeman?"

The Gentlemen swept their hats from their heads. Fortuna smiled down at them beguilingly from her high seat in the Phaeton.

"How do you do," she said shyly. "I feel I ought to curtsy instead of being perched so far above you!"

"You look entrancing as you are," Sir Guy Sherrington said.

He was a good-looking young man dressed in the very *ton* of fashion, the points of his collar so high that it seemed impossible for him to move his chin.

"Thank you," Fortuna said quietly.

"I call that a very banal compliment," Lord Worcester protested. "Let me tell you, Madam, that the Gentleman who has just spoken has clearly no soul. I should describe you as a Goddess of beauty and light descending from Olympus on a cloud to bless us poor mortals with your presence."

"Now I must thank you, My Lord," Fortuna said. But she blushed with a little embarrassment as

61

she spoke and looked so utterly adorable that the Gentlemen could only watch her with bemused eyes.

"My horses are restless," the Marquis said sharply. "I will bid you good-morning, Gentlemen."

"No, pray do not leave us," his friends cried almost in unison.

"You will receive an invitation from me to dine tonight," he said. "I hope you can be my guests."

With that, before they could reply, he had left. They had not moved far before a lady riding a spirited roan came trotting alongside the Phaeton.

"Good-morning, Sylvanus."

"Good-morning, Charlotte," the Marquis answered. "You should not be talking to me."

"But I want to talk to you," the rider replied. "Listen, Sylvanus, I must see you. I expected you last night and—the night before."

"I was engaged," the Marquis said briefly.

"So I understand," the lady answered. "And the Duke is a good enough excuse for last night, but not for the night before, nor for the fact that you had said you would be calling on me."

"Charlotte, people are looking at you," the Marquis said. "Continue your ride, I swear this will do you no good."

"I have to see you, Sylvanus! Can you not understand? I cannot go on wondering, waiting—longing for you."

Fortuna could not help listening to the conversation. Now she looked at the woman who was speaking and thought she had never seen anyone so beautiful. With raven black hair against a camellia-white skin, she had dark passionate eyes and her red lips curved invitingly.

She was so lovely that Fortuna found it difficult to understand why the Marquis should say sharply:

"We will talk another time, Charlotte. I beg of you to behave, more circumspectly."

"I hate you, Sylvanus! Do you hear me? I hate you!"

Though the words were violent, at the same time her very tone belied their meaning. Then the Lady turned her horse and riding undeniably well cantered away in the opposite direction.

"Who was that?"

Fortuna could not help asking the question, even though she felt the Marquis might snub her for being curious.

"The Lady's name," he said coldly, "is The Lady Charlotte Hadleigh."

"And she loves you?" Fortuna enquired.

The Marquis's expression darkened.

"That is not the sort of question you should ask."

"I am sorry," Fortuna apologised, "but it is obvious, is it not? I suppose when people are as handsome and attractive as you, ladies cannot but fall in love. Does she wish to marry you?"

"I have told you, Fortuna," the Marquis said in his most uncompromising voice, "that those are not the sort of questions that a young lady of any sensibility would ask a Gentleman."

Fortuna signed.

"But I am not a young Lady," she said, "not in the true sense of the word. I do not really even possess a name of my own. I use that of a farmer whose wife abandoned me at birth because she had no liking for me."

She sighed.

"It is obvious from Gilly's letter to you that she thinks I am, in fact, not Mrs. Grimwood's child. I am just Miss Nobody. And so I feel I can say the things which a Lady should not say and it does not really signify."

"You are the most extraordinary girl I have ever met in my life," the Marquis asserted. "I am beginning to question if Gilly has brought you up in the way she should have done."

Fortuna laughed.

"She did her best, I assure you. She was always telling me what a lady should and should not do. But I came to the conclusion that it was no use bemoaning the fact that I had blue blood and was therefore of no consequence.

"Instead I thought to myself that if I were clever I could contrive to have the best of both worlds. I would know what was the right thing to do, but if I did the wrong thing nobody was likely to be in the least surprised."

The Marquis's lips twitched at the corners.

"I can see one thing," he said, "there is every likelihood of your becoming a problem.'"

He turned his horses as he spoke and drove back down the Row.

"Are you letting them have another look at me?" Fortuna asked.

"Now what do you mean by that?" the Marquis demanded, considerably startled.

"Well, you have not told me anything I want to know," Fortuna said, "and I suppose I am really too frightened to ask you. But I have thought to myself that you must have some reason for dressing me as you have and bringing me into the Park. Mrs. Denvers says you have not driven with a lady in the Row for nearly a year. She was very surprised when she heard where you were taking me this morning."

"I really think we should get along better," the Marquis said crushingly, "if you did not gossip with the servants, or at any rate ceased to discuss me and my actions with them."

There was silence for a moment, and then in a very small voice Fortuna said:

"I will try to do what you want, but it will be very dull if you do not tell me anything. It will be rather like walking blindly through a fog, not knowing where one is going and feeling terribly lost and frightened."

"What do you want to know?" the Marquis asked coldly.

"First of all, I would like to know what you won last night?" Fortuna answered.

"I never discuss my game," the Marquis replied harshly.

"How dull that must be!" Fortuna exclaimed. "You must really long to do and tell someone . . . someone who cares, who wants you to win, who wants you to defeat the wicked Duke! I am sure it is not good for you to bottle it all up inside you."

"Very well, as you are so curious," the Marquis capitulated, "I won Lambeth."

Fortuna knitted her brow.

"I am not quite certain where that is," she said.

"Would you like to see it?" the Marquis asked.

She felt somehow from his tone that there was something unpleasant behind the invitation.

"Yes, I would," she said eagerly. "Can we go there now?"

"As you wish," he said.

Again she felt that while he had acquiesced in her curiosity there was something sinister about it.

They drove through Hyde Park Corner, down Constitution Hill and into Birdcage Walk. Fortuna was disappointed with Buckingham House, she had expected it to be more impressive and less drab.

65

The Houses of Parliament, however, lived up to her expectation of them, and when they crossed Westminster Bridge she exclaimed with delight at the barges moving up and down the Thames and at the ships, their sails billowing in the wind coming in on the tide.

They passed some nondescript, rather dingy houses, and then the Marquis swung the horses away from the river and down a narrow street. Dirty and squalid, it was flanked with high ugly houses, the panes of their windows broken, many of them with their doors hanging awry.

There were ragged children playing in the road who ran screaming out of the way of the horses or were snatched from the filthy gutters by their mothers or by an older child. They were all bare-footed, and many of them were naked enough to show the sharp prominence of their ribs.

Grim, rough men were leaning lazily against the walls of the houses or clustered together on the street corners. Bawds, with their cheeks roughed, reddened lips and crimped hair, leant out of the windows and called invitingly to the passers-by or screamed abuse at a more successful rival.

The Marquis drove the whole length of two streets without speaking. They emerged into a small market cluttered with barrows laden with whelks and winkles, tripe and the red flesh of unidentifiable animals, and he manoeuvred his way through the crowds with difficulty into a better class road where at least the windows had panes of glass and there were fewer children occupying the muddy roadway.

It was then with an almost cruel expression in his face that he turned to look at Fortuna.

"This is what I have won," he said. "I hope it meets with your approval."

Fortuna did not speak for a moment. Then she said slowly as if she considered every word:

"I am sure the houses are sound structurally. What has happened, of course, is that owing to the rents being raised again and again until the tenants could no longer afford to meet the demands of the rent collectors, they have been forced to overcrowd every room with lodgers.

"What is more, I only saw one pump in the whole length of each street. As you know, it is impossible for these poor people to keep clean unless there is water.

The ugly look on the Marquis's face was replaced by one of sheer astonishment.

"How do you know about such things?" he asked.

"There are very much the same conditions in Waterless," Fortuna answered.

"Waterless?" the Marquis questioned.

"Yes, do you not remember? It is, or was, a small market town, originally, of course, on your father's estate. Owing to the fact that the Duke allowed farms in the surrounding countryside to fall into disrepair, a large number of people left the land and moved into Waterless hoping they would find work."

"The result being overcrowding," the Marquis said sharply.

"Of course," Fortuna agreed. "Quiet little streets became a seething mass of children, of old people, of men who could not get work, of tired women who just could not keep a house clean. There is lack of water and hunger, conditions which invariably lead to disease."

"But how do you know all this?" the Marquis asked.

"Even country bumpkins," Fortuna said with a

little flash in her eyes, "can take an interest in the conditions which exist around them."

"But Ladies do not interest themselves in squalor and poverty," the Marquis said almost as though he tried to excuse her knowledge to himself.

Fortuna smiled at him as one might smile at a rather petulant child.

"Have you no idea what Gilly has been doing all these years?" she said.

Then before the Marquis could reply she added:

"No, of course you have not, there is no reason why you should know. Gilly studied herbs. She told me she had always been interested in them, even when she was looking after you. And your mother, I understand, had a famous herb garden."

"That is true," the Marquis murmured almost beneath his breath.

"Gilly collected all the recipes," Fortuna went on, "that were used in the still-room at Thane Castle, and when she retired she went on finding remedies in old books. She searched through the Squire's library, which was very extensive, through the Vicar's and through the Doctor's.

"Then gradually, though I was too young to know about it, she started to treat people in the village. Of course they talked and said how amazing her remedies were, and soon people came from miles away to ask Gilly's advice."

"I could hardly guess at anything so unusual," the Marquis exclaimed.

"She was really quiet famous," Fortuna told him, "and once a week we used to go into Waterless, she and I, to help the people in the bad streets like the one we have just been through.

"It was extraordinary how much her tisanes and salves could help children with bad eyes and

68

gathered ears, the women with ulcers and the men with boils and skin eruptions. But, of course, as she always said herself, what such people really need is decent housing, food and water."

"And you helped her!" the Marquis exclaimed, glancing down at Fortuna incredulously.

He could hardly believe that he was listening to this exquisite, transparent-skinned girl talking as if the filth of the slums through which he had just taken her was not something to be shuddered at but to be tackled as a problem.

"And what would you do to sweep away the squalor we have just seen?" he asked.

"I think you know the answer to that," Fortuna said. "Repair the houses, lower the rents, install more pumps and, if possible, find the men work."

"And you think all that is easy?" the Marquis asked with once again a sneering, sarcastic note in his voice.

"Not easy," she answered, "but possible. Of course, it depends on how long you can remain the owner, does it not?"

"And you believe that if I were the permanent owner, not one who could lose the property again on the turn of the cards, I would do those things?" the Marquis enquired.

"Of course you would!" Fortuna declared. "Once you gain back all you have lost, you will not only try to put Lambeth right, but you will make good the farms on what were once the Thane lands.

"Do you realise that even during the war the Duke would not help the farmers by repairing their barns or even the roofs of their houses? What was more, when they asked if he would lower the rents so that they could buy new equipment to make their farms more efficient, his only reply was to put the rents up.

69

"They hate him. They too pray for the day when you will become their landlord."

"And suppose I tell you," the Marquis said, "that I have no longer any desire to concern myself with their well-being, that I have ceased to be interested in their problems and their tribulations. They would whine whatever one did for them."

He paused.

"If I told you that, would you believe me?"

"No, of course I would not," Fortuna answered. "You are are only saying such things to tease me because you think I have been a trifle presumptuous in telling you what you should do. But you know far better than I what should be done. Think how wonderful it would be, Apollo, if all these people could be happy and content again!"

Her name for him slipped out unconsciously, and though he noticed it he made no comment. Instead he kept his eyes firmly on the road ahead of them, seemingly deep in his own thoughts.

They drove back again over Westminister Bridge, but now they passed through Horse Guards Parade and turned up St. James's Street.

The Marquis was well aware that the Gentlemen going in and out of the Clubs stopped to stare as they passed. Behind the bow window at White's recently installed by Beau Brummel he saw Lord Hornblotton and knew that the members would soon be buzzing with speculation as to who Fortuna might be.

She was quite conscious of the interest she was provoking as she looked around her with delight, her eyes as wide and excited as a child's, the sunshine revealing the exquisite purity of her skin and finding the few thiny threads of gold in her almost white hair.

When they drew up at Merrill House in Berkeley Square Fortuna turned impulsively to the Marquis.

"Thank you," she said, "it was a lovely morning, and I know, however much you pretend to be indifferent, that you will look after those poor people. I have a feeling—you may think it very stupid of me—that things are going to come right for you very, very soon."

"Perhaps you have brought me luck," the Marquis said in his deep voice, and for once he was not sneering.

"I hope so," the answered softly, "I hope so with all my heart."

Fortuna saw nothing of the Marquis for the rest of the day. Madame Yvette was waiting for her and she spent most of the afternoon standing while gown after gown was pinned into place.

"I cannot want so many things," she exclaimed at last.

"You will want many, many more," Madame Yvette said in her fascinating French accent. "You would not wish the so handsome Marquis to be ashamed of you, no?"

"He certainly will not be ashamed of me in all these gowns," Fortuna smiled. "But you are right, Madame, I wish to do him credit. You think he will be pleased?"

"I am sure he will," Madame Yvette said. "M'Lord has—how shall I say—*toujours* an eye for a pretty girl!"

Fortuna did not answer, and with a little laugh Madame Yvette added:

"And the pretty girls have an eye for him, yes?"

Fortuna remembered the passionate entreaty in Lady Charlotte's voice. It was absurd, of course, but she could not help feeling a little jealous of all the women that she could picture reaching out their arms to the Marquis, longing and yearning for him as Lady Charlotte did.

Then with some of Gilly's common sense she gave herself a shake. Why should she worry about anyone else?

She was here in the Marquis's house as his guest. He was spending a great deal of money on her clothes, he was interested enough to take her driving in the Park, as no other woman had been privileged for a long time. And tonight there was to be a party.

It was Madame Yvette who had informed her that she was to be present at the dinner to which she had already heard the Marquis invite his friends.

"This gown has to be the loveliest of them all," Madame Yvette said.

"Why?" Fortuna enquired.

"Because it is always first impressions that are the most important," the Frenchwoman replied. "Once fix the idea in a gentleman's mind that *vous êtes ravissante*, then after that—*voila!*—he will always believe it so."

"Then I do perceive it must be a very special gown," Fortuna replied seriously.

She wondered if the Marquis would think her lovely, if not lovelier than all those woman who were yearning for him, begging for his attention. Perhaps he was with Lady Charlotte now, she thought, and then remembered that the Duke was in London.

No, he would be at White's, she was sure of that. Somehow her spirits rose at the thought.

It was Mrs. Denvers who finally shooed Madame Yvette away.

"The young lady is dead on her feet," she said. "She will not do your gown, or anyone else's, any credit tonight unless you let her rest. She's to have an hour's sleep at least before we start dressing for the dinner. Why it all has to be done in so much haste I can't imagine. The whole household is running about like demented rabbits. But there, that's His Lordship all over."

"How many to dinner?" Madame Yvette asked.

"Thirty, and as many, if not more, coming in afterwards," Mrs. Denvers replied. "And His Lordship insisting it should be held in the Ballroom which has not been used to my knowledge for nigh on ten years."

"Where is the Ballroom?" Fortuna asked.

"His Lordship's grandfather built it at the back of the house," Mrs. Denvers answered. " 'Tis lucky I've always kept it clean and ready for use at any moment; otherwise we'd be in a nice pickle with His Lordship giving orders this morning, if you please, for a big party to be held there tonight."

"That is the way to have a party!" Fortuna smiled. "It is so much more exciting than worrying about it months beforehand. Why, in Little Waterless they used to start planning the May Fair a year ahead. And by the time it happened we were all so sick and tired of hearing about it that we could hardly enjoy the festivities, not even the dancing round the Maypole."

"Mademoiselle is right," Madame Yvette said. "The things that happen quickly are always the best, like falling in love."

Mrs. Denvers sniffled.

"That is for them who are interested in such things," she said. "All I am concerned with, Madame, is that Miss Fortuna should have a lie-down."

"Very well, I will release her into your hands," Madame Yvette consented, "because tonight I want her to look *ravissante,* and then my little shop will be crowded with order. *Alors,* the grand ladies will imagine that my gowns will have the same magic where

73

they too are concerned, *C'est fou*—no one will look so beautiful as Mademoiselle!"

"I will try to be a good advertisement for you," Fortuna smiled.

Then she was whisked away by Mrs. Denvers to lie in a darkened room. But she found that she was far too excited to sleep.

What would the party be like? she wondered. Would they dance? And if they did, would the Marquis dance with her? She felt a little breathless at the thought of being close to him. He was so wonderful, the Apollo she had dreamt about ever since she was a child, driving across the sky in his chariot.

How well he drove, she thought sleepily, and knew that even the real Apollo could not have looked more handsome than the Marquis with his tall hat at an angle on his dark head . . .

The Anteroom to the Ballroom already contained a number of guests before the Marquis appeared, magnificently attired in a new coat of midnight blue satin.

There were wines of every description for his guests, but as the butler announced one Gentleman after another it was Sir Guy Sherrington who voiced the question which trembled on all their lips.

"Great Heavens, Sylvanus, do not tell us this is an all male party? We were expecting something very different."

"I hope you will not be disappointed," the Marquis replied. "I have invited the whole of the Corps de Ballet from the Opera to join us as soon as their performance is over. Many of the dancers, you know, are new to England, and I thought new faces were what is needed to disperse the jaded, or should I say surfeited, look in your eyes."

"Sylvanus, you dog!" one of his friends ejaculated. "We might have guessed you would have something original to offer us. The Corps de Ballet! Well, you certainly do things on a grand scale. There is a little French piece dancing in the second row who I am told is absolutely entrancing—though I dare say she's above my touch."

"That's the trouble with these foreigners," an older man complained. "They think the British are all millionaires. That wide-eyed Parisienne I took under my protection last year made a hole in my pocket which I have not yet been able to repair."

"Well, personally I always think women are over-rated at dinner," a Tulip of Fashion drawled. "When one is eating one should be beguiled by sensible and, if possible, witty conversation. A giggling woman should be kept for dessert."

"You have a point there," the Marquis agreed, "but at the same time this is not entirely an all male dinner party. I have asked a lady who I am sure you will be delighted to meet to join us."

It was at that moment the butler announced in unnecessarily stentorian tones:

"Miss Fortuna Grimwood, M'Lord."

There was an almost audible sound of surprise or interest as all heads turned towards the door. Fortuna stood there.

Just for a moment she was still, looking a little anxiously amongst the sea of faces for the Marquis. There was no doubt, he thought, that Yvette had done well.

Fortuna wore a gown, not as might have been expected of white or one of the pastel shades so popular at the moment, but of emerald green.

It was ornamented with hundreds and hundreds of

tiny pearls sewn skilfully onto the soft gauze-like material with just a shimmer of silver behind the pearls themselves.

The depth of the colour made her skin and her hair seem almost dazzling in contrast, and the high-waisted gown with its velvet ribbons under her tiny breasts and the pearls shimmering in the light of the candles made her appear like a nymph that had risen from a stormy sea.

There was something so lovely and so unusual about her that for a moment she silenced the chattering tongues of the most critical audience in the country, the Beau Ton of St. James's, the most ardent gossipers of Clubland.

Then Fortuna saw the Marquis, who was standing some way from her, and with a smile almost like the sun coming out she sped towards him. It was the impulsive movement of a child running towards security and safety.

But as she reached his side she remembered her manners, and stopping suddenly dropped him a curtsy. She raised her grey eyes to his.

"Good evening, Fortuna," the Marquis said formally. "I trust you are rested."

"Yes indeed, My Lord."

"And now you must meet my friends," he said, and taking her by the hand he led her round to each of the Gentlemen.

"We met this morning," Sir Guy Sherrington said, "and I swear to you that I have thought of nothing else all day. I had a suspicion that we should meet you here this evening, and if we had not met you I would have indeed challenged Sylvanus to a duel for daring to deprive us of your presence."

Fortuna dimpled at him.

"Do Gentlemen in London always make such pretty speeches?" she asked.

"Only when they have someone as pretty as you to inspire them," Sir Guy replied.

She laughed at that.

"Be careful of this fellow," Lord Worcester, who had come up while they were talking, said. "He is dangerous, Miss Fortuna, I warn you."

"Dangerous?" Fortuna asked. "In what way?"

"He will attempt to steal your heart," Lord Worcester asserted, "but I promise you I will do my best to prevent it."

"I do not think anyone can steal a heart," Fortuna replied. "A heart—and if by that you mean love—must be given, must it not?"

The Gentlemen laughed as though she had said something very witty, and indeed as dinner progressed Fortuna began to feel that she was acquitting herself admirably.

Seated on the Marquis's right, she had Sir Guy Sherrington on her other side and she found herself making both him and the Gentleman next to him laugh, while some of her remarks were repeated down the table.

When on going into dinner she looked around the Ballroom she had exclaimed with sheer delight at the beauty of it.

All day florists had been decorating the walls with garlands of flowers, and the Major-domo to the Marquis's household had been supervising the laying of the long table, the setting out of the gold ornaments, the arrangements of the candelabra, the Sèvres dinner service, the snuffboxes of enamel set with diamonds.

It was all incredibly grand, and it seemed to Fortuna that the Gentlemen in their brightly coloured evening coats, their snowy cravats, their glittering jewels, their fobs and their high starched collars gave the room an elegance such as she had never expected to see, and which filled her with an excitement she had never known before.

Halfway through the meal she turned to the Marquis and said impulsively:

"It is all so beautiful! It is just how I hoped so fervently you would live."

"What do you mean by that?" he asked.

"The gold, the silver, the porcelain, the wine and, of course, your guests. They are all the right background for you. It is all so elegant, so beautiful in its own way, like a picture by a famous artist. I am explaining myself badly, but somehow by the way everybody talked about you, I expected to find you living in mean circumstances, poor, impoverished, and that was not how I wanted to find you."

"Did it matter?" the Marquis asked.

"Very much to me," she answered. "You see, for Apollo everything must be shining and glorious, not a dim sun or one suffering eclipse, but brilliant, burning, glorious, giving light to those who need it. That is how I think of you."

"Let us hope that nothing will happen to destroy the picture you describe so graphically," the Marquis said rather sourly.

"Could anything happen?" Fortuna asked anxiously, "Could the Duke hurt you any further?"

"No, that indeed would be impossible," the Marquis replied with a note of bitterness in his voice.

"Then things must get better," Fortuna said positively. "When one has reached the bottom, one can go no further. We know that."

"As I have already remarked, perhaps you have brought me luck," the Marquis replied.

"Oh, I hope so, I hope so indeed!" Fortuna said. "Did you win this afternoon?"

Her voice was very low so that no one else could hear.

"I have told you, I do not . . ." the Marquis began, then met her eyes. "Yes, I did!"

He saw the expression of joy which seemed almost to transform her face so that for a moment he was bemused by it. Then he said harshly:

"You are neglecting Sir Guy, I think," and obediently Fortuna turned her head away from him.

As the long and elaborate menu came to an end the door was suddenly flung open and the ladies from the Opera arrived. There was a flutter of colour, the glitter of jewels, the chatter of high voices, and it seemed as if a flock of colourful humming-birds had invaded the dining-room.

The Marquis rose to greet them, extra chairs were set down at the table, and the chattering and laughing newcomers sorted themselves out until every Gentleman had beside him a pretty face and an elegant little figure wearing a daringly low-cut evening-gown.

Fortuna had not been told what to expect, and she watched with surprise and interest the manner in which the Corps de Ballet managed to infuse a new gaiety and excitement into the company.

Wine was brought, and though the ladies protested that they had already dined, many of them chose to eat the purple muscat grapes or the huge peaches which had been brought up that day from the gardens at Thane.

But wine was something they would all accept. They toasted their companions, they toasted each other and they toasted the Marquis.

The servants, with their powdered wigs and their colourful livery, were kept busy filling up the crystal glasses from the napkin-covered bottles which had been kept cool in a great bath of ice behind the screen which led toward the kitchens.

"Your health, Sylvanus!" Sir Guy Sherrington exclaimed. "May you always have as many good ideas with which to entertain us as this party this evening."

"I will drink to M'Lord's health," a pretty dancer cried with a beguiling French accent, "for this is le brave I have been so longing to meet, *le Monsieur* who they tell me is so bad and wicked that they call him *le jeune* Devil! Me—Odette—I have a grande passion for *le diable*."

She jumped to her feet as she spoke, and running round the table to the Marquis bent forward to kiss him French fashion on both cheeks.

"Voila, Monsieur!" she said. "Now I am, how you say, a disciple of ze Devil himself."

There was a shriek of laughter at this, and from that moment the party seemed to grow more unrestrained and noisy.

In the Musicians' Gallery at the end of the room the music which had been playing softly for some time became louder and gayer. Chairs were pushed away and some of the gentlemen began to dance with their pretty partners, swirling them around in the waltz which at the beginning of the century had been declared immoral but which was now accepted even at Almack's.

But the polka which succeeded it was certainly not tolerated in correct social circles. But Fortuna was not to know this. She only thought it was a mad romp and wondered what Gilly would have thought of it.

"Will you dance with me?" Sir Guy asked when the band started yet another waltz. "Or will Sylvanus call me out for asking you?"

"I do not see why he should do that," Fortuna replied innocently.

She was, in fact, a little piqued that no one had asked her to dance, not realising that most of the Marquis's friends would have thought it impudent to encroach on his preserves. Sir Guy, however, was prepared to presume on a long-standing friendship.

Fortuna looked to where the Marquis was deeply engaged in a conversation with the vivacious Odette.

"I would like to dance," she said, "but I wonder if I am good enough. I have had dancing lessons, but my steps will seem rather staid and perhaps old-fashioned compared with what they are doing here."

"I will teach you," Sir Guy said eagerly.

They waltzed, and Fortuna was glad to find that she could follow him quite competently. Only once did she hesitate and lose a step as she glanced towards the end of the table and saw that Odette was once again kissing the Marquis, this time on the mouth.

When Sir Guy took Fortuna back to the table, it appeared he had broken down the barrier which had kept the other gentlemen from approaching her. She was overwhelmed with invitations to waltz or polka, and she received so many extravagant compliments that she found herself blushing and becoming a trifle confused.

"You are utterly adorable!" Lord Worcester said when finally she consented to waltz with him.

"I am not sure that you should speak to me like that," Fortuna replied shyly.

"So long as His Lordship does not hear me, I shall speak the truth," Lord Worcester asserted. "That may sound yellow-livered, but Sylvanus is a Nonpareil with a pistol."

Fortuna laughed.

"Sir Guy also was frightened of His Lordship's

81

calling him out, but I do not think that the Marquis would duel over me."

"You are too modest," Lord Worcester answered, "and perhaps too young to realise that men will not only fight and maybe die because of your beauty, but they will also languish in misery—as I shall do because you are a star twinkling out of reach!"

"How I wish I could believe such things were true!" Fortuna cried. "But thank you, My Lord, for saying them. Even though I know you are but roasting me, it is exciting for me to think I am a success!"

"You are very sweet and unspoilt," Lord Worcester said in a different voice. "It is a pity . . ."

He stopped and looked towards the Marquis. Then his lips tightened and he said no more until the dance was finished.

As Fortuna sat down she realised that many of the candles in the room had been extinguished. The light was low and more seductive, and while the dancing was still gay, many of those who had started to dance were now sprawled on the sofas which lined the walls or were sitting with their arms on the table as though it were impossible for them to stand, let alone dance.

Suddenly a dancer sprang onto the floor alone and started pirouetting round and round, her skirts twirling wildly. With a burst of laughter two Gentlemen pursued her, snatching at her dress as she danced, pulling at the soft material until it tore.

"Salome of the Seven Veils!" one of them shouted. "And there are only two left!"

Clutching at her, but slipping on the parquet, they rendered her almost naked amidst the cheers of their friends, until with cries of pretended dismay she ran away from them.

She managed with great dexterity to dodge round

the table and chairs until finally she was caught, and screaming with delight was carried away into the shadows.

"Poses! Poses!" came the cry from several Gentlemen, and an attractive Austrian from Vienna stood alone in the centre of the dance floor.

Slowly with exaggerated gestures she began to unrobe, taking off her garments one by one in the manner of the *"Poses Plastiques"* which was the rage in Paris but had only recently arrived in London.

Only when, amid shouts of applause and cries of "Bravo", she was almost completely naked, did the Marquis glance at his watch. Turning to Fortuna, who was watching wide-eyed, he said:

"I am leaving now, I have an appointment at White's. Do you wish to stay?"

He asked the question as though it were not of the least concern to him what she did, and Fortuna said quickly:

"I too would like to leave, My Lord!"

"You are not deserting us," Sir Guy cried.

He had been flirting with an attractive Venetian with red hair, but now he left to take Fortuna's hand.

"Come and dance with me again," he pleaded. "There are many things I wish to say to you, especially if Sylvanus is not listening."

"Thank you, but I must retire to bed," Fortuna answered. "It sounds ungrateful, but so much has happened to me in the last twenty-four hours that I am really fatigued."

"How can you be so cruel?" Sir Guy exclaimed. "But I understand! Is it imperative for you both to leave us, Sylvanus?"

"I think you will fare quite well without me," the Marquis said.

"It is certainly an excellent party," Sir Guy answered, "and I do not blame you for wishing to be alone with Fortuna. She is entrancing! I only wish I had seen her first."

The Marquis without answering turned away as if the subject bored him.

"Good-night," Fortuna said to Sir Guy, "and thank you very much."

He kissed her hand and would have whispered something in her ear. But before he could speak she had run after the Marquis. His Lordship had reached the door when Odette sped across the room to take his arm.

"You will come and see me tomorrow, Monsieur?" Fortuna heard her ask. "I wish to see you—verry, verry much. You understand? Yes? There is no one else—not yet."

"I perceive I must not waste time," the Marquis answered.

He would have raised her hand to his lips but she flung her arms round his neck and kissed him.

"I am 'appy—verry 'appy," Odette cried. *"A demain, mon brave."*

It seemed to Fortuna there was some deeper meaning in the words which she could not understand.

Then she and the Marquis were walking alone down the long corridor which led from the Ballroom to the main part of the house. When they entered the Hall a sleepy footman started to his feet.

"Order my carriage," the Marquis said.

"Very good, M'Lord."

The footman opened the door.

"Good-night Fortuna," the Marquis said. "I imagine you will sleep deeply after so much excitement."

"Good-night Apollo," Fortuna said in a low voice, "I will pray that you win."

The Marquis turned towards the door, then as Fortuna did not move but stood watching him he turned back.

"You have enjoyed tonight?" he asked. "The party did not shock you?"

"Shock me?" Fortuna asked. "N . . . no, it was most . . . enjoyable. But I liked last night the best, when I was alone with you."

She spoke simply, stating a fact. The Marquis looked down into her face and he was scowling.

"Good-night Fortuna," he said coldly and turned away quickly.

There was a sudden hurt in her eyes as she watched him go and wondered what she had said to annoy him.

4

The Marquis was stepping into his curricle when he saw Colonel Alistair Merrill hurrying down the pavement towards him.

"Good-morning, Alistair," the Marquis said. "I expected to see you last night at my party."

The Colonel drew the Marquis aside so that they were out of hearing of the servants.

"I posted to Eton," he said in a low voice. "I wished to have a look at my so-called cousin—the Viscount Merr."

"And what was your impression of him?" the Marquis asked.

"When I was cogitating over what you had related to me and what had been written in that letter from your old governess," the Colonel answered, "I remembered Grimwood quite clearly. I used to be at Merrill Park a great deal when I was looked on as the heir presumptive."

The Colonel's lips tightened for a moment, then he continued:

"I remembered more than once calling at the Grimwood's farm when I was hunting in that direction. On one occasion my horse went lame and I sat in the farmhouse to wait while the groom fetched another. Mrs. Grimwood gave me a glass of beer and a slice of homecured ham, and Grimwood came in from the fields."

"What did he look like?" the Marquis asked.

"He was a thick-set, strong looking fellow," the Colonel replied, "with dark hair. He was obviously a true countryman—a man born and bred in the fields."

The Colonel paused, and after a moment the Marquis said, tapping the top of his snuffbox with his finger:

"Well?"

It was a question.

"The Viscount Merr is the spitting image of him," the Colonel said impressively.

"It was what I expected," the Marquis said, "and now you are convinced, I hope, that this is no piece of moonshine."

"No, of course not!" the Colonel exclaimed. "I believed you anyway. But I wanted to have a look at the boy, and it was only with the greatest difficulty that I prevented myself from denouncing him. When I think of the way my uncle has managed to commit his damned crime and get away with it I . . ."

The Marquis held up his hand.

"Be careful, Alistair, you are raising your voice. No one must know what we suspect until we can prove conclusively what at the moment could be dismissed as the mere imaginings of a fertile mind."

"Proof!" Colonel Merrill said angrily. "Have a look at young Merr, and if you can find the very slightest resemblance to the Old Devil or to his wife it would be a miracle."

"And Fortuna?" the Marquis asked softly.

"Fortuna is my aunt's child," Colonel Merrill declared. "She is, therefore, the key to the whole problem. What trick have you up your sleeve at the moment, Sylvanus?"

"I will tell you in due course," the Marquis replied evasively. "In the meantime, instead of posting down to Eton or anywhere else, you should be talking. I expected you to be at my party last night."

"I returned too late to be present," the Colonel replied, "From what I hear it was a great success. Is is true that an Italian dancer took off her clothes and appeared in a naked pose such as we hear so much about on the Continent?"

"She performed most admirably," the Marquis answered coolly.

"And Fortuna was there?" the Colonel asked. "Good God, Sylvanus, surely . . ."

"Fortuna informed me she was not in the least shocked," the Marquis interrupted.

"Not shocked—that child!" Colonel Merrill ejaculated.

The Marquis smiled unpleasantly.

"Have you not realised, my dear Alistair, that Fortuna is indeed her father's daughter."

"I do not believe it," the Colonel said incredulously. "If, as I suspicion, you have a dislike of her because she is the Old Devil's daughter, do not punish her for his sins. I cannot credit she is anything but what she looks—pure and innocent."

"My dear Alistair, you are very trusting, are you not?" the Marquis sneered. "Anyway, the only thing we need concern ourselves with is the downfall of the Old Devil, and Fortuna, as you have already said, is not only our key to the problem but also our ace— an ace, remember, which the Duke so far does not realise we hold."

"And when are you going to confront him with it?" the Colonel asked.

"When I am ready," the Marquis replied. "In the meantime, instead of wasting your time at Eton post to Merrill Park. The Duke is in London, it is imperative that the Duchess should learn about Fortuna and be curious about her before the Duke returns."

Without waiting for a reply the Marquis turned away abruptly to enter his curricle and take up the reins. The Colonel stood still to watch him go until the smart turn-out was out of sight.

Then he walked away in the direction of St. James's.

The Marquis had not far to tool his horses. In Park Lane he drew up outside an imposing mansion, and on enquiring for Lady Charlotte Hadleigh he was told that Her Ladyship would receive him immediately.

Lady Charlotte was still in her bedchamber having her hair arranged by Monsieur Antoine, the most fashionable hairdresser of the moment, and being entertained as she did so by two elegantly attired gallants who were busy relating to her the latest news in the social world.

It had been the fashion during the late 1700's and at the beginning of the nineteenth century for ladies of fashion to receive their beaux in the morning while they performed their toilette and suffered the endless administrations of hairdressers, couturiers, milliners and abigails.

During the war the vogue had almost lapsed, and while Gentlemen met in each other's chambers and gossiped, the women bedecked themselves more modestly. Now the war was over Lady Charlotte, copied by many of her friends, had revived the custom of receiving while she robed.

When the Marquis was announced she jumped up eagerly.

"Sylvanus!" she exclaimed. "I was not expecting you at such an early hour. I was just hearing of your revels last night. They must have been extremely entertaining."

"They were indeed," the Marquis replied without enthusiasm.

"But I have no desire to speak of last night," Lady Charlotte went on, "it is today that matters, and you particularly."

She looked up at him seductively before turning to her other guests.

"You will forgive me, Gentlemen," she apologised, "but I have much to discuss with His Lordship. So I know you will grant me your pardon if I ask you to take your leave."

"It is always the same, My Lord," one of the gallants grumbled as he rose to his feet. "You pick the ripe plums while we are left with those for which you have no partiality."

"You flatter me," the Marquis replied drily.

"He is piqued, My Lord," the other Beau exclaimed. "He did not receive an invitation from you last night. May I on the other hand thank you for a most delightful evening."

"It was my pleasure," the Marquis answered conventionally.

The Gentlemen took their leave, the hairdresser bowed himself from the room, and Lady Charlotte and the Marquis were left alone. She was looking very lovely in a negligee which being of flame coloured chiffon set off her dark-haired beauty at its best.

As the door closed she held out her arms to the Marquis with an exaggerated gesture of surrender, and he realised that beneath the negligee her voluptuous figure was unashamedly naked.

"Sylvanus," she murmured invitingly.

He looked at her with an expression she could not fathom.

"I have desired so ardently to see you," she said,

"but now you are here I find it difficult to express my feelings."

"You must behave more circumspectly, Charlotte," the Marquis said reprovingly. "Your speaking to me in the Park yesterday will undoubtedly occur the disapproval of the patrons of Almack's."

"Do you think I care what those old hens say about me?" Lady Charlotte asked passionately. "Besides, what does a bit o' muslin matter where you and I are concerned?"

"You thought her attractive?'" the Marquis asked. Lady Charlotte shrugged her shoulders.

"I do not look at creatures like that," she replied, "and anyway, they are of no consequence. You can have as many lovebirds as you please, Sylvanus, but I wish to be something very different in your life."

"Am I allowed three guesses?" the Marquis enquired.

Lady Charlotte turned away from him and walked towards the window. She was aware that her figure was silhouetted against the light, and the Marquis was also aware that her action was deliberate. She stood for a moment looking out into the sunshine, then she turned and faced him.

"Listen to what I have to say, Sylvanus," she answered, "for it is of import both to you and to me."

"Your sense of hospitality is somewhat lacking this morning," the Marquis said. "May I be seated?"

"Of course," she replied.

She moved from the window to stand in front of him, steadying herself with one white hand against the carved and gilded cupids which ornamented the foot of her bed. White muslin drapery fell from a carved gold corolla; the sheets and pillow-cases edged with wide Venetian lace were embroidered with her monogram.

91

"Are you interested in what I have to say?" she asked when the Marquis had seated himself and drawn out his snuffbox.

"I am listening," he replied.

"You drive me wild, Sylvanus," she complained, her voice thickening with passion. Then with an effort she continued: "But we will speak of that later. What I have to tell you now is that at last poor George's Estate has been settled."

"It appears to have taken an unconscionable time," the Marquis commented.

"In fact three years," Lady Charlotte said. "After George was killed at Waterloo we discovered an endless tangle which has taken the lawyers until now to settle. Two days ago I was told the result."

"It is pleasant news, I hope," the Marquis said.

"Very pleasant," Lady Charlotte answered. "I am a very rich woman, Sylvanus. Does that mean anything to you?"

"Should it?" he enquired.

"Sylvanus, do not pretend to be so dense," Lady Charlotte cried impatiently. "I am rich, do you understand, perhaps one of the richest women in England. Marry me and every penny of it is yours!"

The Marquis shut his snuffbox with a snap.

"You were always unconventional," he said.

"What does it matter what I am?" she asked. "I love you, Sylvanus, I love you and I want you. Marry me and you can forget all this endless, boring chase for the money and lands the Duke tricked away from your father. I have vast estates in Leicestershire, but you can sell them if you wish and we will buy others.

"You can purchase anything that will please you, and you need no longer spend your time speculating as to whether you will gain or lose, conquer or be conquered."

The Marquis rose to his feet.

"I think this is the first time, Charlotte," he said slowly, "that I have actually received in so many words a proposal of marriage."

"What does it signify if I ask you or you ask me?" she enquired. "All I want, Sylvanus, is to be your wife. I attract you, I know that, and we shall deal well together. What more can you want than to be the possessor of many millions. And if it pleases you, you can keep your little lovebirds, so long as you kiss me when I ask it and let me know the thrill of your body close to mine."

Lady Charlotte moved nearer to the Marquis as she spoke, and reaching out her arms put them round his neck.

"What is your answer?" she asked, her lips very near to his.

The Marquis's arms went round her and she gave a little shudder of delight.

"Tell me," she whispered urgently, "tell me."

"My answer to your proposal of marriage," the Marquis said suavely, "is no. My answer to your second proposition is yes."

He crushed her close to him as he spoke and his lips were on hers, hard, brutal, passionate. He moved her backwards as he kissed her without her being aware of it, and only as he tumbled her onto the bed did she give a little cry of surprise.

But her arms were still round his neck and she drew him down with her.

Fortuna spent a lonely day in the house hoping that the Marquis would take her driving or return for lunch. When he did neither she went out into the courtyard and played with his Dalmatian dogs, who were also waiting for his return.

Madame Yvette came with more gowns, and Chambers enquired not once but half a dozen times if there was anything she would like to eat or drink.

The afternoon passed without a sign of the Marquis. Fortuna, feeling low and forgotten, had gone sadly upstairs to change for dinner, wondering if she must eat alone, when a footman came hurrying upstairs to find her lady's maid.

Fortuna was drying herself in front of the fire in her room after enjoying a scented bath when the maid knocked on the door.

"Who is it?" she asked.

" 'Tis me, Miss," the maid replied, entering and dropping a curtsy. "His Lorship's compliments, and will you dine with him in half of the hour."

"The Marquis is back!" Fortuna exclaimed, the joy in her voice making the words sound like a peal of bells.

"Yes, Miss, His Lordship's just come in. And he says, if you please, Miss, will you wear one of your best gowns."

"It means His Lordship will be taking me somewhere, perhaps to a party," Fortuna exclaimed. "Oh, how exciting it is! Quick, Mary, open the wardrobe and let us decide which of Madame Yvette's dresses is indeed my best. Thank goodness Mrs. Denvers sent for the hairdresser and he has arranged my hair in a new fashion. I wonder what I should wear?"

"Perhaps I had best decide for you," a voice remarked in the doorway.

Fortuna gave a little cry.

"I am so glad to see you, My Lord," she said. "I was half afraid you had forgotten me."

"It is unlikely I should do that," the Marquis replied.

94

He walked across the room to inspect the gowns hanging in the open wardrobe.

It was then Fortuna realised that she was draped only in a large white bath towel. It completely enveloped her, and she was less naked than she would have appeared had she been wearing an evening-gown.

At the same time she blushed a little, worrying not because it might seem indecent but because she felt she did not look attractive enough.

She cast a despairing look at the maid and went towards the chair on which lay an elegant robe of pale pink satin trimmed round the sleeves and hem with wide lace.

Mary realised what was required, and in a moment had held out the gown with her back to the Marquis so that Fortuna could slip her arms through the wide sleeves, letting the bath towel fall to the ground as she wrapped the robe tightly around her slim body.

The Marquis appeared quite unaware of what was occurring. He was concentrating on the gowns in the wardrobe, looking first at this one and then at another. Finally as Fortuna reached his side he held out the skirt of one.

"Wear this," he said briefly, and walked from the room as swiftly and as unexpectedly as he had entered it.

Fortuna stared after him and for a moment there was an expression of disappointment on her face. Then she exclaimed gaily:

"Quick, Mary, we must not keep His Lordship waiting. And this new gown may be difficult to fasten."

But when finally she was dressed, there was no doubt that the Marquis had chosen what she should wear with the eye of a connoisseur. The gown was of deep hyacinth blue embroidered with tiny dewdrops of diamante and ornamented with velvet ribbons the same colour.

There were tiny puff sleeves, and the bow of velvet ribbon sprinkled with diamante which she wore in her pale hair gave her a look of being very young and yet so surprisingly beautiful that it seemed as if the gown was part of the sky itself and ornamented with stars.

The Marquis made no comment when Fortuna came into the Salon before dinner, but she was woman enough to know that while his lips were silent he could not repress a sudden flash of admiration in his eyes. The knowledge that he found her attractive took away her shyness, and looking up at him under her dark eyelashes she said:

"Am I really to be honoured by having dinner alone with Your Lordship this evening? I am hoping that you will not find it exceeding dull after the many attractions that were provided for you last night."

"I regret I cannot promise you parties on such a lavish scale every evening," the Marquis replied.

Fortuna laughed.

"I hope not indeed. It was a wild extravagance, and I am persuaded that by the end of the evening half your guests had no idea whether they were drinking good or bad wine."

"The wine in my home is always the best," the Marquis replied, "but I regret that apparently it did not please you."

Fortuna dimpled at him.

"You noticed that Chambers brought me lemonade," she said. "He whispered to me that I would not like champagne, and he was quite right. To be honest I do not care particularly for wines."

"Having a vast experience of them, of course," the Marquis said sarcastically, "amongst your other accomplishments."

"Now you are being unkind," Fortuna protested. "But Gilly thought it was part of the education of every woman to know a little about wine, and I can order a proper menu without making obvious mistakes."

"You have so many talents!" the Marquis remarked.

It did not sound like a compliment.

"It was kind of Chambers to realise that I would not like to drink much," Fortuna said reflectively. "But then your staff are all so considerate and understanding. Do you know that Mrs. Denvers is so afraid that I might be disturbed by robbers, who she says are becoming a constant menace to the rich houses in the neighbourhood, that she locks the door of my bedchamber every night so that I shall not be frightened or disturbed."

She paused and went on:

"It is kind of her, is it not, because it means she has to stay up until after I have gone to bed."

She looked at the Marquis as she spoke, and to her surprise she saw a sudden frown between his eyebrows and the squaring of his chin which she knew by now signified that he was annoyed. Then the humour of it struck him.

That Fortuna should be looked after and protected against himself by his own servants brought a twist to his lips even as the door into the Dining Room was opened and dinner was announced.

Although dish followed dish, each more elaborate and delicious than the last, the time seemed to pass so quickly that not only Fortuna but even the Marquis discovered with some surprise that they had been talking for over an hour and a half when finally the servants left the room.

"I need not withdraw, need I?" Fortuna asked anxiously.

"Not if it pleases you to remain," the Marquis replied.

"Gilly told me that was the right way to behave," Fortuna said, "but I felt it could not matter when you and I were alone. Oh, Apollo, how nice this is! You have not been bored, have you?"

"No, you have interested me," the Marquis said truthfully.

Fortuna had been telling him of the country round Little Waterless, of the Duke's influence on the neighbourhood, and of people Miss Gillingham had treated with herbs. She had chattered away unselfconsciously and she had even argued with the Marquis on some subjects.

He forgot to be bitter or to sneer, and found indeed it was impossible to do either with Fortuna's eyes looking adoringly at him and being so certain that when the time came he could undo the harm that the Duke had perpetrated in a thousand ways since he had taken over the Thane estates.

Finally, as the Marquis finished his glass of port, he said:

"Now I am taking you to the Palace of Fortune."

"A party?" Fortuna asked.

"Not exactly," the Marquis said.

His voice seemed to change, becoming reserved and hard again as it had not been during the past hour.

"What is the Palace of Fortune?" Fortuna asked. "Do people game there?"

"They do indeed," the Marquis replied, "and it is a new meeting place of amusement. I have been told that the Duke will be there tonight."

"And I am to come with you?" Fortuna asked excitedly. "Shall I see you play?"

"You will," the Marquis said, "but I have something I wish you to do for me, Fortuna."

"You know I will do anything you ask," she said quickly.

"Then if you would please me you must carry out my instructions very carefully," the Marquis told her. "When we reach this place I will tell you exactly what I require."

"Will I meet the Duke?" she asked.

"I will present you to His Grace," the Marquis said.

"I suppose I cannot tell him how much I hate him?" Fortuna asked. "Or how greatly I despise him for how he has ill-treated those poor people in Waterless, and the farmers who have watched their roofs fall in over their heads and found they could not afford to till their fields?"

"You will not speak of such matters," the Marquis replied, and his tone was sharp. "You will curtsy, and I have a feeling His Grace will not ask you many questions. If he does, be careful what you say. And no rudeness, Fortuna! That I absolutely forbid."

"I understand," Fortuna said in a low voice. "But I loathe the Duke for all he has done, you realise that."

"It is apparently almost a personal problem where you are concerned!" the Marquis said enigmatically, rising to his feet. "Get your cloak."

"We are leaving at once?" Fortuna asked.

"At once," the Marquis replied.

They drove to their destination in the Marquis's closed landau, an elegant vehicle, the interior padded comfortably and lit by a candle in a silver lantern.

"This is very exciting," Fortuna said happily.

The Marquis noted that she was wearing not a cloak but a wrap of the same material as her dress and edged

99

with marabou. It made her appear very young, almost like a small fluffy new-born chick.

"Now you must do exactly what I tell you to do, Fortuna," the Marquis admonished her.

She had the impression, although she was not sure why, that he was nervous.

"You know I only desire to please you," she replied.

"This is all I ask," the Marquis said.

The landau drew up outside an impressive-looking entrance where linkmen with torches were helping guests to alight, and there appeared to be innumerable powdered flunkeys in flamboyant uniforms of purple, rather vulgarly bedecked with gold braid and sparkling buttons.

The Marquis alighted first, and taking Fortuna by the arm walked through the open door and past the bowing menials. Without pausing for Fortuna to see the murals of naked gods and goddesses, he took her quickly up a narrow carpeted staircase which led to the first floor of the building.

She found as they reached the top that they were on a balcony which encircled a huge hall. On each side were a number of doors, each one numbered, but at the far end there was a break in the symmetry of the balcony.

It was towards this that the Marquis led Fortuna.

She tried to see what was happening beneath them. There was a sound of laughter, of music and the chatter of many tongues.

Then before she had time to perceive what was happening, the Marquis had opened the door of a tiny room and led her into it. She found that it was little more than a cupboard save that it had a window overlooking the gaieties below.

"This belongs to the proprietor," the Marquis explained, speaking for the first time since they had left the carriage, "but he has lent it to me this evening and no one will disturb you. Lock the door on the inside and on no account leave here until I give you a signal."

"What signal?" Fortuna asked.

The Marquis took her to the small window and let her look below. There were six large alcoves, or rather rooms in which one wall had been taken away, opening on a centre hall in the middle of which a small fountain threw scented water into a carved bowl.

In four of the alcoves there were gaming tables, some large, some small, and already they were thronged with people throwing golden guineas on the green cloth or watching the turn of the cards on which it appeared immense sums of money were changing hands.

In another alcove, which was barely lit except by a few candles cunningly concealed behind coloured shields, there was dancing.

In the sixth there were tables groaning under succulent dishes, and flunkeys passing amongst the guests filling to the brim the crystal glasses they held in their hands.

It was all very colourful, and Fortuna looked first this way and then that until finally she felt the pressure of the Marquis's hand on her shoulder and knew that he intended to look at one alcove where the tables were smaller and intended for four players only.

This place was not so occupied as the others. At the far end Fortuna could see with his back to a long red curtain an old man.

She could feel the tension in the Marquis and knew without asking who it was.

The Duke, she thought, was just how she had expected him to look—old, ugly and sinister, his claw-

101

like hands resting on the table, his hooded eyes staring down at the cards. He was not playing, although two men were sitting on either side of him.

They were waiting, Fortuna felt, waiting for one person to join them.

"Now listen carefully," the Marquis said. "I shall leave you and go downstairs to play with the Duke. You will watch me, and in about an hour or perhaps longer I shall drop my handerchief on the floor. When that happens you come downstairs. Do you understand? When you see the handkerchief, that is the signal. Just come and stand beside me. Do not speak, wait for me to speak to you. Stand in silence at the side of my chair."

He spoke sharply as though he were on the quarter-deck of a man-o'-war giving his orders.

"I understand," Fortuna answered.

"And when I have departed, lock the door," the Marquis said. "You are not to open it whatever you hear, whatever happens, until you come down to me."

"I will lock it," Fortuna told him.

"Then watch carefully," the Marquis admonished her. "Do not miss the signal because when I drop my handerkerchief a flunkey will pick it up almost immediately. You must be watching, Fortuna."

"I promise I will watch you all the time," she answered.

The Marquis opened the door of the small room.

"Lock this door," he said again, and then he was gone.

Fortuna did as she had been told and drew the hard chair which was the only furniture in the room besides a small desk up to the window and sat looking below.

It was gay and colourful, but she noticed that the women were even more décolleté than the dancers of the Corps de Ballet had been the night before. Their dresses seemed cheap and rather tawdry, while they themselves had a flamboyant vulgarity she had never seen before.

It was obvious that some of the Gentlemen had already wined too well.

They walked unsteadily, and when any of the ladies threw her arms around their neck they were drawn easily and without protestation to one of the comfortable sofas which Fortuna now saw were standing in many secluded places and sometimes screened with flowers.

The decorations were garish but attractive. There were innumerable mirrors, statues of naked goddesses and murals crudely executed on the walls and ceilings. The dancing was rough and noisy.

Many of the dancers fell down, embracing each other where they fell. At the gambling tables there seemed often to be altercation and noisy exchanges of words, only in the alcove where the Duke was waiting was there comparative peace and quiet.

Fortuna watched the Marquis cross the floor. He looked tall and handsome, but at the same time proud, disdainful and disinterested in the noise and gaiety around him.

People seemed instinctively to clear a path for him, he had no need to push his way through the crowd. When he reached the gaming table where the Duke was sitting the other two Gentlemen rose, bowed and retreated into the background.

The Duke did not even look up. A fresh pack of cards was put on the table and he took it between his bony fingers.

"Apollo must win tonight, he must," Fortuna said beneath her breath, clasping her hands together.

She found herself willing him to win, to beat the

dissolute old man who faced him. It became a prayer. She could not tell from where she was sitting if he was gaining or losing, she only felt as if a power within herself went out towards the Marquis to protect him, to bring him luck—a luck which he thought had changed when she had come to London.

She was so intent on sending her thoughts towards the Marquis that it was some time before she realised that quite distinctly she could hear someone crying.

"Help . . . oh help me!"

It was a pathetic sound, a sound of someone very young in distress.

"Help me . . . oh please . . . help!"

The voice was choked with tears, and yet there was no doubt it was desperate in its appeal. Fortuna tried not to hear. The Marquis had said she was not to open the door whatever she heard or whatever happened.

"Help . . . h . . . help."

Fortuna rose to her feet. The Marquis would be angry, but she knew she could not remain aloof when that cry of help came to her ears so piteously.

She turned the key in the door and opened it a little. There appeared to be no one about. Then she saw a little to the right that a door opening onto the balcony at the other side of the passage was half open. In the aperture there stood a girl.

"Help . . . help . . . help me," she whispered, and the tears were running down her face.

Fortuna slipped onto the balcony, closing the door behind her.

"What is it?" she asked. "What is the matter?"

The girl who was crying was very young. Her round face was blotched with tears, the mascara on her eyelashes had run, her lips which had been reddened were smudged, and her hair which was a golden brown was falling about her shoulders in disarray.

104

"How can I help you?" Fortuna asked as it seemed almost impossible for the girl to speak.

"I don't . . . know what to . . . do," she sobbed. "He be . . . dead, I'm sure he be . . . dead. It weren't my fault . . . I swear to you, Miss, it weren't . . . my fault."

"Who is dead?" Fortuna asked.

The girl, who was clinging to the doorway as if to support herself, moved back and Fortuna entered the room.

She had a quick impression of a table laden with food and wine, of a bed at the far end draped with curtains, of two chairs which had been upset and a wine-bucket knocked over.

Lying among the debris was the body of a Gentleman.

"I didn't . . . mean to kill . . . him, I swear . . . I didn't," the girl cried. "He were achasing . . . me and I were . . . feared. I tried to . . . push him away. I struggled and . . . suddenly he went all . . . queer. He made a . . . choking sound in his . . . throat and fell down . . . on the floor . . . breathed heavy-like, then . . . was . . . still."

She whimpered like an animal.

"He be . . . dead . . . I knows he be . . . dead, and she'll say . . . I killed him."

Fortuna stood looking down at the man on the floor. He was very old, she thought, with white hair, and he had a cruel and unpleasant face. There were bags of dissipation under his eyes, and his lips were thin and drawn back over decayed teeth.

"Who is he?" she asked.

"I don't know," the girl answered in a voice which had a country burr in it. "I were told I had to . . . dine with him and . . . do as he . . . asked. I know nawt about . . . him. I comes to London from Waterless

105

three days ago and . . . she kept me locked up. I wants to go back to my Ma, that's what I wants. But she'll say I killed him . . . I knows she will."

Tears fell afresh.

"You come from Waterless?" Fortuna asked. "Stop crying, you must tell me about yourself."

Her voice was a command, and the girl made an effort to stop her frightened sobs.

"M' family lives in Waterless," she said. "But there be no work for my Pa there . . . so as I be nigh on fifteen I comes to London to be a housemaid or work in the kitchens of the Quality. But a Lady speaks to I when I steps off the coach and tells me she has employment for me. 'I'll give you good money,' she says, 'money you can send home to your family.' "

There was a pause and the girl covered her face with her hands.

"I didn't know it'd be this sort of . . . place, I swear I didn't. The Lady gives I somewat strange to drink. It made me that sleepy I didn't know what be ahappening. Then tonight her dresses me up . . . says I be a lucky girl and brings me in here to . . . him."

Fortuna said nothing, and after a moment the girl went on:

"I was . . . feared . . . feared by what he says to me. Then he starts atearing my gown. There'll be trouble . . . over that . . . too."

She moved her hands from her face and Fortuna saw the white gown she wore, trimmed with a coarse white lace, had been torn from one breast, leaving her partially naked.

"She'll blame I for . . . that," the girl said, still in that frightened plaintive voice, and Fortuna could see she was shaking. "I don't know what she'll do to me . . . the other girls told I she be real cruel . . . when she be angry."

106

"What do you want to do?" Fortuna asked.

"I wants to go . . . home . . . I wants to go back to my Ma. This place be . . . bad . . . and I didn't know there could be . . . Gentlemen who'd behave like . . . him.'

She glanced at the dead man lying on the floor and once again burst into tears.

"She'll say I done it . . . I swear she'll say I done it," she sobbed. "He were bad . . . I tell you . . . the things he said and . . . his hands. I had to try and . . . escape . . . I had to."

"Yes, of course you did," Fortuna said.

It seemed as though she suddenly made up her mind.

"Come with me," she said.

Taking the girl by the hand she led her out onto the balcony, closing the door behind them. She glanced to the right and to the left, but there was no one in sight, only the noise coming up from below which seemed to hit her like a tidal wave.

She drew the girl into the small room on the other side of the landing. She shut the door and locked it.

"Sit down," she said, indicating the only chair.

The girl obeyed her, trying to wipe away the tears from her cheeks with the knuckles of her hands—strong country girl's hands, freckled in the sun and hardened by work.

There was something intensely pathetic, Fortuna thought, in the way that the girl, who ought to have been a milkmaid or in charge of the chickens on the farm, had been decked out in a vulgar white dress, her hair arranged in some semblance of a fashionable style, her face coated with powder and painted with rouge and lipsalve to make her appear fashionable.

Now that the cosmetics had run and been smudged by her tears, she looked exactly what she was—a

107

country girl who had got lost in a strange world of which she had no comprehension or knowledge.

"I am going to find someone to help you," Fortuna said.

"She'll have I up for . . . murder when she finds . . . him," the girl gasped. "She'll never believe I didn't kill . . . him."

"I am going to find someone who will make her understand," Fortuna promised her. "Now stay here. Lock the door when I have gone and do not let anyone in unless you hear my voice."

She remembered guiltily that the Marquis had told her to lock the door and not open it. She glanced through the window. He was still sitting opposite the Duke, but there was no sign of his handkerchief on the floor.

It was useless to wait, she thought, he may even have given the signal while she was away. She must go to him, she must help this frightened girl.

"What is your name?" she asked.

"Emmeline . . . Emmeline Higgins," the girl replied. "Oh Miss, can you really help me? I be feared . . . I've never been so feared as I be now."

"Do not be frightened," Fortuna said. "I promise that I will bring you help. Now, do exactly as I told you, Emmeline. Lock the door and clean your face."

She handed her own handkerchief to the girl, then leaving her wrap on the chair she opened the door to go downstairs.

"Do not let anybody in," she turned to say.

"I won't . . . I swear I won't," the girl answered. "Oh Miss, God bless you for being kind to me. I thought I were done for . . . I did really."

Fortuna smiled at her; then she shut the door, heard the key turn in the lock inside and walked towards the staircase.

5

As Fortuna reached the stairs she saw that there were two people ascending it. Realising she would be unable to pass them she waited on the landing.

She noticed that the girl, who was dressed in white, seemed shy or reluctant to walk upstairs, and the Gentleman put his arm through hers as if to urge her upwards.

Then as they came nearer Fortuna saw that the girl, who had a pretty but vacant face, was, in fact, only a child.

She could not have been more than twelve years of age, and it appeared as if she were half asleep, moving almost as if she was drugged.

Only as the couple stepped from the stairs onto the landing did Fortuna look at the Gentleman. At the same time his eyes met hers and he gave an exclamation.

"Surely," he said in a silky voice which she remembered all too well, "it is the little Lady who ran away from me?"

Fortuna was suddenly tense. She recognised the heavy florid face, the lustful eyes and the licentious mouth of the man who had frightened her in the street off Berkeley Square and from whom she had escaped only to be nearly run down by the Marquis in his Phaeton.

109

"Are you accompanied?" he asked, his voice seeming to grate on every nerve of her body. "Or are you here in search of an escort?"

"I am with the Marquis of Thane," Fortuna said coldly, striving not to feel frightened, not to run away as she had done before.

"So you have sold yourself to the Young Devil," the Gentleman said sneeringly. "Well, he will soon tire of you, and then you can come to me. My name is Sir Roger Crowley—let me give you my card."

He fumbled in the breast pocket of his evening coat. Then, as Fortuna stood silent, he added—and every word seemed a threat:

"I will make good provision for you, but you will not escape me again."

He would have put out his hand to touch Fortuna but the child who was with him seemed about to collapse. She swayed on her feet and Sir Roger was forced to hold her up.

This made room for Fortuna to squeeze past him and run down the stairs. She did not speak or look back but hurried as quickly as she could away from the man who filled her with revulsion as no one in her life had ever done before.

She felt he was staring after her; she imagined his lewd eyes scrutinising every movement of her body, his thick lips smiling as if he knew she could not evade him for long.

She reached the floor below and pushing her way through the crowd sped towards the alcove where the Marquis was playing.

Several Gentlemen as she passed attempted to arrest her flight, but she shook herself free and reached the Marquis's side somewhat breathless, her heart pounding, but nevertheless with the feeling that now she was

110

safe because he was there, because she was close to him.

The Marquis was so intent on his game that he was not for the moment conscious of her presence. Then with a catch in her breath she said in a whisper:

"My Lord . . . I must speak . . . with you."

He glanced up and she saw first surprise and then anger in his face.

"I am . . . sorry," she said in a low voice which only he could hear. "I know I should not be here . . . but there is . . . someone who needs your help . . . needs it urgently. Please come upstairs. You know that I would not disturb you if it were not a . . . matter of life and . . . death."

"I told you, Fortuna . . ." the Marquis thundered, only to be interrupted by a voice from the other side of the table.

"It is your play, Thane."

The Duke's tone was impatient.

"Please . . . Apollo . . . please," Fortuna pleaded.

For a moment she thought he was going to refuse her, then his expression changed and he looked towards the Duke.

"Your Grace must grant me your pardon," he said, "but I am informed that something has occurred which most urgently requires my attention."

"It is your play, Thane," the Duke repeated querulously.

For the first time since Fortuna had reached the Marquis's side the Old Devil raised his eyes.

"It would seem inconceivable, Your Grace," the Marquis said clearly but without raising his voice, "that anything should be more important than our game. But apparently we are mistaken. May I present Miss Grimwood?"

The Duke's eyes, which had been fixed on the Mar-

111

quis, turned indifferently to glance at Fortuna. For a moment he stared at her and it seemed as if she made no impact upon him.

Then he was seemingly frozen into immobility, but the Marquis, watching him closely, saw the fingers of his old blue-veined hands lying on the table contract.

Fortuna sank down in a curtsy.

"I understand," the Marquis continued, "that Miss Grimwood was actually born on Your Grace's Estate."

The Duke did not answer. His eyes were fixed on Fortuna, and he was so still that there was something uncanny about it.

The Marquis rose to his feet and threw his cards down on the table.

"I think, Your Grace," he said, "it would be simpler if our game up this moment was held of no account. I am, I reckon, at this moment the gainer, but since I must inconvenience you by leaving you must permit me to erase this play from the record."

"You—are—leaving?"

The words, slow and hardly audible, showed that the Duke was not really aware of what he was saying.

"Miss Grimwood says she has need of me," the Marquis replied. "I may be able to return to challenge Your Grace this evening, but if not I hope we will encounter each other on another occasion which will not be too long delayed."

He bowed. Once again Fortuna realised she must curtsy, and she swept to the ground hoping that her dislike of the Duke did not show itself in her expression. Then she turned impulsively to the Marquis, reaching out both her hands to hold on to his arm.

They moved away, and only as they left the alcove did the Marquis glance back to note with satisfaction that the Duke's eyes were still on Fortuna's hair.

They had some difficulty in manoeuvring themselves

through the crowds in the main Hall. When they reached the staircase the Marquis asked:

"What has occurred? Why did you not carry out my orders?"

"Forgive me . . . please forgive . . . me," Fortuna pleaded, "but you must help someone in . . . dire distress. There is a Gentleman who is . . . dead."

"Dead!" the Marquis ejaculated. "And if he is, what is that to do with you? I told you not to leave the place where I had put you until I gave you my signal."

"I . . . I . . . know," Fortuna faltered, "but I heard someone crying . . . for help . . . it was . . . desperate and I could not . . . ignore it."

"Whatever has happened is nothing to do with us." the Marquis said. "Come, we will leave."

They were only a few steps up the stairway and he turned as if to descend.

"No! no!" Fortuna cried, putting out her hands to hold onto him. "You cannot desert this girl, Apollo. She comes from Waterless . . . she is one of your people . . . your responsibility."

"Waterless," the Duke said firmly, "as you well know is on the Duke's Estate. No one there is any concern of mine."

"They are, of course they are!" Fortuna contradicted. "Can you not understand? It is only a question of time before you will be in a position to help people like Emmeline Higgins. She came to London to seek employment because there was not work for her father in Waterless. Oh, Apollo, you must help . . . you must!"

"I will not involve myself . . . the Marquis began loftily, but as he looked down into Fortuna's eyes he found the words dying on his lips.

There was the same look of trust in them, he

113

thought, that he had seen so often in his dogs, an expression of unquestioning faith.

Though he knew that if he had any commonsense he would take Fortuna away at once and leave behind whatever unsavoury situation she had discovered, he could not do so.

"Very well, I will see this girl," he said disagreeably.

Fortuna slipped her hand into his and drew him up the stairs. She opened the door of the room from where she had rescued Emmeline. The body of the Gentleman was lying on the floor. His sightless eyes were wide and staring, his fingers clenched together as if in a last spasm of pain.

"Lord Beaslow!" the Marquis said almost as if he spoke to himself.

"Do you know him? Fortune asked. "He is dead . . . I think."

The Marquis made no effort to investigate. He had seen enough men die in battle to know when it was too late to help them in any way.

"He is dead," he said briefly.

"Emmeline was afraid she had . . . killed him," Fortuna whispered. "He was struggling with her . . . tearing at her . . . gown. But I think that . . . there must have been something wrong . . . with his . . . heart."

"I am not a physician," the Marquis said, "but I imagine Lord Beaslow died either of a stroke or a heart attack."

"Then will you tell Emmeline so," Fortuna begged. "She is terribly distressed . . . and please . . . we must take her . . . away from here."

"That is impossible!" the Marquis said firmly. "The women here,"—he paused, and it was obvious he chose his words with care—"are under—er—contract to the proprietress."

114

"No, that is not true!" Fortuna protested. "The proprietress, if that is who it was, inveigled Emmeline into this place with the promise of employment. She came to London to become a housemaid or to work in the kitchens of some Lady's or Gentleman's house. A woman met her when she stepped off the stage-coach and promised her money that she could send back to her family."

Fortuna paused and looked at the Marquis. It seemed to her that his expression was forbidding, and she said pleadingly:

"Oh, please . . . let us take her away . . . she is only fifteen, and wishes to return to her mother . . . perhaps you could find her a place in your household . . . but whatever else we do . . . she cannot remain . . . here."

"Where is the wench?" the Marquis asked.

As he spoke he moved from the room. Fortuna followed him, closing the door behind her. In the passage the Marquis said:

"I imagine you have put her in the place where I left you, Fortuna. Let me inform you that this is none of our business. I cannot interfere with the internal arrangements which are made here."

His lips tightened.

"You would not understand, but it is something which cannot be done. A suggestion of that sort would, I promise you, involve me in a great deal of unpleasantness."

"But we cannot . . . leave her . . . we cannot . . . Apollo! She belongs to you . . . she is one of your people . . . Waterless was your father's and it will be yours. It is impossible for us to leave her here in a state of terror. Besides, if that woman does not punish Emmeline for the death of the Gentleman . . . will

115

she not make her dine with . . . others . . . like . . . him?"

There was sheer horror in Fortuna's low voice. The Marquis, with his mouth set in a grim line, crossed the passage. Fortuna followed him with a sudden gleam of hope in her eyes.

"Emmeline," she cried, "Emmeline, open the door."

There was the sound of a key turning in the lock and the Marquis entered the small room. Emmeline had cleaned her face with Fortuna's handkerchief, but she had obviously continued crying for the tears still glistened on her cheeks and her eyelashes were wet.

Without cosmetics the tawdry, low-cut evening-gown looked even more incongruous. It was obvious that at fifteen Emmeline had not yet grown to maturity, and with her untidy hair and pale tear-stained face she looked nothing but a frightened child.

"You are Emmeline Higgins?" the Marquis asked.

Emmeline bobbed him a curtsy.

"Yes . . . Sir."

"And you came to London to seek employment."

"Yes . . . Sir."

"Have you signed any piece of paper since you have been in this place?"

"No, Sir . . . I can't write . . . Sir."

The Marquis did not speak for a moment and Emmeline, her voice suddenly broken with tears, cried:

"I didn't kill him, Sir . . . I swear I didn't . . . kill him!"

"I believe you," the Marquis said, and turned to Fortuna.

"Stay here," he commanded, "do not dare to open the door again until you hear my voice. And this time obey me."

He was gone before Fortuna could reply. Locking

116

the door behind him she turned to the sobbing Emmeline and put her arms round her shoulders.

"It is all right," she said soothingly. "I knew His Lordship would help you, I knew in my heart that he would . . . understand."

It was over an hour later that the coachman tooled the Marquis's landau from the Palace of Fortune back towards Berkeley Square.

Inside the carriage the Marquis and Fortuna sat on the cushioned seat while opposite them with her back to the horses sat Emmeline Higgins. Attired in her own clothes, a dress of thick cambric, a woolen shawl, a plain straw bonnet and thick laced boots, she looked what she was—a decent girl from the country.

They drove in silence. Only as the lights from the Palace of Fortune flickered out of their sight did Fortuna slip her small hand beneath the rug into that of the Marquis. She did not have to say the words, he knew that she was thanking him.

As he did not take his hand away she felt he understood.

When they arrived at Berkeley Square and moved into the brilliantly lighted Hall, the Marquis said to his Major-domo:

"Send for Mrs. Denvers."

He turned to Fortuna.

"Go into the Salon and wait for me."

Fortuna hesitated and glanced at Emmeline, who was staring around her with an awed expression on her face.

"At once, Fortuna," the Marquis said commandingly, and she obeyed him.

A footman came into the Salon, lit the fire and brought in a large silver tray on which there were drinks and crystal glasses.

"Mr. Chambers said I was to ask if you wished to partake of any refreshment, Miss?" he enquired respectfully.

"No, thank you," Fortuna answered.

She found it impossible to sit down, wondering what the Marquis was saying to Emmeline, what arrangements he was making about her. At the same time Fortuna asked herself again and again whether the Marquis was very incensed with her for disobeying his command?

She felt so afraid that her mouth was dry and her knees felt weak. She remembered the anger in his voice and the forbidding expression on his face as they had left the Palace of Fortune."

"Please God, make him forgive me," she prayed.

It seemed to her as though she waited a very long time before finally the Marquis appeared, coming into the room without hurry.

She could not read from the expression on his face what he was feeling, but she felt it was ominous that he did not look at her!

She stood waiting as he approached the fireplace. He went to the grog tray and with what appeared to be deliberate slowness helped himself to a glass of brandy and sat down in the chair he habitually occupied, a tall, wing-backed armchair to the right of the fireplace.

Fortuna waited trembling for him to speak. Finally, when he had sipped his brandy and placed the glass beside him on a small polished table, he looked at her and said sternly:

"I expect to be obeyed."

"I know it was wrong of me," Fortuna said in a low voice, "but I could not help it . . . I swear to you I could not . . . help it."

118

There was a pause, and because she could contain her curiosity no longer Fortuna asked:

"What have you arranged about Emmeline?"

"Mrs. Denvers knows of a position which she believes will suit the girl," the Marquis answered. "It is, I understand, that of fourth housemaid in the residence of one of my relatives, who wrote to Mrs. Denvers recently to ask her assistance in finding someone suitable."

Fortuna gave a little sound that was half a laugh and half a cry. Then she flung herself down on the hearth-rug at the Marquis's feet.

"Oh, Apollo," she said joyously, "I knew you would not fail! I knew you would help that poor girl. It is wonderful of you! Now she need not go home and admit that she is a failure. She can do what she came to do, work in a respectable household and send the money back to her family. Thank you, thank you more than I can ever say."

"You can show your gratitude another time," the Marquis replied coldly, "by not disobeying my orders and thereby involving me in such an unpleasant and extremely expensive situation."

"It cost you money?" Fortuna asked anxiously.

"Quite a considerable sum," the Marquis said sourly. "The proprietress, as I quite rightly assumed, considered that the chit was her property."

"But how could she be?" Fortuna enquired. "Emmeline did not wish to go to a place like that or be decked out in a vulgar gown and have her face painted to please that horrible old man."

She stopped and after a moment said in a low voice:

"There is . . . something I do not . . . understand."

"What is that?" the Marquis asked.

119

The fire which had been lit by the footman had kindled brightly and the flames made an iridescent halo for Fortuna's pale hair.

She looked very ethereal as she sat at the Marquis's feet, her gown glittering as if it was flecked with tiny stars, but her eyes, which were raised to him, were dark and troubled.

"What do you not understand?" he asked surprisingly gently.

"L . . . last night," Fortuna said a little hesitatingly, "I thought that the ladies you had . . . invited to come in after dinner were like the . . . Hetaerae of Greece. I had read about them in a book."

"I cannot credit that Gilly thought that was a suitable subject for your studies," the Marquis said drily.

"Gilly did not give me the book," Fortuna answered, "I found it in the Squire's Library. I think it was by Lucian."

"I have an idea of the volume you read," the Marquis said.

"Then you will remember," Fortuna went on, "that it said there were intelligent and lovely women who were called Hetaerae who consorted with politicians and statesmen. A large number of them amused and entertained Alexander the Great after he captured Persepolis."

She made a little movement with her hands and added:

"I thought last night that . . . you were like . . . Alexander."

"The Hetaerae of Greece!" the Marquis said almost beneath his breath. "So that was why you were not shocked."

He looked down at her and his expression hardened.

"And what about the woman who undressed?" he enquired.

"Gilly always told me," Fortuna replied, "there was nothing . . . wrong or . . . wicked in . . . nakedness as long as it was . . . beautiful."

Then her eyelashes flickered for a moment and a faint colour rose in her cheeks.

"It is rather . . . different," she continued in a low voice, "'. . . seeing such . . . things . . . rather than reading about them."

"So I imagine," the Marquis remarked.

"But the . . . Ladies last night were gay and pretty," Fortuna went on, still in a hesitating voice as if she were puzzling things out to herself, "and I could . . . understand Gentlemen wanting to . . . look at them and to . . . talk to them, but I cannot believe that . . . anyone would want to talk for long to poor Emmeline. And the girl . . . the very, very young girl that . . . Sir Roger Crowley was with . . . tonight seemed . . ."

"Sir Roger Crowley?" the Marquis interrupted abruptly. "You saw him?"

"He came up the stairs when . . . I was seeking you," Fortuna explained.

"Did he speak to you?"

Fortuna dropped her head so that he could not see her face.

"I asked you," the Marquis said sharply, "did he speak to you?"

"Y . . . yes."

"What did he say?"

"I would . . . rather not t . . . tell . . . you."

"I insist! Do you hear me? Tell me what he said."

"He . . . said," and Fortuna whispered so low that the Marquis could hardly hear her, "that you would . . . weary of . . . me, and then I should . . . go to . . . him. He wanted to give me . . . his card. I ran away from . . . him . . . once again. But he told

121

me . . . I would be . . . unable to . . . es . . .
escape . . . him."

There was silence, then suddenly Fortuna laid her
cheek against the Marquis's knee and in a small
broken voice whispered:

"If you weary of . . . me, please do not . . . send
me . . . away. I will do anything you say . . . I
swear I will . . . obey you. But if you turn me . . .
from the . . . house I would be . . . frightened . . .
very, very . . . frightened."

"That will not happen," the Marquis said, and his
voice was firm. "And I promise you, Fortuna, that
whatever occurs in the future, I will see that you are
provided for."

"He . . . said that . . . I would be . . . unable
to . . . escape him."

"If Crowley approaches you again I will deal with
him," the Marquis said, and his voice was grim. "Forget him, forget what happened tonight."

"Can I?"

Fortuna looked up at him and he saw her eyes were
full of tears.

"You will never go to such a place again," the Marquis told her, "that I promise you."

"It was evil!" Fortuna said slowly. "That is why I
cannot understand why . . . someone like you . . .
should want to go . . . there."

"I have told you, Fortuna, forget about it," the
Marquis commanded. "Are you already disobeying
me?"

"No . . . I promise you I am . . . not," she answered. "It is just that I did not expect to find so many
things in London which puzzle me. I will try not to
think of . . . them, but I keep remembering that . . .
horrible man who frightened . . . Emmeline and the

face of that . . . child with . . . Sir Roger Crowley."

The Marquis suddenly rose to his feet.

"If Gilly were alive," he said harshly, "I should send you back to her now and at once."

"You would send me . . . away?" Fortuna cried. "Oh, please do not say . . . that. You are angry with . . . me, and indeed everything has gone wrong this evening. I was so . . . excited when I thought you were taking me out to a . . . party, and it was so wonderful that we dined together . . . alone."

She gave a little sob.

"Now everything is . . . ruined. You are incensed and it is . . . my fault for not obeying you. Please . . . forgive me . . . I will not ask any more nonsensical questions. It is only that I want to be clever and intelligent and not to make stupid mistakes so that you are . . . bored with me."

The Marquis turned round to look at her, a small glittering figure on the floor with tragic grey eyes.

"I think it is time," he said, "that you went to bed."

"No! no!" Fortuna protested, "I could not sleep. I should lie awake thinking of all the foolish things I have done to annoy you, unless . . ."

It seemed as if a sudden thought had struck her.

". . . unless you wish to go out to play cards with the Duke or perhaps to find some lovely Hetaera to amuse you as . . . I am unable . . . to do."

The Marquis sat down again in the chair he had recently vacated.

"You are very young," he said in a surprisingly gentle voice. "Will it please you if I say I have no longer any wish for gaming this evening, and that I find you quite as amusing as any Greek Hetaira, who I have the suspicion may have been over flattered by Lucian and Aristophanes."

Fortuna gave a little cry.

"Oh, you have read his comedies. I was wondering whether I dared confess that I had read them too."

"In the Squire's Library?" the Marquis enquired.

Fortuna nodded.

"I have the idea," the Marquis said, a twinkle in his eye, "that you were not only a somewhat rebellious pupil of Gilly's, but also a deceitful one."

"I did not really mean to be deceitful," Fortuna protested, "but Gilly was always so busy with her herbs, and sometimes when she grew older she used to get impatient when I asked too many questions. And so I tried to puzzle things out for myself."

"And did you succeed?" the Marquis asked in an amused voice.

"Sometimes," Fortuna answered, "but not always. There was one word in those particular books I could never translate."

"And did you ask someone to help you?" the Marquis enquired.

"Yes, I asked the Vicar," Fortuna replied. "He was a Greek scholar, but somehow I think I must have shocked him. Anyway, he looked embarrassed and I felt as if he debated in himself whether he should answer me or not. Then he decided he would do so, and he said: "The word means to ravish". And with that he shut up the books and I knew it was no use asking him any more."

"And did that explain what you wanted to know?" the Marquis enquired.

"Not exactly," Fortuna answered, "because when I looked up ravish in the dictionary it said—'to enrapture, charm, fill with delight'. And ravishment means—"ecstatic delight'."

She was silent for a moment, a little frown between

124

her eyebrows as though she was concentrating on a tangle. The Marquis watched her.

"You see," she said at length, "I thought that was what the Hetaerae would give to the men they entertained. But there was no "ecstatic delight" about poor Emmeline tonight, and somehow I feel that she would not . . . enrapture anyone, however nice and hardworking she may be."

The Marquis bent forward to take Fortuna's chin in his fingers and turned her face up to his.

"Will you listen to me?" he asked in a deep voice. "Stop worrying your head over what happened in Greece or what happens here. In such places as we went to tonight you may be Miss Nobody, as you call yourself, Fortuna, but you are still a Lady. You have been brought up as one, and while you are under my roof you will behave like one. And Ladies do not talk of such things, or indeed think of them."

"I understand what you are saying to me," Fortuna replied, "and you are being kind because, Apollo, like the Sun-God you try to bring light and happiness to those who need it.

"But I realise that I really am a nobody, hanging, as it were, between Heaven and earth—not a lady like Lady Charlotte and not of the same uneducated class as Emmeline.

"And however much you may forbid me to think of it, I cannot help wondering if when your time indeed comes when you do . . . weary of me, where I shall go or what shall . . . become of . . . me."

Fortuna's voice held a note of fear, and her eyes looking into the Marquis's were troubled. Then suddenly something strange seemed to happen between them as they looked at each other.

They were both very still, and it seemed to Fortuna

125

as if the touch of his fingers gave her a strange feeling within her breast and it was hard for her to breathe.

Then as something awakened and quivered within her the Marquis released her chin and turned his head away.

"You are right, Fortuna," he said, and his tone was harsh, "at the moment you are nobody and you do indeed hang precariously between Heaven and hell."

She felt as though he had thrown a glass of cold water in her face. She sat back on her heels staring up at him. The Marquis rose to his feet again.

"Tomorrow morning early," he said, "we will leave for Thane Castle. I will give the orders now."

"We will go to Thane?" Fortuna cried incredulously, "Oh, but that is something I have wanted to do above all things—to see the Castle, to see where you lived when you were young and where Gilly taught you."

"We are going," the Marquis said, and his voice was uncompromising, "because I believe it will accelerate matters quicker than if we remain in London."

"What matters?" Fortuna asked bewildered.

"If you will cease asking questions," he said in an irritated tone, "I am convinced events can proceed a lot more smoothly."

He tugged at the bell-rope.

"You rang, M'Lord?" Chambers enquired.

"Miss Fortuna and I will be leaving for Thane Castle first thing tomorrow morning," the Marquis answered. "Post a groom there immediately to inform the household of our arrival. We will travel in my Phaeton, the baggage cart can follow with Miss Fortuna's maid."

"Very good, M'Lord."

"And now, Fortuna," the Marquis said as Chambers left the room, "I suggest that as we shall be leaving

126

early you should retire to bed. I do not wish to be kept waiting."

"I will not do that," Fortuna answered, "although I doubt if I shall sleep tonight. I shall be too excited at the thought of seeing the Castle. I feel as if I know it well already from Gilly's descriptions, and perhaps if there is time you will show me some of the places where you used to play when you were young."

She anticipated that the Marquis might answer her sharply, instead of which he said with a faint smile:

"There might be time for that, and perhaps for you to ride my horses which I am convinced are under-exercised. So bring a habit if you have one."

"It was delivered today," Fortuna replied happily. "Madame Yvette said she was certain that sooner or later you would ask me to ride with you."

"Yvette knows my tastes," the Marquis said. "She herself used to look well on a horse."

"She rode with you?" Fortuna asked.

"On several occasions . . ." he replied, then stopped abruptly. "Will you not be so damned inquisitive! I have told you before that you should not ask such questions."

"So Madame Yvette was one of your . . . Hetaerae," Fortuna said in a low voice. "I rather suspicioned it from the way she talked so wistfully of the past. Oh dear, there must be so many of them, because like Alexander the Great you are so . . . very, very attractive."

She curtsied as she spoke, and then before the Marquis could think of a suitable reply she had gone from the room. For a moment he stared after her, then turning to the grog tray he poured himself out a large glass of brandy.

He lifted it to his lips, then suddenly with an oath

127

which seemed to echo around the walls he flung the glass into the fireplace where it smashed into a thousand pieces.

"Damn and blast! Curse his black heart!" he cried. "May he rot in hell!"

6

"It is wonderful!" Fortuna exclaimed. "Almost more wonderful than I had imagined possible!"

The beauty of the Castle took her breath away. Seated beside the Marquis in his High Perch Phaeton they had turned through the great wrought-iron gates and came down the long drive, which was bordered on either side with high chestnut trees, their pink and white blossoms pointed like candles towards the sky.

Then suddenly the Castle stood in front of them, its grey Norman tower as impregnable as it had been when it was first built.

Other parts of the Castle had been added down the centuries. The second Earl of Thane had erected the Elizabethan wing, and his son and grandson had built before and after the Restoration.

It was the first Marquis returning from the wars fought under Marlborough who had contributed the great Banqueting-hall with its colourful murals, the long Gallery hung with family portraits, and the Library which made Fortuna almost speechless with delight when she saw its five thousand books stretching from floor to ceiling.

But her first impression of the Castle was of a fairy-tale loveliness. Sheltered by dark pinewoods and surrounded on three sides by an ancient moat, it appeared to stand full square against its enemies, and it seemed impossible that one man's jealousy and vengeance could have humbled and humiliated its hereditary owner.

"It is magnificent!" Fortuna exclaimed. "Just the Castle that you, M'Lord, should have as your own."

"A Castle without lands, without anything to provide its maintenance save what I have won on the turn of a card," the Marquis said harshly.

There was so much pain in his voice that instinctively Fortuna put out her little hand to lay it on his arm.

"It will all come back to you," she said. "You may think it foolish of me, but I believe I will, in fact, bring you good luck."

"That remains to be seen," the Marquis said indifferently.

But Fortuna felt, although she could not explain it even to herself, that there was some hope in him that had not been there before.

As soon as they arrived he took her over the Castle, showing her, as she had longed to see, the Schoolroom where he had done his lessons with Gilly, the Norman Chapel where Sunday services were said by the Marquis's private Chaplain, the great Ballroom shrouded in dust-sheets, and the fine Salons with their exquisite furniture and impressive family portraits.

To Fortuna it was like walking back into history. Gilly had described the Castle to her so often, but no words could portray the feeling of age, or what she knew to the Marquis was so important, the continuity of succeeding generations, who century after century had made the place their home.

"How can you ever bear to leave here?" she asked.

They stood waiting for luncheon to be announced and the Marquis poured himself a glass of Madeira before he answered.

"Do you really think it amuses me to be confined within a few hundred acres," he asked harshly, "when my father owned thousands?"

There was a violence in his words which made Fortuna wince, feeling that she had been tactless in asking the question.

Yet she knew that because she was a woman she would have been content with the wonder of the great house, the exquisitely laid out gardens and the lakes with their nests of wild swans and geese, where the Marquis had swam and boated when he was a child.

She found herself welcomed to the Castle by the staff in the same manner that she had been welcomed at Thane House because they had known Gilly.

The elderly butler, Bateson, had served not only the Marquis's father but his grandfather when he was an old man; the housekeeper had known Gilly as well as Mrs. Denvers had; and there were many other servants who told Fortuna how much they had loved and respected "Master Sylvanus's" governess.

So many of them spoke of the Marquis as if he were still a boy that Fortuna could visualise him running around the house, sliding down the balustrade to the Grand Staircase, calling for his dogs, then racing towards the stables with a pack of spaniels at his heels.

There were several dogs at the Castle, and they greeted the Marquis uproariously. As he bent to pat them it seemed to Fortuna for a moment as if the cynical expression on his face changed and he looked happy and carefree.

Yet all too quickly the bitterness returned. When they looked at the portrait of his father the Marquis's only remark was:

"Thank God he never knew what happened after he died."

It was hard for Fortuna to keep the conversation

131

going at luncheon, but somehow she managed it and even contrived to make the Marquis laugh once or twice.

At the same time she was glad when as the meal was finished he said:

"I thought you would wish to ride this afternoon. We cannot go far unless we trespass on other people's property, but nevertheless if it pleases you I have ordered the horses to be ready in a quarter of an hour."

"I will take less time than that," Fortuna answered, and she ran upstairs to her bedchamber.

The Housekeeper and two housemaids were waiting for her, not, Fortuna knew, because she needed so much assistance in changing her clothes, but because they wished to talk of Gilly and the old days.

"What a lovely room!" Fortuna had exclaimed when she first saw where she was to sleep.

There was a high four-poster carved, gilded and ornamented with ostrich feathers which rose above a canopy of exquisite embroidery that had been stitched in the reign of Charles II. The furniture was ornamented with angels, and everywhere there were great bowls of flowers from the garden which Fortuna had already seen was a miracle of beauty.

She went to the window to look out on the lilacs purple and white, the laburnums with their golden chains moving in the breeze, the trees of almond blossom shedding their pink petals on the velvet lawns and the great banks of syringa which she knew would be scenting the air with their exotic fragrance.

It was all so beautiful that Fortuna felt she must cry at the thought that the Marquis could not be happy here.

"Do possessions matter so much?" she asked herself beneath her breath.

Then she turned to smile at Mrs. Summers, the

Housekeeper, who was exclaiming over the style of the habit which Fortuna had brought with her from London.

Madame Yvette had certainly done her best to make Fortuna look elegant on a horse. The habit had, in fact, been intended to be worn in the Row and was, Fortuna thought, too smart for riding in the country-side.

However, she was glad that the Marquis could see her in emerald green velvet, her tiny waist accentuated by the tightness of the coat, her hair pale under a high hat draped with a veil of green gauze, the ends of which flowed out behind her when she moved.

There was little time for her to think of clothes; for when she was mounted on the horse the Marquis had chosen for her, she found it was a thrill beyond words to be riding a piece of horseflesh which responded to her slightest touch and which she knew had an Arab strain in him.

The horses were fresh and inclined to be restless, and as they moved away from the Castle Fortuna felt that the Marquis was watching her critically to see if she could ride well enough to handle his animals.

Fortuna was not afraid, she was completely con-fident of her ability not only to ride well but to prove herself the equal of any other woman who had been privileged to partner the Marquis.

"I cannot have you clumping about on the only type of old rocking-horse that I can provide for you," Gilly had said when Fortuna was still quite small.

She had gone from the tiny cottage where they lived to visit the Squire in his great ugly mansion which lay on the outside of the village.

He was an old man even then and crippled so that he himself was unable to ride—indeed he seldom left his bedchamber. But he had always kept a good stable and had refused to part with his horses, even though he never used them.

Gilly had charmed him, as she had charmed so many people, into doing what she wanted.

Fortuna had been taught to ride by the Squire's head groom. She progressed rapidly from a quiet, well-behaved pony to horses which even the stable-boys found tricky to ride. When Gilly asked after her prowess the groom had replied:

"A lady, Miss, be either born with hands, or nawt that Oi can say or do could teach her how to handle horseflesh. Miss Fortuna be one of them as needs no teaching."

As she grew older, Fortuna knew that the Squire was regularly carried to the window so he could watch her riding in the Park.

He had jumps erected, and she would take his horses over them knowing that they had often been raised during the night so that they became a new test not only for her but for the horses which the Squire continued to buy, principally, she was convinced, because it pleased him to see her on them.

Now because she sensed that the Marquis was watching her she looked towards him with a mischievous smile.

"I believe you are a gambler, My Lord," she said in a demure voice. "Dare I wager that I will beat you in the gallop that I see ahead of us?"

Without waiting for his answer she gave her mount a little flick with her whip and they were off, galloping wildly across the park, their horses neck and neck, the thunder of their hooves in their ears.

It brought Fortuna a sense of exhilaration which made her long to cry out aloud at the joy of it. She had known that the Marquis would be a magnificent rider, and although she had a slight start she soon realised it would be hard to be the winner.

On and on they galloped, until seeing the parkland ending ahead of them in a high wall Fortuna started to rein in her horse, even as she saw that the Marquis was half a length ahead of her and she could not beat him.

He drew his horse to a standstill and turned to smile at her.

"How much do you owe me?" he asked triumphantly.

She laughed up at him, her cheeks flushed with the exercise, her eyes shining.

"The terms of the wager were not fixed," she replied.

"Then surely I can ask for anything I want," he suggested.

"It will be difficult for me to pay you anything, whatever it may be," Fortuna answered, "As you well know, I have nothing—nothing to give anyone."

"A reckless statement for a pretty woman to make," the Marquis said with a twist of his lips.

Then as he realised she did not understand his meaning he added:

"If you cannot pay me in gold—the usual forfeit is a kiss."

Something in his eyes and in the tone of his voice made Fortuna feel shy. She had a sudden vision of Odette with her lips pressed eagerly against his mouth and the colour rose in her cheeks.

"I do not think," she said slowly, "that kisses should be given lightly or . . . without meaning."

"There usually is a meaning," the Marquis remarked.

"I may be . . . mistaken," Fortuna faltered, "and doubtless you will think it foolish . . . but I would not wish to kiss a man . . . or for him to kiss me . . . unless I . . . were . . . in love."

135

"What is love?" the Marquis asked harshly. "You are very young, Fortuna; in a year or so you will doubtless distribute your favours more generously."

"No," Fortuna said firmly, "on this I am convinced I shall not change my mind."

"Then you will be very different from most young females," the Marquis sneered.

She realised that she must keep him from being serious, so with an effort she managed to say lightly:

"In the meantime, I am in your debt, My Lord, and my pockets are to let."

"A most reprehensible manner of gambling," the Marquis said severely, but there was a faint twinkle in his eyes.

"I will think of something with which to pay you," Fortuna promised, "but in the meantime it was worth the risk, was it not?"

"You ride amazingly well," the Marquis said.

"I know that you suspected that I was boasting when I told you that I could ride," she challenged him.

"I could not imagine that Gilly could provide you with a very expensive stable," he replied.

"Someone was kind enough to mount me," Fortuna answered.

"I thought you told me you had no beaux," the Marquis said sharply, and there was again that hard, suspicious note in his voice which invariably made her afraid.

"I rode the Squire's horses," she said quickly. "As I have already told you, he was an old man. In fact, I seldom saw him."

She wondered as she spoke why the Marquis was so quick to find fault, almost eager, it seemed, to catch her out in some falsehood or prevarication. Then she told herself it was because he had been deceived so often that he expected deceit in everyone he met.

136

To make him forget his suspicions Fortuna asked: "Where shall we go now?"

"We have come, as you see, to the boundary of my Estate," the Marquis replied. "We will ride towards the woods, there is not much left to see."

Fortuna gave a little sigh. She knew all the bitterness and cynicism had returned and he was no longer the man who had smiled triumphantly at the end of their gallop.

They rode soberly side by side, and then coming towards them they saw two Huntsmen wearing the traditional pink coats and velvet caps. They were accompanied by a dozen hounds who were kept together by the sound of a horn which seemed to ring out in the clear, still air.

"Foxhounds!" Fortuna exclaimed. "Are they yours?"

"They are what are left of my father's pack," the Marquis explained in a hard voice. "He bred a special strain which we hunted over our Estate. Now unless I encroach on my neighbour's property, there is nothing for the hounds to do during the winter months except to pine away in their kennels."

They drew level with the Huntsmen, who took off their caps politely.

"Good to see Your Lordship," the older Huntsman said, and there was no doubt that his words were sincere.

"There seem to be fewer hounds than usual," the Marquis remarked, looking down at the pack.

"Deborah and Juliet are in pup, M'Lord."

"Again?" the Marquis replied. "Well, it will be pointless to keep their litters."

"As you say, M'Lord," the Huntsman replied. "At the same time Colonel Fitzgibbon has suggested that if Your Lordship would wish to hunt his land next winter, you are very welcome."

137

There was an eagerness in the man's tone which told Fortuna all too clearly how much he wanted the answer to be in the affirmative. The Marquis was frowning.

"I will hunt on my own ground," he said sharply, "or I will not hunt at all."

"Very good, M'Lord."

The Huntsman was disappointed, and as if to hide his feelings he blew his horn and with a polite "Good afternoon, M'Lord" he led the pack away, the hounds carrying their tails high, their noses to the ground, a look of alertness about them which Fortuna could realise was to the Marquis almost a reproach in itself.

The Marquis spurred his horse into a quick trot and there seemed no chance of conversation. They came to the wood and rode down a moss-covered path which wound through the centre of the pine trees.

There was an air of mystery, the coo of wood-pigeons, the sudden scamper of a rabbit through the undergrowth, a glimpse of a deer in flight.

"When I was a little girl," Fortuna said, "I believed that dragons lived in pine woods."

"Now you are more likely to find dragons in the streets of Mayfair or—the Palace of Fortune," the Marquis replied.

She knew he referred to Sir Roger Crowley and wondered why he tried to hurt her by reminding her of someone she longed to forget.

"You have forgotten that in the story-books," she answered, "the Princess is always rescued by the Prince!"

"How distressing if the Prince had been otherwise engaged," the Marquis scoffed. "I expect in many cases that was the true tale."

"But how disconcerting for his self-conceit if he were in a coil and the Princess rescued him!" Fortuna smiled.

"Do you think you can rescue me?" the Marquis asked, and he was not being sarcastic.

"I shall try," Fortuna answered in all seriousness, then added: "And what will you give me if I succeed?"

"So mercenary?" the Marquis questioned. "But of course I shall offer you half my kingdom!"

"And I shall accept!" Fortuna smiled, and held out her hand.

She looked very lovely silhouetted against the dark green of the pine trees, her grey eyes seeking his with an unselfconscious appeal in them.

The Marquis had to admit that she rode a horse as well as any woman he had ever met. He knew too how hard she was trying to coax him from the blue devilled mood which being at the Castle always induced in him.

Suddenly ashamed he took her hand and raised it to his lips.

"My fate is in your hands, Princess!" he said gently, and saw the flash of gratitude in her little face that he had responded to her fantasy.

"*A votre service, Monsieur!*" she replied, using the age-old pledge of a French soldier.

He smiled and did not relinquish her hand. For a few moments they rode side by side linked together.

"This wood is enchanted!" Fortuna thought.

She wondered why despite the fact they were in the shadow of the trees she felt dazzled by sunlight.

The bluebells made a carpet of colour as they emerged from the pines, and then in front of them Fortuna could see an amazing vista of fields green and golden, of woods, streams and a winding river stretching far away to the horizon. The Marquis reined in his horse and Fortuna stopped beside him.

"All that belonged to my family for centuries," he said quietly. "It was ours to fight for, to defend against the enemy—an enemy who came openly in armour, an enemy one could fight, an enemy one could defeat."

He paused.

"Could anyone have been perceptive enough to expect guile, deceit, perfidious treachery from a neighbour?"

"It is hard, very hard for you to bear," Fortuna said sympathetically, "but are you not letting the Duke win an even greater victory than he has won in the past?"

"What do you mean by that?" the Marquis asked.

"You are letting him destroy . . . you," Fortuna answered. "I know he has taken your lands and he has hurt your pride, but possessions are not so important to a man as himself."

"I know what you are trying to say," the Marquis said in a low voice, "but it is too late for sermonising, too late, Fortuna, to save me from myself. I am, if you like, what the Duke has made me. You have heard my nickname, 'the Young Devil', and it is, I can assure you, very apt."

"Not to me," Fortuna said quietly.

Before he could reply she urged her horse forward and moved away from him almost as though she wished him no longer to look at the lands which he could not now claim as his own and from which he was shut out.

The Marquis followed her, but slowly, making no effort to draw level. Then as they rounded the side of the wood Fortuna gave an exclamation.

Down below, in a sheltered clearing, was a gypsy camp. She turned to look back over her shoulder at the Marquis.

"Gypsies!" she cried. "Do look at their pretty caravans. I can remember them at Little Waterless ever since I was a child. Gilly learnt some of her special herbal medicines from them. I wonder if they could by any chance be the same clan?"

"What were they doing in Little Waterless?" the Marquis asked casually as though he was not particularly interested in the answer.

"They used to arrive every summer to work on the farms," Fortuna replied. "They came to pick the strawberry crop and the peas, and to lift the potatoes and, of course, for the hay-making."

There was a sudden interest in the Marquis's eyes.

"And you think these might be the same gypsies?" he asked.

"I can soon find out," Fortuna answered, "I speak a little Romany."

Without waiting for the Marquis she urged her horse forward and rode down the side of the hill towards the camp. There was the traditional fire in the centre of the caravans, with a large black pot suspended over it from a tripod of sticks.

There were a number of gypsy children seated around it obviously waiting for their meal, and the women who had been washing their clothes in a nearby stream were hanging them out to dry.

The children jumped up when Fortuna appeared on her horse. She looked round the camp and then said to one of the women:

"Surely you are the Bucklands? I visited you once with Miss Gillingham."

A dark woman who had been eyeing her suspiciously gave a cry of excitement, and then with a chatter of tongues the women came crowding from the caravans and surrounded Fortuna.

As the Marquis drew nearer he could hear them saying "Little Waterless" and "Gillingham", while Fortuna answered them in a strange, soft language of

141

which he could not understand a word. She stopped speaking to smile at him.

"They are the same clan," she explained unnecessarily. "They are the Bucklands, and they have camped in and around Little Waterless for years. It was their mother, Leonora, who gave Gilly some of the very best remedies she ever had."

"Ask them," the Marquis said, "if anyone here remembers the Grimwoods."

Fortuna was suddenly still and the smile faded from her lips. For a moment the Marquis thought she was going to refuse to obey him; then in a different voice to the gay lilting tones she had used before she asked the question.

One of the women replied and she translated to the Marquis:

"They say their mother, Leonora, who is still alive, will remember the Grimwoods. These women are too young."

The Marquis dismounted.

"Take me to Leonora," he said.

The gypsy boys ran forward to hold the horses as Fortuna and the Marquis were escorted to an elaborately painted caravan standing a little apart from the others.

A gypsy woman ran up the steps and opened the door. She spoke to someone inside, then turned to beckon to Fortuna.

"We can go in," Fortuna said to the Marquis.

The caravan was spotlessly clean. The walls were painted with signs of pattern in vivid colours. There were pans and horse brasses which were polished until they shone as brightly as mirrors.

There were lace curtains over the small windows, and lying on a low bed was Leonora, the mother of the Clan.

She had the high cheek-bones and black eyes of her race. There were dark ringlets falling on either side of her face, huge gold earrings in her ears, and the wrist of the thin hand she held out to Fortuna was weighed down with bracelets.

"Do you remember me, Leonora?" Fortuna asked, sitting down beside the bed on a rush-bottomed chair.

The Marquis, who was unable to stand upright inside the caravan, seated himself on another.

"Ye be Miss Gillingham's little girl," Leonora answered in English, and in the slow, far-away voice of the very old.

"This is the Marquis of Thane," Fortuna said, indicating the Marquis, "on whose land you are camped."

"We thank Your Lordship."

"You know that Miss Gillingham is dead?" Fortuna asked in a low voice.

"No one told me, but I knew it as ye came through the door," the gypsy replied.

"She was grateful to you," Fortuna said, "you helped her to help other people."

"Her were a good Rriena," Leonora replied. "Ye'll miss her, but Cham will protect ye now ye are alone."

Fortuna noticed she used the Romany word which meant Sun, but her eyes turned towards the Marquis.

"There is something I want to ask you," the Marquis said. "Do you remember the Grimwoods? They lived at Little Waterless over seventeen years ago."

"Ay," the gypsy replied after a moment. "We went to their farm every summer—they were kind people. There was never any trouble."

"You remember Miss Fortuna being born?" the Marquis enquired.

"I remembers th' night Mistress Grimwood gave birth to her sixth child," the gypsy replied.

"And three days later they left the farm," the Marquis said. "Where did they go?"

"They went over th' sea. I remembers Farmer Grimwood telling my man he were agoing. He paid us what we were owed, every penny."

"But did you hear the name of their destination?" the Marquis insisted. "It is important for you to remember."

Leonora was silent and there was an expression in her eyes which made Fortuna feel that she looked back into the past, seeing rather than remembering.

It was as if her spirit bridged the years and was no longer confined by the restrictions of time.

"They—go—to an—island," Leonora said at length, and her words came slowly as if from a long distance away, "an island to which they must travel—west—an island between two other islands—but small—very small. The farmer—didn't tell us—th' name, but 'tis th'—island which has th'—face of a cat."

"A cat!" the Marquis exclaimed, wrinkling his brow.

"Some land's like animals—some like birds," Leonora explained.

"An island between two other islands," the Marquis repeated to himself, "with the face of a cat."

Fortuna was watching Leonora and somehow she too could almost see the symbols by which the gypsy used her powers.

"A cat without a tail," she said suddenly, "a manx cat!"

"The Isle of Man!" the Marquis cried. "Is that the island you mean?"

"Ay—that'll—be it," Leonora answered.

"Thank you," the Marquis said, and there was a note of excitement in his voice, "thank you for your help."

He put his hand into his waistcoat pocket and brought out a golden guinea. He would have given it to the gypsy, but before he could do so Fortuna put her hand over his and he knew that what he was about to do was wrong.

"May we thank you for your help, Leonora," Fortuna said gently. "His Lordship and I wish you good health."

"Soon they'll carry me from my caravan," Leonora replied.

Fortuna knew this meant she was going to die, because the gypsies died in the open-air and their caravans were burnt.

"Then may you find peace," she said.

"My people'll not forget Miss Gillingham's kindness," the gypsy murmured, "they're your friends for all time."

"I know that," Fortuna answered, "And if I can ever help them you know I will do so."

"One day—you'll be in th'—position to help many—people," Leonora said, and again her words were those of clairvoyant.

Then she closed her eyes as if she could no longer make an effort to speak.

Fortuna said no more. Very quietly she left the small caravan and the Marquis followed her.

"They are our friends, they do not expect money," she told him, "but you can give the children who have held our horses a small piece of silver each."

She said good-bye to the other gypsies in their own language, and she and the Marquis rode back towards the wood.

"Why did you ask Leonora where the Grimwoods had gone?" she enquired.

"I was curious," the Marquis replied.

She knew he was hiding something from her, but

145

because he obviously did not wish to confide in her she would not press him.

They rode back to the Castle almost in silence. She had the feeling that the Marquis's thoughts were preoccupied with the information he had received from Leonora.

As they dismounted and walked into the house he said:

"I expect you would wish to rest. I have invited four friends to dine with us tonight."

"A party!" Fortuna exclaimed. "Oh, I did so hope we would be alone."

"I wish my friends to meet you," he replied brusquely.

He saw the look of disappointment on her face.

"You do not wish them to stay long," he went on, stating a fact, "nor do I. What we will do, Fortuna, is to speed them on their way at eleven of the clock."

"How can we do that without being impolite?" Fortuna enquired.

"After dinner—when you retire," the Marquis replied, "go into the Library. The Gentlemen will not join you. When the hands of the clock touch eleven send Bateson to me with a note. It matters not what you write, it will be my excuse for ending the party."

"That is indeed a splendid plan!" Fortuna cried happily.

Then something in the Marquis's expression, or perhaps in his voice, told her that he had another reason for asking her to send him a note.

She could not imagine what it would be, but she was absolutely convinced it was not because he wished to be alone with her, or even to rid himself of his friends.

146

There was, however, nothing she could say, and she realised he was waiting for her to go upstairs to rest. She was not tired, she would rather have been with him, but she thought that perhaps he desired to be alone.

She therefore went to her bedchamber, where she took off her habit and put on a loose robe, to sit at the window looking out over the gardens.

"How happy," she told herself. "I could be at Thane if only the Marquis was not so bitter, if only he did not so much resent everything that reminded him of the Duke's treachery."

She thought of the great acres stretching towards the horizons she had seen from the wood.

"It is cruel," she thought, "but he has, in fact, so much for which to be thankful."

Then she knew that was something she would never be able to convey to the Marquis. He was obsessed with the thought of what he had lost—nothing else mattered to him, nothing else was of consequence save that he would have his revenge upon the Duke and win back from him all that was rightfully his.

"If only I could help him," Fortuna whispered to herself, and felt suddenly insignificant and helpless.

How could she comprehend what a man would suffer under such circumstances? How could she understand the bitterness that ran like poison through his veins, distorting everything he saw, everything he did, everything he thought?

He was so handsome with his clear-cut features, deep set eyes and square forehead. His face, so harsh and cynical in repose, could be transformed by the fascination of his smile.

He had a twinkle in his eyes when he was amused which she found irresistible, but she knew that she

147

dreaded the moments when his voice sharpened and there was that hard, almost cruel expression in his eyes.

"Help him, please, God, help him," she prayed.

Somehow she must find a way to heal him as she and Gilly had healed the sick children in the slums of Waterless.

But how often Gilly had said:

"A sickness of the mind is often far more painful and more difficult to cure than a sickness of the body."

What the Marquis was suffering from was even worse than a sickness of the mind—it was a sickness of the soul.

How right she had been when she said that the Duke was destroying him! But how could she ever find the right potion to make him well?

She remembered years ago hearing Gilly talk of the Herb of Grace. She could not now remember what it was, but she felt that that was what the Marquis needed—the Herb of Grace to take away his misery, his bitterness and his hatred, and to give him peace and happiness.

"Show me how I can help him," Fortuna whispered, "show me the way."

She felt as though her prayer winged out over the garden like the flight of a bird, that it went towards the sun that was setting behind the pine trees, the sun which reminded her of Apollo, the god that she had loved ever since Gilly had taught her about him, the god she subconsciously linked in her mind with the Marquis.

A sudden flutter of wings startled her, then she saw a white dove had settled on the window-sill. It stood there, unafraid, putting its head first on one side, then on the other as it looked at her with its round bead-like eyes.

"It is a sign to tell me that my prayer will be answered," Fortuna told herself.

The dove spread its wings. White as purity against the green of the trees it soared into the sky and disappeared against the radiance of the sunset.

"Somehow I will be shown the way, I am sure of it," Fortuna cried, and felt her spirits rise irrepressibly.

The maids brought a bath in her bedroom, the water scented with the oil of roses, and she dried herself on towels which smelt of lavender.

When she was dressed in a gown of leaf green trimmed round the neck and hem with tiny frills of lace held by little bows of green velvet, she went downstairs.

She expected that the Marquis would still be changing, but he was already in the Salon. As she entered he rose from the desk at which he was writing and she saw that he wore a coat of emerald green satin cut by a master hand, which fitted him to perfection.

"We look as if we were the spirits of the woods," Fortuna cried, "Were you aware that I would be wearing green?"

"I had no idea," the Marquis replied, "I did not choose your gown this evening. But may I say you look very charming in it."

Fortuna dropped him a curtsy.

"You are paying me compliments," she said. "If you are not careful they will go to my head and I will become overbearingly conceited."

"Is there really any fear of that?" he asked.

"Not really!" she replied. "I am extremely conscious of all my shortcomings, even when you do not point them out to me."

"You are determined to make me an ogre," he said with a twinkle in his eyes.

149

"Is that not the sort of person one expects to find in a Castle?" Fortuna asked, looking at him from under her eyelashes. "But I cheer myself with the thought that according to the fairy-tales ogres invariably have a *penchant* for pretty young women."

He laughed almost as if he could not help it.

"I cannot imagine what sort of lessons Gilly gave you to turn you into a minx," he said, "but that is what you are rapidly becoming."

His words were spoken in such a pleasant tone that Fortuna felt her heart leap.

"I must make him laugh," she thought to herself, "I must not let him become so depressed . . . so introspective."

"Shall we have a glass of wine before our guests arrive?" he asked, then added as he walked towards the bell-rope: "But I forgot, you have no liking for wine."

"I will have some if it pleases you," Fortuna answered. "I am sure that a Gentleman feels there is something rather depressing in drinking alone."

"How do you know a man feels that?" the Marquis enquired. "Is that another axiom from one of your lesson books?"

"No, it is something I have thought out for myself," Fortuna answered. "I am sure that most people, if they are truthful, would rather do things in the company of someone else. It is so much more fun. It must be very lonely receiving no congratulations if one is successful and no sympathy if one is not."

"I prefer to be alone," the Marquis said firmly.

"That is not true," Fortuna contradicted. "For instance, you could not have enjoyed racing your horse today if I had not been there. And, although Your Lordship will not admit it, I would swear you enjoyed showing me round the Castle and relating the escapades of your boyhood."

She paused.

"There was also, surely, a few seconds of happiness when we rode together in the pine-wood?"

The Marquis looked away from her pleading eyes.

"You have an answer to everything, have you not?" he asked crushingly.

"There would not be much use talking to me if I did not answer," Fortuna replied. "At the same time, you are certain to say I talk too much, just as, if I do not talk, you will say how 'damned' dull I am."

The Marquis threw back his head and laughed.

"You are incorrigible!" he exclaimed.

The footman crossed the room with a salver on which was a glass of wine and beside it another glass containing a liquid at which the Marquis looked suspiciously.

"What is that?" he enquired.

"It is peach juice for Miss Fortuna," the man replied. "Mr. Bateson thought the young lady would prefer it to wine."

"How kind!" Fortuna exclaimed.

"Another example of my considerate staff," the Marquis said with lifted eyebrows.

"They all were so fond of Gilly," Fortuna said simply. "They have made me feel very welcome."

"And have I not done so?" he asked.

He was not sneering as he asked the question, and Fortuna looked up at him.

"Do you like having me here?" she replied in a low voice.

Her grey eyes were anxious and there was also a touch of fear in them. She could not guess from his expression what his feelings were.

The harsh, cynical lines on either side of his mouth were deeply engraved, and yet she felt that for the moment at any rate he was not feeling bitter.

"Fortuna! . . ." He spoke her name as if he were about to say something momentous.

Then the door was opened and the butler announced in stentorian tones:

"Sir Hugo Harrington, M'Lord."

7

Sir Hugo Harrington was an elderly man who had once been extremely handsome. His bearing belied his years as he advanced across the Salon, his fob and the diamond tie-pin in his elegantly tied cravat glittering in the light of the candelabra.

"It is good to see you back here, Thane," he said to the Marquis.

He then looked at Fortuna, who was standing by the mantelshelf, and exclaimed:

"Good Heavens, Your Grace! I was not expecting to meet . . ."

He stopped suddenly and in obvious astonishment raised his quizzing-glass to his eye.

"I thought . . ." he began, only to be interrupted by the Marquis.

"I do not think you know Miss Fortuna Grimwood," he said, accentuating the surname. "Fortuna, this is an old friend of mine, Sir Hugo Harrington, who, I can assure you, is one of the most important men in the county."

"Your servant, Miss Grimwood," Sir Hugo said politely.

His eyes took in every detail of her pale hair, her large grey eyes and the shape of her little pointed face.

"It is extraordinary!" the Marquis heard him mutter almost under his breath.

But before he could say more the butler announced:
"Lord Trevor and General Rexford-Stirling, M'Lord."

They too were men of advancing years, and Fortuna could not help being aware that they also stared at her in an incredulous fashion as the Marquis introduced them.

At the same time they all seemed delighted that the Marquis was at the Castle.

"It is too long since you have paid us a visit, my boy," the General said. "I began to think the furniture would be perpetually in hollands. I never ride past without looking up at the Tower and hoping to see the flag flying."

"I doubt if it will fly for long," the Marquis replied, "this is but a short visit. Nevertheless, I could not return home without having a word with good friends like yourself."

"Mr. Colin Fitzgibbon, M'Lord," the butler announced from the door.

The Marquis looked up in surprise. A young man crossed the floor to say apologetically:

"We are not acquainted, My Lord, but my father is regrettably indisposed and has sent me to make his apologies and, if you wish it, to take his place at dinner."

"Of course, Mr. Fitzgibbon, I am delighted to welcome you," the Marquis said, "but I am indeed sorry to hear the Colonel is not in good health."

"It is but a touch of gout," Mr. Fitzgibbon said with a smile, "but it makes my father exceedingly peppery and in no mood for company."

"That I can understand," the Marquis said, and turned towards Fortuna. "May I present Mr. Colin Fitzgibbon?—Miss Fortuna Grimwood."

Fortuna curtsied, the young man bowed; then they proceeded into dinner.

The Marquis placed Fortuna at the end of the dining-table with General Rexford-Stirling on one side of her and Mr. Colin Fitzgibbon on the other.

The table, as usual, was decorated with candelabra, gold ornaments and an arrangement of flowers so that it was difficult for Fortuna to perceive the Marquis clearly.

She liked to see him at the top of his table, and had thought on other occasions how elegant and supremely at ease he appeared in the high-backed velvet armchair which he told her had been brought into the family in the reign of Queen Anne.

Tonight, because she felt he was genuinely glad to be with his friends, he seemed relaxed, talking more easily, responding to their jokes and not seeming to mind when they chaffed him about his gay life in London.

"When are you going to get tired of the bright lights and the lure of lovely women, Sylvanus?" she heard Lord Trevor say to him. "My wife has been hoping, like so many other county Ladies, that you would soon bring a Châtelaine back to live at the Castle."

"A Châtelaine?" the Marquis enquired, raising his eyebrows. "My dear George, you must be sadly out of touch with the prattling of the upper crust if you imagine I would bring home the type of wife that Lady Trevor would find comfortable."

"Well, I cannot blame you, my boy, at the moment, for having other interests," Lord Trevor said with a glance at Fortuna.

She was puzzling exactly what His Lordship might mean by that when Mr. Colin Fitzgibbon on her left side said tentatively:

155

"Do you enjoy the country, Miss Grimwood?"

"I have lived in the country all my life," Fortuna answered.

"Your appearance belies such a statement," he said with a glance of admiration that was unmistakable.

"Must a country maiden, to proclaim her rural interest, come to dinner with mud on her shoes and a milk-pail on her arm?" Fortuna asked.

He grinned at her.

"Usually she need not proclaim her origin so loudly," he replied, "the freckles on her nose are evidence enough."

"You are being unkind," Fortuna complained, but she was laughing. "And what are your interests?"

"Would you really like me to tell you?" he asked.

"Of course," she replied.

"What I would wish to do above all else," he said, "is to design houses."

"You mean you desire to be an architect?" Fortuna enquired.

He nodded.

"And I have as much hope of realising my ambition as journeying to the moon," he said.

"Why?" she enquired.

"Because my father is determined that I shall go into politics, which is something for which I have no aptitude and no inclination."

"What sort of houses would you like to design?" Fortuna asked politely.

Though hearing the bitterness in his voice she felt that she could not bear to listen to the frustrations and unhappiness of yet another man.

There was a sudden visionary look in Mr. Colin Fitzgibbon's face which she knew all too well meant that he was going to unburden his heart to her.

156

"My father recently added a new wing and a new façade to our house," he said. "I spent much time both with the designers and the builders, and I learnt a great deal. It made me sure that this was something I could do and do well.

He sighed, then continued:

"But when I asked my father if I could study the subject further he refused categorically. But I have gone on working alone, not on big houses like this but on cottages for workmen."

"What sort of cottages would you build?" Fortuna enquired.

"Those that could be built cheaply," he replied, "because I am quite certain that as the population increases we will be short of houses all over England. And we will require such as will stand the wear and tear of time far better than those which are being erected at the moment."

"You have new ideas perhaps?" Fortuna questioned.

"Far too many for me to tell you them all," Mr. Fitzgibbon answered.

"Tell me one," Fortuna said.

"Well, I have been thinking . . ." he began, then paused. "I beg your pardon, Miss Grimwood, this must be incredibly dull for you."

"As a matter of fact it interests me profoundly," Fortuna answered. "Pray continue with what you were saying."

There was no mistaking the sincerity in her voice and he continued eagerly:

"I was thinking as I was driving here tonight that the trouble with a great number of our workmen's cottages, especially those that are built near the river, is that they are so damp."

He moved a pepper-pot towards him as if to use it to demonstrate what he was about to describe.

"I believe," he continued, "that if it were possible not to put the floor straight onto the ground, but to raise it a little so that the air could percolate underneath, one would in that way eliminate much of the damp that rises from the ground itself."

"But of course!" Fortuna exclaimed. "I am sure you are right about that. We drove through Lambeth two days ago and though I did not enter any of the houses there, which at the moment belong to the Marquis . . ."

She sighed.

"I am convinced that because they are near the river every wall on the ground floor will not only be damp but doubtless growing a fungus of some sort or other."

"I am sure of it," Mr. Colin Fitzgibbon said, "and my idea would, I believe, do a great deal to eliminate ground damp."

Fortuna was so interested in her conversation that it was with reluctance she turned towards the General on her other side.

To her relief she found he was deep in conversation with Sir Hugo about some horses they had recently purchased, and she turned again to Mr. Fitzgibbon with an eagerness that was unmistakable.

"Tell me more," she said.

They talked until dessert was finished and Fortuna realised it was time for her to withdraw. She rose to her feet, and as she did so Sir Hugo from the other end of the table raised his glass of port.

"Should we not drink a toast," he said, "to the most attractive young woman it has been my good fortune to meet for a very long time."

"Yes, yes, of course," Lord Trevor agreed. "Your health, Miss Grimwood."

The General and Mr. Fitzgibbon also raised their glasses. Fortuna, looking adorably shy, thanked them in a sweet little voice before she moved towards the door.

To her surprise the Marquis rose and walked beside her.

"We shall miss you, Fortuna," he said, and taking her hand raised it to his lips.

Her eyes widened for a moment in astonishment, and then as the footman shut the door of the Dining-room behind her she told herself it was a bit of play-acting to impress his friends.

As he had instructed her, she went to the Library. The fire had been lit and the Marquis's dogs had already made themselves comfortable on the hearth-rug. She sat down amidst them and they made her welcome with an exuberance that was almost over-whelming.

But when at length they were quieter, she found herself puzzling over the dinner party she had just left.

Did not the wives of the gentlemen who had been present, like Lady Trevor and Mrs. Rexford-Stirling, think it strange that their husbands had been asked without them?

And who had Sir Hugo thought she was when he first entered the Salon?

There had been a similar expression of surprise on the faces of the two other older men when they had first seen her.

They had stared at her hair as if they could not believe it were real, and she felt that there were a dozen questions trembling on their lips which they were too polite to utter.

Only Mr. Fitzgibbon had seemed to think that there was nothing particularly unusual about her, save that she was prepared to listen to his plans for building houses and to sympathise with him for being thwarted in his ambition to become an architect.

"I wonder," she thought to herself, "why nobody seems to get exactly what they want from the world."

Then she remembered Gilly saying to her:

"If you wish for something hard enough, it will come true. Be careful, therefore, that you wish for the right thing."

She thought then that perhaps Mr. Fitzgibbon could attain his wish. When the Marquis's lands were restored to him, would not the building of new houses be a necessity?

The population would have grown both in the rural areas and in the town. Perhaps he would see that Mr. Fitzgibbon had ideas that were worth trying out as an experiment.

Excited by the idea of helping the young man, Fortuna looked at the clock and realised that it was already twenty minutes to eleven.

She went to the desk and picking up the big white quill pen drew a piece of writing-paper from the drawer. She wondered if the Marquis liked her writing. Gilly had once told her that it was distinctive.

She took tremendous pains with the one sentence she wrote:

Come quickly, I have Something of Import
to relate to Your Lordship.

Fortuna.

The words were well formed and she signed her name with a flourish. She folded the paper, sealed it with a wafer and waited impatiently for the hands of the clock to reach the hour.

When they did so she rang the bell.

It was, however, nearly half an hour later before the

160

Marquis appeared. Fortuna was sitting once again on the hearth-rug, a spaniel had his head on her lap and the other two dogs lay asleep on either side of her.

They all looked up as the Marquis entered the Library, and instantly the dogs were bounding towards him, wagging their tails and jumping up in welcome.

"You have been a long . . ." Fortuna began, and felt the words die in her throat.

She looked at his face and realised as he came towards her that he was in a towering rage.

There was a frown between his eyes and his lips were set in a hard line which she knew with a sinking of her heart preluded his most cynical and sarcastic utterances.

It seemed to her that he took a very long time to walk from the door to the fireplace, and when he reached her he stood looking down at her with an expression which she could only describe to herself as one of contempt.

"May I inform you," he said, and his voice was biting like a lash of a whip, "that it is not usual when a young woman is under the protection of one Gentleman for her to accept favours from another. I thought that you had some elementary knowledge of behaviour, but I find that I am mistaken."

His voice deepened.

"I imagined too that you were different from other women," he went on, "whose greed is insatiable and whose hands are always stretched out claw-like to extract everything possible from any man they meet, whoever he may be. But again it appears I was mistaken."

He paused, and his voice when he spoke again was even more harsh and biting.

"Perhaps you would care to inform me what it is that I have omitted to provide for you, and which

161

apparently you require so urgently that you must accept it from the first stranger who happens to pass your way."

"What are you saying?" Fortuna asked as the Marquis appeared to pause for breath. "What have I done? Why are you angry?"

"Angry!" the Marquis exclaimed. "That is indeed a mild word for it. I am disgusted, if you like, ashamed and perhaps humiliated that the woman who is in my keeping should have to beg from a guest at my table."

"This makes no sense to me," Fortuna said, "I swear to you I do not understand what you are saying."

"Then perhaps it will please you to explain what Mr. Fitzgibbon meant when, as he bade me farewell, he said: 'Will you thank Miss Grimwood and tell her I will ride over tomorrow bringing with me what I promised her.' What was it he promised you? Is it jewellery? Some gem that had taken your fancy? And what indeed have you promised him in return?"

The frightened look on Fortuna's face faded a little. Her eyes were still dark and worried, her cheeks were very pale, but a little of the colour came back as she said:

"Of course I did not ask Mr. Fitzgibbon for jewels! As though I wanted such things! Now I understand. He is coming tomorrow to show you some plans he has made for building workmen's houses. Cheap ones, but houses where people can be free of damp and enjoy some comfort."

She spoke slowly to make him understand.

"Yet they would not cost more than those now being built which are often badly constructed and which do not last more than a few years without needing a vast number of repairs."

"Houses?" the Marquis asked as if he had never heard of them.

162

"Yes, houses that you will be able to build in Lambeth, in places like Waterless and other parts of the country where the population has increased."

"Houses," the Marquis said almost beneath his breath and sat down in an armchair. "Was that what you were discussing so intently at dinner?"

There was still a note of suspicion in his voice, but the anger had gone from his eyes and he was no longer scowling.

"Yes, it was," Fortuna answered. "Apparently Mr. Fitzgibbon has always wanted to be an architect, although his father is determined he should go into politics. But he has many clever ideas and he promised me that he would show me his plans tomorrow. I thought that you would find them interesting."

"I suppose I must believe you," the Marquis said reluctantly.

"You can always believe me," Fortuna said, "because I invariably tell the truth."

"I think you do," he said slowly.

"You are so suspicious," Fortuna said in a low voice, "that it makes me wonder what sort of women you have known in the past."

"Perhaps perfidy comes with sophistication," the Marquis said.

"I think I have always told the truth," Fortuna persisted.

"Perhaps you have not had many occasions when it would be more convenient or more advantageous for you to lie," the Marquis suggested.

"Yes, that is true," she agreed, "at the same time I do not think I would ever lie to someone I loved. That would be a betrayal, would it not?"

"And how many people have you loved?" he asked.

She gave him a mischievous smile.

"Not very many," she answered. "That is what you
163

want me to say, is it not? You are making me look foolish. It is stupid of me to try to cross swords with you."

"Is that what you are doing?" the Marquis asked.

"In a way it is enjoyable," Fortuna answered. "I have always thought I would like to argue with a man, to talk with somebody clever and perhaps take an opposite view just so that we could reason things out, debate them, bring ideas we did not even know we had to the surface."

"You will not be a success in society if you are clever," the Marquis said.

"What sort of society?" Fortuna asked.

She realised as she said the words that it was a mistake to ask such a question. There was a frown between the Marquis's eyes as he looked away from her into the fire.

He knew he should feel that the evening had been a success. It had gone entirely according to his plan.

He had asked the four most important men in the county to dinner, and they were also the four greatest gossips. Three had come, and he knew that already they would be chattering away about what they had seen at the Castle.

The older men had immediately seen the astounding likeness of Fortuna to the Duchess of Accrington. Merrill Park lay only twelve miles away, and the Marquis was quite certain that at least one of his dinner guests would make an excuse early the next morning to ride there and relate what they had seen at Thane Castle.

They were also captivated by Fortuna herself, by her grace, her charm, her delightful manners; and it was something, the Marquis knew, which would not remain untold when they recounted their evening's entertainment.

And then to make quite certain that they talked, Fortuna's note, brought by the butler as the port was passing round the table, for perhaps the sixth time, was a titbit of gossip which would lose nothing in the telling.

"From Miss Grimwood, M'Lord," Bateson had said.

The Marquis opened the letter, conscious that four pairs of eyes watched him do so.

"Thank you, Bateson."

The butler withdrew, and then Sir Hugo expressed the curiosity that was in the minds of all the guests.

"Not bad news, I hope," he remarked.

The Marquis laughed and slipped the note into his breast-pocket.

"No indeed," he said, "merely that attractive young women, well aware of their charms, are often impatient."

"You mean that Miss Grimwood is inviting us to join her?" Lord Trevor enquired.

The Marquis raised his eyebrows.

"I think," he said quietly, but a little hesitatingly as if he were half-embarrassed, "that Miss Grimwood has retired."

He had no need to look at the knowing smiles on the faces of his friends. They glanced at their watches, they made plausible excuses that they should return home early; in fact, they thought exactly what he wanted them to think.

He knew that by the next morning half the county would be buzzing with the story of how Thane left the dinner-table almost before the port had been passed round because his "little bit o' muslin" demanded it of him.

He had wanted gossip and had supplied the material, and yet now looking down into Fortuna's grey eyes he felt ashamed. It was a feeling he had not experienced for some years, and for a moment he did not recognise it for what it was.

Then as she put out her hand to touch his knee he felt like a small boy who has been caught out cheating.

"You are no longer angry with me, are you, Apollo?" he heard Fortuna ask softly.

"No," he answered, "and I owe you an apology."

"Do you really think that I would accept presents from a stranger?" Fortuna enquired. "I know that you have given me these wonderful gowns; but surely that is different, because Gilly sent me to you. And it is not as if you were really a stranger."

She looked at him pleadingly.

"Gilly talked so incessantly of you and I have thought of you so often that I feel I have known you all my life."

"Yes, it is different," the Marquis admitted.

She gave a little sigh of relief.

"Then you will look at the plans that Mr. Fitzgibbon is bringing tomorrow?" she said.

"If it pleases you," the Marquis replied. "What did you think of him, Fortuna?"

"I thought him an interesting young man," she replied.

"And you liked him?"

"Yes, I suppose so," she answered in a puzzled tone. "Why?"

"Is he the type of young man you would wish to marry?"

Fortuna's eyes widened for a moment, then she looked away towards the fire.

"I have no wish to marry anyone," she answered.

"But you will do so one day," the Marquis persisted.

"Only if I fall . . . in love," Fortuna answered.

"What do you want of life?" the Marquis said. "All

women want to be married. Surely that is what you want?"

Fortuna thought for a moment.

"Of course I have dreamt of being married, of falling in love with someone who loved me. But I think if I am truthful I want more than that: I want to love and marry someone with whom I can do things."

She paused, but as the Marquis did not speak she went on:

"It is difficult to put into words exactly what I want, but although it would be wonderful to be in love, I feel that women should have other interests."

She frowned as she concentrated in trying to explain her feelings.

"I know the average Gentleman," she went on, "would not want his wife to interfere in his affairs, but perhaps there would be some things they could do together. I know politicians depend on their wives to dispense hospitality, but there must be other ways in which a woman can be useful and help, and not just in being a housekeeper who is left at home and forgotten when her husband is out enjoying himself."

"And who told you that that is what happens in marriage?" the Marquis asked.

"I have read books, I have heard people talking, I know what Gilly has told me," Fortuna said. "So I know that when I marry I want to share with my husband his interests so that they become mine too."

"Do you think he will share yours?" the Marquis asked. "What are a woman's interests? Gowns, hats, gossip, food, babies? They do not sound very masculine to me."

"That is just the point," Fortuna said, "I do not wish to spend my life thinking of clothes. I hate gossip, it bores me, I want to do something real which would

167

help other people. For example, I would like to assist someone like Mr. Fitzgibbon to build his houses."

"So that is where your interest lies," the Marquis said sharply. "I think perhaps I was right in the first instance."

"You are not right," Fortuna asserted, and there was a note of anger in her voice. "You are deliberately misunderstanding me, you are trying to force me into saying I have a tenderness towards a man whom I have seen for the first time this evening and who means nothing more to me, except that he was kind enough to explain to me something which I feel would be of use to you in the future."

She rose to her feet.

"Will you cease attempting to twist what I say," she asked sharply, "trying to force me into admitting I am enamoured with someone who is not of the least consequence to me now or ever? Why must you be so unkind? Why must you deliberately search for things that I do wrong?"

Her eyes seemed to flash fire. She stood facing him, her breasts moving beneath the thin silk of her gown, her small hands clenched together. She looked so lovely and so fragile that the violence of her words seemed somehow in contradiction to her appearance.

Suddenly the Marquis capitulated, and with a smile that she found irresistible he held out his hand.

"I seemed to have engendered a storm," he said gently. "Forgive me, Fortuna. I am apologising once again."

She took his hand and sank down at his feet.

"I am sorry too," she said. "I have a temper, but it is not often aroused."

"You had reason," he said, "I am at fault. It is just that sometimes I find it impossible to believe that there can be someone so different from other women I have known, so perfect in many ways."

She stared at him as if she felt she could not have heard him right, then she asked in a very soft voice:

"Do you mean that?"

"I mean it," he replied.

She was leaning against his knees, her face only a little lower than his. She looked at him and she had the strangest feeling as if he had but to put out his arms and she would be held close against him.

She was almost sure that he was thinking the same thing. She felt the colour rise a little in her cheeks, and without consciously doing so she swayed a little nearer to him.

She held her breath and she felt that he held his too.

The clock on the mantelpiece chimed midnight and the spell—if that is what it was—was broken. Fortuna looked towards the clock.

"Do you feel it is time for bed?" the Marquis asked, and his voice was very deep and low.

"It is twelve o'clock," Fortuna said. "I feel a little guilty because your head housemaid is waiting up for me. I insisted I could unrobe myself, but she said it was her duty to wait on me."

"And does she intend, like Mrs. Denvers, to lock you in?" the Marquis asked.

"I do not think so," Fortuna replied, "but Mrs. Summers has said that she will come along to enquire if I would like a glass of hot milk."

She wrinkled her small nose.

"It is something I dislike above all things, but it seemed ungrateful to tell her so when she has taken so much trouble."

"My most considerate staff," the Marquis said almost as though he spoke to himself.

"I have no wish to go to bed yet," Fortuna said, "indeed I would far rather stay here and talk to you."

"About life and perhaps—love?" the Marquis said.

"I would like you to tell me about love some time," Fortuna said. "Is it very wonderful to be in love?"

"It is a long time since I have been in that much vaunted and over-estimated condition," the Marquis answered.

"A long time?" Fortuna questioned.

"Many, many years," the Marquis replied.

There was a sudden light in her eyes and he felt the softness of her body against his knee was suddenly tense.

"Then you are not," she half whispered, "in love with the French lady from the Corps de Ballet . . . the one called . . . Odette."

"No, not in the slightest," the Marquis answered. "In fact, I have not even seen her since the party in Berkeley Square."

He saw a sudden radiance light Fortuna's face.

"Oh, I am glad," she said almost involuntarily.

She rose to her feet but still stood beside his chair.

"I think I should go now," she said. "There will be much to do tomorrow, and I am, in fact, a trifle fatigued. Good-night, Apollo."

She curtsied, and as she rose she pressed her lips, soft and warm, against his hand which rested on the arm of his chair.

"There is my . . . forfeit," she whispered, and before he could reply or even rise she had gone from the room, closing the door softly behind her.

Fortuna woke early with a feeling of intense happiness. The sunshine was streaming through the windows of her bedroom, she could hear the song of the birds outside.

170

"There is so much to do today," she thought.

Then she remembered that when they had returned from their ride the day before the Marquis had ordered the horses early.

She came down to breakfast to find he had already eaten and left the room. But when she went to the front door it was to find him mounted on the big black stallion he had ridden before, and her own horse was waiting.

He was smiling as he greeted her, and she felt that the sun was more golden than she had ever known it and the flowers in the garden more vivid.

There was a faint breeze which brought a crispness to the air and had already swept away the mist which habitually lay over the lake in the early morning.

"This will be a wonderful day," Fortuna told herself as they galloped across the park, and as the day progressed she felt that it was, in fact, magical.

She had never known the Marquis in a better humour. They rode together for two hours, and then he took her on the lake, swearing that it was years since he had rowed a boat, at the same time managing the oars most skilfully.

They found a number of wild ducks, swans with broods of cygnets, and a pair of pink-footed geese which the Marquis told Fortuna were rare in that part of the country.

They talked and laughed over luncheon, and the hours sped by so quickly for Fortuna that she was astonished when Mr. Fitzgibbon arrived with his plans to find it was already three o'clock in the afternoon.

The Marquis greeted him most pleasantly, and when the plans were spread out on the Library desk the conversation became really animated as the Marquis asked for explanations of this and that, and Colin Fitzgibbon, full of enthusiasm, explained his ideas.

171

They all three discussed the possibilities of how such a house could be built and what improvements could be made or what alterations effected.

"I cannot help feeling," Fortuna said, "that in years to come something will have to be done about the disposal of sewage in our great cities. Gilly was convinced that a great deal of disease comes from the fact that drainage is not properly taken into account when houses are erected, and that in many places sewage accumulates, causing outbreaks of typhoid and even worse epidemics."

"You are right, of course you are right," Colin Fitzgibbon said. "Do you not agree, My Lord?"

"It is certainly a point that ought to be considered." the Marquis said. "I know that in many places like Lambeth there are courtyards built round a centre pump, with perhaps only one privy to serve them all."

"That is a scandal and a disgrace!" Fortuna exclaimed.

"I cannot help feeling that you ought not to be talking about such subjects at all," the Marquis suggested.

"Nonsense," Fortuna answered. "If disease and the health of a family is not a woman's consideration, what is?"

"Perhaps what we need," Colin Fitzgibbon said, "are women in public life. In many ways I feel they would be much more practical than the men."

"Thank you," Fortuna smiled, "but I feel, Sir, that yours is a still, small voice to which no one will listen."

It was nearly five-thirty of the clock before Colin Fitzgibbon departed, and when the Marquis had seen him off he came back into the Library. He found Fortuna halfway up the mahogany steps taking a volume from one of the upper shelves.

"What are you seeking?" he asked.

"I have just found that you have on your shelf of Latin books one by Juvenal," she replied. "He is an author I have always wished to read."

"And this is one you will not read," he replied, "so long as you are in my house."

"Are you really forbidding me?" she asked, the book in her hand.

"Absolutely," he answered. "Give it to me."

"I think you are being overbearing and autocratic," she complained.

"It is not a suitable book for a young girl."

"I am sure it is no worse than many others I have read," she protested.

He reached up his arms and lifted her from the steps. He took her by surprise and she gave a little gasp.

"Have you really the right to choose what I shall read as well as what I shall wear?" she enquired, pretending an anger she did not feel.

He did not set her down on her feet but held her for a moment in his arms.

"I have the right to do anything I wish," he replied.

"Have you?" she asked.

"Have I not?" he insisted.

There was something in his eyes and in his voice which made her blush and feel shy, yet at the same time she felt more excited than she had ever felt before.

"Answer me, Fortuna."

She looked up at him, but before she could speak the door behind him opened.

"Lady Charlotte Hadleigh, M'Lord."

The Marquis set Fortuna down. She moved a little way from him, still holding the book in her hand.

Lady Charlotte was looking exquisitely beautiful in a ruby-red driving coat with feathers of the same colour in her bonnet. The Marquis walked towards her.

173

"Charlotte! This is indeed a surprise!"

"I thought you might think so!"

Lady Charlotte gave him her hand, which he raised perfunctorily to his lips. Then she looked with cold, hostile eyes at Fortuna.

"Send that creature away," she said, "I wish to speak to you, Sylvanus."

The Marquis stiffened and it seemed for a moment as though he would refuse to do what Lady Charlotte asked. Without waiting for his command Fortuna turned and ran swiftly through the open window out onto the Terrace.

She meant as she reached it to re-enter the house by another window, but some pride or perhaps anger prompted her to stay where she was.

"I will not be treated like a servant girl," she told herself.

She stood within sight of the window, leaning against the balustrade looking out over the garden.

Lady Charlotte watched her go, then turned to face the Marquis. There was a firey anger in her dark eyes.

"Are you as mad as Bedlam, Sylvanus?" she enquired.

"Not that I am aware of," the Marquis replied.

"Then how could you do anything so stupid, so irresponsible as to bring a doxy of whom all London is talking to the Castle."

The Marquis did not reply and she went on:

"I am on my way to Merrill Park to stay the night with Her Grace. And when I heard you had come here, I planned to see you, before I learnt from people who were only too willing to inform me that you had left for the country with the Cyprian who has been living with you in Berkeley Square. That was bad enough!"

She turned to the Marquis and walked across the room in an agitated manner as if it relieved her feelings.

174

"You have never before, as far as I know, had a woman of that sort living in your house. Such behaviour might be tolerated in London, but not in the country, Sylvanus. No one knows that better than you. Can you imagine what they will say."

"What will they say?" the Marquis enquired.

"They will say that you have lost every semblance of decency and honourable behaviour," Lady Charlotte snapped. "Nobody cares how much time you spend with lovebirds or where you entertain them, so long as it is not in your home—the house which you will share with your wife."

"I have no wife," the Marquis expostulated.

"Do not prevaricate, Sylvanus," Lady Charlotte admonished him. "You know perfectly well that I intend to marry you and will live here as I will live in your house in Berkeley Square. I do not want it soiled with the memories of creatures that are beneath my notice."

"Then why notice them?" the Marquis asked.

"Sylvanus, you are being deliberately provocative," Lady Charlotte said. "You know exactly what I mean. As my father used to say so very wisely—'No Gentleman fouls his own nest.' And that is what you are doing, Sylvanus. Can you imagine how the county will gossip."

"I have an idea," the Marquis said with a faint smile on his lips.

"Why you should do such a thing I cannot fathom," Lady Charlotte went on, "unless, of course, it is deliberately to infuriate the Accringtons. People in London are saying that this lovebird of yours closely resembles Her Grace."

Her voice was acid.

"I cannot credit such a thing is true," she snapped, "but if it is so then she must obviously be a by-blow in the family, a bastard who is trading on her facial

175

similarity to a great Lady. My advice to you, Sylvanus, is to forget her, and quickly."

"And if I do not?" the Marquis asked.

As if his words were a danger signal Lady Charlotte turned to him with her hands outstretched.

"We are quarrelling, Sylvanus," she said in a very different tone, "and you know that is something I have no wish to do. I love you, and as I have already told you I intend to marry you."

She lifted her lovely face to his.

"Your lovebirds are of no consequence to me," she went on softly, "or indeed to our feelings for each other. But surely you must see it is indecent of you to bring one of them here. Take her away, do what you like with her, but do not let such an insignificant piece of nonsense come between you and me."

"If indeed you are considering my reputation," the Marquis said, "I assure you, Charlotte, it has already sunk so low that there are no further depths to which it can descend."

"That is fustian!" Lady Charlotte replied. "For you know full well that to a man who is rich and powerful everything will be forgiven. It is just that you overstep accepted bounds when you come here—here of all places—with some wench you have picked up in the gutter."

"I feel sure you are only thinking of my interests," the Marquis said.

"And my own," Lady Charlotte replied. "Oh, Sylvanus, do let us stop playing with each other and come to some sensible solution about ourselves. I would adore a summer wedding, and you will make a breath-takingly handsome bridegroom."

"You flatter me," the Marquis said.

"I must go," Lady Charlotte said regretfully. "As it is I shall be late for dinner at Merrill Park. When shall I see you again? I shall be back in London within two days."

"Then I must undoubtedly await your pleasure," the Marquis said and bowed.

There was a sarcastic note in his voice which made her glance at him suspiciously. Then she went from the room and he followed.

Her coach was waiting outside, drawn by four white horses with emblazoned panels on the doors and its outriders wearing their green and orange livery. It was a spectacular entourage.

On the steps of the Castle Lady Charlotte paused a moment and put her hand on the Marquis's arm.

"Please, Sylvanus," she said in a low voice so that the servants could not overhear, "send that creature away. You know full well that it is not right for you to have brought your mistress to your home—if indeed she is your mistress."

The Marquis stiffened.

"May I enquire what you mean by that last remark?"

"It is only that Lord Worcester, who is enamoured with her and indeed talks of no one else," Lady Charlotte said, her voice sharp, "is proclaiming to all and sundry that she is too pure and unspoilt to be anything but a virgin. Yet I believe you are credited with being a ladykiller, Sylvanus!"

She swept down the steps and into the coach without waiting for the Marquis to assist her. The footman closed the door, the coachman whipped up the horses and with a clatter of hooves and a jingle of harness Lady Charlotte drove away, leaving the Marquis staring after her, a scowl between his eyes.

He walked slowly back to the Library. Fortuna did not hear him enter.

She had come back into the room and was standing

177

framed in the open window, her head thrown back against the curtain, her features silhouetted against the sky outside.

Her pose revealed the rounded loveliness of her white neck, the soft curves of her breasts, the outline of her lips. For a moment the Marquis stood looking at her and a fire smouldered in his eyes.

Then purposefully, as if he suddenly made up his mind, he walked towards her.

He stood at her side and knew that she was tinglingly aware of him. His hand went out towards her, but before he could touch her she said in a low voice:

"I was thinking when you were not here how very beautiful the Castle is and how much it owes to your mother."

The Marquis was suddenly still and his hand fell to his side.

"You may think it fanciful of me," Fortuna continued, "but somehow I feel she is close to you, loving you and wanting your happiness just as she must have wanted it when she was alive."

There was a silence. Then abruptly the Marquis crossed the room and pulled at the bell.

"We are leaving for London," he announced, and his voice was so loud that it seemed to echo round the Library.

"For London!" Fortuna exclaimed.

"That is what I said," the Marquis snapped. "Get your cloak, the luggage will follow us. I am ordering my Phaeton immediately."

"But why . . . why are we going back?" Fortuna said. "We have been so . . . happy here."

"Happy?" the Marquis asked, and his voice was harsh. "Happy in this dull spot? I assure you, Fortuna, that I need gaiety, I need people, the companionship of my friends and, of course—an Hetaira to amuse me as you are unable to do."

He walked from the room as he spoke and the Library door closed behind him with a slam. Fortuna stiffened as if turned to stone. Then as the tears welled into her eyes there was an unbearable pain in her breasts and she realised for the first time that she was in love with him.

She loved him as a woman loves a man, and she had—lost him.

8

As dawn broke Fortuna rose from her bed and went to the window to look out into Berkeley Square.

The faint light silhouetted the roofs and the tops of the trees, which still had the purple shadows of the night beneath them, while the flares outside the great houses had burnt low or were extinguished.

She had not slept even after she had wept until she was utterly exhausted, but had lain restless in her bed knowing an agony that was all the more poignant because of the happiness she had experienced that last day at the Castle.

She thought now how foolish she had been not to recognise that she had been in love with the Marquis almost from the first moment she had seen him.

She had always loved him in her heart. He had been in her dreams and her imagination ever since she could remember, but then he had been the idealised Apollo, no human but a being as mythical as the god with whom she connected him.

Now it was the man she loved. Bitter and cynical, enraged or sarcastic, she still loved him so overwhelmingly that she felt her whole body throb with the agony of it.

"I love him!" she whispered aloud in the darkness of the night.

She thought despairingly that she had nothing to offer him save a heart in which he was not interested.

She went over and over again that moment when he had come back to the Library and he had turned upon her speaking in that harsh, cruel voice which seemed to strike through her as if he had stabbed her with a sword.

What had she done? What had she said?

They had been so happy that long enchanted day when she had made him laugh, when they seemed closer to each other than ever before.

She knew now that her happiness had been based on her love for him and it seemed as golden and wonderful as the sunshine itself.

"I . . . love . . . you."

She could hear her voice broken with tears repeating the words over and over again, and she thought regretfully how foolish she had been not to kiss the Marquis when he had demanded it as a forfeit.

What nonsense she had talked about wanting to kiss only a man with whom she had fallen in love, when she was already in love!

She knew now that she wanted above all else in the world to feel the touch of his lips, to know his arms were round her.

She could imagine nothing more wonderful, nothing nearer to Heaven, and she recaptured again and again that moment in the Library when he had held her and said:

"I have a right to anything I wish."

She could recall all too vividly that strange excitement which rose within herself, an excitement which seemed to make her feel as though she was unable to breathe, that there was something thrilling throbbing in her breast and something constricting in her throat.

That was love and she had not recognised it.

Was it something Lady Charlotte had said to him which had made him so angry? For it was after her visit that he had changed.

The young man who had rowed her on the lakes, who had ridden at her side across the Park, who had made the luncheon they had enjoyed together a meal of enchantment had changed into a man who seemed almost to hate her.

"Oh God, what can I do?" Fortuna asked, and buried her face in her hands . . .

The Marquis had driven her back to London in silence, indeed it would have been difficult to talk even if she had wished to do so; for he had driven like a maniac, and only his superb skill in tooling his horses had prevented not one accident but a dozen.

If Fortuna had not been so miserable she thought there would have been a strange exhilaration in moving faster than she had ever moved before in her life with a man who seemed determined to bring them to the very brink of destruction.

And yet somehow they had survived and arrived in Berkeley Square in what must have been record time.

The horses were steaming and Fortuna had felt breathless and exhausted, not only from apprehension during the drive but also from sheer physical fatigue. She had been thrown from side to side and had to cling tightly to the box of the Phaeton for fear of falling from her high perch into the road.

Regardless of good manners the Marquis had stalked ahead of her in through the doorway of his house.

"Order my London landau," he said to the butler, "I shall be leaving immediately I have changed."

"Very good, M'Lord," the man replied. "Will Your Lordship be dining here tonight?"

"I shall not—I shall be out," the Marquis replied,

and without even glancing at Fortuna walked up the stairs towards his bedroom.

She stood in the Hall feeling wretchedly bereft.

"Would you wish for dinner in the Dining-room, Miss, or upstairs?" the butler enquired.

"I want nothing, thank you," Fortuna answered in a voice that was perilously near to tears.

Somehow she managed to control her feelings until Mrs. Denvers and the attentive maids had left her and she was alone.

Then at last she had buried her face in the pillow and cried hopelessly and tempestuously as she had never cried in her whole life.

The sky grew a little lighter and she thought how only yesterday she had believed the sunshine on the gardens at the Castle was the most beautiful thing she had ever seen. And yet now its very light seemed to mock the darkness within herself.

A sound down below in the street made her lean forward.

A carriage was drawing up outside the house. She drew in her breath as from it stepped the Marquis. He was carrying his hat and the dawn sun touched the darkness of his hair, the white elegance of his frilled cravat and the shining lapels of his evening-coat.

There was an elegance about him which made her feel that in the company of other men however distinquished, however smart, he would stand out. There was something in the breadth of his shoulders which however fashionable his attire made him look intensely masculine.

"I love him," she whispered. "He is the best looking man I have ever seen in my life, yet I believe I would still love him if he were maimed and ugly. I love him because I cannot help it; whether he wants me or not I belong to him."

The Marquis disappeared into the house, the carriage drove away, and then Fortuna realised with a sudden stab of her heart that it must be nearly four o'clock in the morning.

There was no need for her to ask herself where the Marquis had been all night, she knew only too well.

Was it Odette that had kept him amused as she was unable to do, or was it some other Hetaira even more beautiful, more attractive, who could press her lips against the Marquis's mouth and feel his response?

She tortured herself by remembering how she had seen Odette kissing him at the party he had given.

There had been a wild gaiety about the slim Frenchwoman, an attraction which rested not entirely on her face, although that was pretty enough, but something in herself, some individual charm, Fortuna felt, that she personally could not emulate.

And yet she had had the chance of kissing the Marquis and refused it! She felt the tears come slowly to her eyes at the thought of what she had missed.

Perhaps now there would never be another opportunity, perhaps after what he had said last night she would no longer be able to sit at his feet and listen to him talking to her. They would not be able to argue about books or plan new housing in Lambeth or Waterless.

He was bored with her, and boredom, Fortuna told herself, was worse than hatred because it was something against which one could not fight.

She felt suddenly very cold and leaving the window went back to her bed.

But the mental agony she was experiencing would not let her lie still; so she rose again, walking around the room, going to the window, sitting in a chair, moving, moving simply because when she was still she felt suffocated with her own misery.

Her breakfast was brought to her at nine o'clock, and when Mrs. Denvers came in half an hour later she exclaimed at the sight of Fortuna's face.

"What have you been doing to yourself, Miss?" she enquired. "Can you be feeling indisposed?"

Fortuna shook her head.

"No, there is nothing wrong," she answered, but seeing the disbelief in Mrs. Denver's expression added: "I have a trifling ache in my head."

"And that doesn't surprise me in the least," Mrs. Denvers retorted in the scolding voice of a child's nurse, "coming home at what I hear was a breakneck speed and then retiring without anything to eat. 'Tis only surprising that you don't ache in every part of your body."

Fortuna longed to reply that it was only her heart that was affected, and then was ashamed that her feelings could show themselves so obviously.

With an effort she managed to ask in a normal voice:

"Has His Lordship any special plans for today?"

Mrs. Denvers looked surprised.

"His Lordship has already left the house," she replied. "Didn't he inform you that he was going out of London this morning?"

"Out of London?" Fortuna repeated. "Where to?"

Mrs. Denvers smiled.

"If His Lordship didn't tell you where he would be journeying, then perhaps he didn't wish you to know," she answered. "But His Lordship's valet tells me there is a very special mill at Wimbledon this morning to which all the Gentlemen of Fashion are aflocking to place their bets on the bruisers, one of whom is His Lordship's own man."

Fortuna felt some of the heaviness of her heart lighten a little. If the Marquis was going to a fight, at least he would not be spending his time with some entrancing Hetaira.

"I hope His Lordship's man wins," she said.

"I understand the betting is on his opponent," Mrs. Denvers said. "But there, I shouldn't be talking to you like this, Miss. But needless to say here in the household we take a great interest in everything that concerns His Lordship, and indeed big sums of money change hands at these mills."

"Perhaps if his bruiser wins the Marquis will be in a good humour," Fortuna thought, and then he might be kind to her again! Perhaps she might even dine with him.

"Madame Yvette has left a message to say she has two of your gowns ready for fitting," Mrs. Denvers said, her voice breaking in on Fortuna's thoughts. "Shall I ask Madam to come here or would you wish, as there is little else to do, to visit her establishment?"

"I will go to Madame Yvette's," Fortuna replied.

She felt that anything was better than sitting alone in the empty house, longing for the Marquis and yet at the same time apprehensive of his return.

"You can't go alone, Miss," Mrs. Denvers said, "and if it be your pleasure I'll accompany you."

"That will be very pleasant," Fortuna smiled, "and perhaps as this is such a nice day we could drive in the open landau."

"I'll order it to be ready in an hour," Mrs. Denvers said, "and I'll send Mary to help you dress, Miss."

"Thank you," Fortuna answered.

She was ready before the carriage came round to the door, and having gone downstairs she went for a moment into the Library.

She remembered how the Marquis had sat in his favourite chair to the right of the fireplace and how when they had returned from the Palace of Fortune he

186

had bent forward to take her chin between his fingers to turn her face up to his.

She felt herself quiver again inside just as she had quivered when he had touched her.

She knew now, though she had not realised it at the time, it was her love that had given her that strange intensity of feeling that she had been unable to explain and had in her ignorance imagined it was but shyness.

She had felt it again at the Castle, when kneeling beside him she had thought how easy it would have been to slip into his arms, to feel herself close against him.

"Apollo!"

Fortuna said his name aloud and wondered if at Wimbledon, or wherever he was at this moment, he could feel her reaching out towards him, calling him with an intensity that had some spiritual force about it because her need for him was so great.

"The carriage is ready, Miss."

The butler's voice made her start. Then walking across the Hall she found Mrs. Denvers waiting, wearing a neat black bonnet and a black mantle over her silk dress.

The landau was open, the horses were flicking their tails to be rid of the flies and shaking their heads so that the harness jingled.

Fortuna sat down on the cushioned seat and Mrs. Denvers sat opposite her, her back to the horses.

"It's a treat for me to be driving in the sunshine, Miss," Mrs. Denvers remarked. "It's not often I've time to get away from the cares of the household."

"You keep everything so beautifully," Fortuna said.

"I've often wondered what His Lordship would do without me," Mrs. Denvers replied in a tone that had no conceit in it. "But there, one doesn't expect a Gentleman to trouble himself with household matters, they just expect everything to run smoothly with someone like myself to keep the wheels arolling until they are wed."

"Do you think the Marquis will every marry?" Fortuna enquired.

"Of course he will," Mrs. Denvers replied sharply. "He needs an heir for the Castle, and what Gentleman in his position doesn't. And it isn't as though things are as bad now as they have been in the past."

"You mean when he first lost all his possessions," Fortuna said.

Mrs. Denvers nodded.

"I thought at first His Lordship would close everything up and dismiss everyone," she said. "Indeed, for one moment he talked wildly of going abroad and never setting foot in this country again. But fortunately it was during the war, and even if he wished to leave it wouldn't have been easy for him. But for a year the staff both at the Castle and in Berkeley Square was halved, and sometimes when the wages were overdue we wondered if we'd ever see them."

Mrs. Denvers pursed her lips as if in memory of those hard times.

"But eventually we were paid every penny of what we were owed," she went on. "His Lordship began to win money at the tables, and those that had been retired came back into service. We had footmen and young housemaids again, and everything seemed back to normal again save that the Marquis himself wasn't the same."

"It must have hurt him terribly," Fortuna said in a low voice.

"Hurt is the right word, Miss," Mrs. Denvers agreed, "and worse than that. It changed him. But as Mr. Clements says so truly, His Lordship's been more like his old self since you've been with us."

Fortuna's eyes seemed to light up.

"Do you mean that?" she asked. "Do you really mean it?"

"I'm speaking the truth, Miss. You seem to have changed His Lordship. He laughs, a sound we haven't heard for years; and I swear he looks younger."

"Thank you . . . thank you for telling me," Fortuna cried.

Mrs. Denvers smiled.

"I think, Miss, if you'll forgive my saying so, it's what Miss Gillingham would have wished you to do. She doted on Master Sylvanus, as he was when she was with him; she thought the whole world of him. She wouldn't have liked to see him as he was when you came. Now I've a feeling things are going to be better in the future, and it's you, Miss, that has done it."

"I hope you are right," Fortuna sighed, "but it is difficult for me. You see, I am so ignorant, so unsophisticated, and the other ladies His Lordship knows are so much more attractive."

"That isn't true, Miss," Mrs. Denvers said quite sharply, "and don't you be comparing yourself with them. You're different, and it's my belief that His Lordship will see the difference if you give him a little time."

It seemed to Fortuna as though the sunshine was a little more golden, and that some of the misery that had encompassed her all night was dispersed.

"Perhaps I am birdwitted to be so depressed," she told herself and felt her spirits rise.

They drew up at Madame Yvette's small shop, which was situated in a quiet street. The Coachman drew the horses to a standstill and the footman jumped down from the box to open the door.

Fortuna stepped out onto the pavement, and then as

she would have walked into the shop she found a lackey barring her way.

"Excuse me, Miss Grimwood," he said in a low voice, "there is a Gentleman in a carriage here who would be deeply grateful if you would have a word with him."

"A Gentleman?" Fortuna asked in surprise.

She glanced round and saw a little further up the street there was a closed landau. It was facing towards her and was drawn by a magnificient pair of horses. The Coachman was wearing a dark blue livery, as was the lackey who had spoken to her.

Apprehensively she wondered if the Gentleman in question, as she knew so few, could be Sir Roger Crowley.

"Who is it who wishes to speak to me?" she said.

The servant lowered his voice.

" 'Tis His Grace the Duke of Accrington," he replied, "and he asked me to say, Miss, that he had something to impart to you which would be of advantage to His Lordship."

Fortuna listened in astonishment. Then she thought that perhaps in some magical way the Duke had had a change of heart.

Perhaps he wished after all to make reparation to the Marquis for his past crimes.

"His Grace will not keep you more than a moment," the servant said insistently.

Fortuna looked back at Mrs. Denvers who had just stepped from the carriage onto the pavement.

"Will you wait for me?" she asked.

She then followed the man up the street to the closed landau.

He opened the door with a flourish. She looked in, saw that it was dark inside, and that there was someone there.

190

Then suddenly she felt herself pulled and pushed into the carriage with a violence that left her gasping. She gave a frightened cry as out of the darkness strong hands held her arms and forced her onto the back seat.

As the Coachman whipped up the horses, a man's hand dragged her head back and she felt the mouth of a bottle forced between her lips.

She tried to cry out and attempted to struggle, but it was useless. A liquid, thick and nauseating, was being poured down her throat, and because of the position in which her head was held she was forced to swallow it.

Then as she thought she must faint with terror, the bottle was taken away and her mouth was free. But she knew even as she struggled against the hands that still held her that she had been drugged.

There was a strange, horrible feeling of drowsiness creeping over her and she could feel first her legs and then her arms become limp so that she was unable to move them.

Last of all, as she fought helplessly against the black tide which was enveloping her, she thought despairingly of the Marquis, and felt she would never see him again . . .

The Marquis, having seen his bruiser, Jem Bart, pummel Bombardier Harris into a bleeding mass, and having collected the very large sums of money he had won, returned to London in a slightly better humour than he had left it.

He realised he was tired, having not slept the night before for more than two hours, and he decided that he would dine at home with Fortuna.

He had been cruel to her the night before, and now his conscience pricked him.

He had seen the unhappiness in her eyes when she

191

had come down the steps at the Castle to climb into his Phaeton, and the devil within him had made him glad that he was hurting her even as he had hurt himself.

He thought now how plucky she had been not to cry out at the manner in which he had driven back to London from the Castle. Only a madman would have taken the risks he had taken, and perhaps only a madman would have survived.

The Marquis was ashamed of himself, and as this was a feeling he did not often acknowledge he decided he would make amends to Fortuna.

He wondered now what she had done the previous evening after he had changed his clothes and gone from the house still in the blue-devilled mood which had brought them back from the Castle so precipitously.

He had not looked back when he had left her standing in the Hall, but he knew without actually seeing her that she was a forlorn little figure, lost, afraid and apprehensive, all because he was behaving like a brute.

He swore softly to himself, not with the violence and the venom with which he usually expressed himself, but gently as though there was an underlying pain which brought the words to his lips, and as though he knew that swearing would on this occasion bring him no relief.

He had gone from Berkeley Square to White's Club. He had asked for Alistair Merrill, and finding he was not there had repaired to the Colonel's lodgings expecting to find that he had returned from Merrill Park.

The manservant informed the Marquis that he was expecting his master but he had not yet arrived; so the Marquis, asking the man to bring him a bottle of wine, had settled himself in an armchair and prepared to wait for the Colonel's return.

It was after two o'clock in the morning before Alistair Merrill, walking into his small Sitting-room, found the Marquis fast asleep in the armchair, his feet raised, a half-empty decanter of claret beside him.

He stood for a moment looking at his friend, and the Marquis stirred and woke with the alertness of a soldier who on waking is instantly in full control of his faculties.

"You are damned late!" he said before the Colonel could speak.

"That was just what I was going to say to you," Alistair Merrill replied with a smile. "I was not anticipating callers."

"Where have you been?" the Marquis demanded.

"Listening to some rather unpleasant stories about you from one of your amoureuses," the Colonel replied.

"Charlotte Hadleigh, I presume," the Marquis remarked.

"Exactly," Alistair Merrill replied. "You appear to have upset Her Ladyship; anyway, she had a deal to say on the subject. And as I was interested I stayed at Merrill Park for dinner. Even so, I would have been here sooner if my cursed horse had not thrown a shoe. I had to wake up a village blacksmith. It all took time, and naturally I had no idea you would be waiting up for me like some anxious Mama."

"Anxious Mama be damned!" the Marquis ejaculated. "I have news for you, and it is not the tittle-tattling of some jealous society wench."

"What is it?" the Colonel enquired.

"The whereabouts of the Grimwoods," the Marquis replied.

"And where are they?" Alistair Merrill enquired. "I have been racking my brains the whole way from

193

Merrill Park to think where my uncle could have sent them."

"Did His Grace at any time speak of the Isle of Man?" the Marquis enquired.

"The Isle of Man," Colonel Merrill repeated slowly, "Now you mention it I believe many years ago he did win a large portion of the island in a game of cards. I cannot recall the name of the man from whom he won the land, but I vaguely recall the jokes about how my uncle would administrate it."

"That is where he sent the Grimwoods," the Marquis answered.

"Of course, it would be a prefect place of hiding, would it not?" Alistair Merrill exclaimed. "And how did you find out?"

"There is no need to go into details," the Marquis answered airily. "What you must do, Alistair, is to hurry there immediately, get a confession from the Grimwoods and bring it back with all speed."

"I will do that," the Colonel agreed. "I regret that I will need gold for horseflesh, and I may even have to hire a ship to carry me across the sea."

"You will find notes of hand for two hundred pounds on your desk," the Marquis said, "and a purse of sovereigns. If the journey costs more you know I will reimburse you."

"I am sorry that I have to ask you for a loan of this kind," Alistair Merrill said, accentuating the word loan, "but at the moment I am under the hatches, as you well know."

"We are in this together, Alistair," the Marquis said curtly, "it is sink or swim for both of us, and, for that matter, for Fortuna."

"How are you going to force His Grace to acknowledge the girl as his daughter?" Colonel Merrill asked curiously.

"We can leave the details until you return with a confession," the Marquis said abruptly.

"You seem so sure that I will get it," Alistair Merrill said.

"There is no reason to anticipate that the Grimwoods will have died meantime," the Marquis said. "One of them surely will be alive at any rate. If you can have their confession witnessed by a Parson or someone of that sort, it will be all the better, though I dare say it will not be of any great consequence. The Duke will find it hard to refute a confession, however it is made, when he is confronted with that and Fortuna at the same time."

"He will certainly learn about Fortuna when he returns home," Alistair Merrill said.

"What happened at Merrill Park?" the Marquis enquired.

"I arrived there this morning," the Colonel replied. "I made the excuse that I was passing and asked quite frankly if I could stay to lunch. The Duchess was charming, then she always is. The Duke was still in London and we talked of various things. Then I related to her how I had met Fortuna and how extraordinary it was that the girl was obviously an O'Keary."

He was silent a moment, remembering the Duchess's grey eyes fixed on his face.

"I had hardly opened my mouth on the subject," he continued, "when an old chap called Sir Hugo Harrington arrived. He told the Duchess how he had dined with you at your Castle the previous evening, and went on to speak of the colour of Fortuna's hair and how he had for a moment imagined it was Her Grace herself who was standing in the Salon."

"What did the Duchess say?" the Marquis asked.

"She said very little," Colonel Merrill replied, "until

195

after Sir Hugo had left. Then she turned to me and said. " 'What sort of person is this girl? You have talked with her, is she educated?'

"I thought it would be best to tell the truth," the Colonel said. "I told her that Fortuna had been brought up by your old governess, and I continued: 'She is little more than a child, Your Grace, young, unsophisticated, with a very sweet and gentle nature. Of course living the life she now leads I suspect she will soon change.'

" 'The life she leads?" the Duchess repeated in a low voice. 'And what sort of life does she lead?'

"I pretended to be embarrassed," the Colonel explained, "I said: 'I should not be talking to you like this, my dear Aunt, but you know how much my father always admired the O'Keary colouring. I think if he could have seen this girl he would have been vastly intrigued as indeed we all are.'

" 'You said just now something about the life she was leading,' the Duchess insisted. 'What did you mean by that?'

" 'Well, to put it bluntly,' I replied, 'she is under the protection of Thane. You know as well as I do that he is nicknamed the Young Devil, and I hardly think that residing alone with him at his house in Berkeley Square and frequenting places like "The Palace of Fortune" is the right environment for a girl of seventeen.' "

"What did the Duchess reply?" the Marquis asked quickly.

"She jumped to her feet," Colonel Merrill related, "and it seemed to me that she had gone very pale."

" 'No, no, not that!' she exclaimed, and went from the room."

The Marquis sat back in his chair.

"So the Duke had not told her."

"No, I do not think Her Grace had heard of Fortuna before I came to Merrill Park," the Colonel agreed. "But she had heard plenty of her before I left. Your lady friend arrived spitting with rage."

"That I can well believe," the Marquis said with a sarcastic note in his voice.

"She was so angry," Colonel Merrill went on, "that she did not choose her words with any care when speaking to the Duchess. She stormed about your behaviour in taking what she termed a 'doxy' into the Castle. She related to the Duchess the story of your party, and how the Corps de Ballet had entertained the guests with *'les poses plastiques'*."

The Colonel smiled.

"By the way she went on," he continued, "you would have thought the whole dinner party, let alone the Ballet, was stark naked by the end of the evening. And then she explained at great length what she had said to you about taking Fortuna to the Castle."

"Pray do not make me listen to it again," the Marquis begged raising his hand.

"I will spare your blushes," the Colonel said with a laugh. "The Duchess listened to her gravely with a look on her face that I could not interpret. She may have been shocked, she may have been disgusted. I honestly do not know."

The Marquis rose to his feet.

"At least by now she is aware of Fortuna's existence," he said. "Get some sleep, Alistair, and post for the Isle of Man as early as possible. I will send you one of my best horses on which to commence your journey."

"That is good of you, Sylvanus."

"Good?" the Marquis ejaculated. "There is nothing good about this whole operation! Do you want to know the truth, Alistair? It disgusts me, but unfortunately there is no other way."

197

The Colonel said nothing, there was something in the Marquis's voice which kept him silent.

The Marquis reached the door and only as he was actually passing through it did he look back.

"Good hunting, Alistair," he said, and then he was gone.

He drove back to Berkeley Square as dawn was breaking. He wondered if Fortuna was asleep. He had half a mind to go up to her bedroom and find out.

Then he remembered that Mrs. Denvers would have locked the door and realised that a very different interpretation would be put on his actions than the fact that he felt penitent for having been so excessively disagreeable.

Now driving back to London he was determined to make amends, and yet how could he explain to Fortuna what had upset him the day before and which had driven him back to London in such a rage that in order to relieve his feelings he had hit out at the one person who he knew was vulnerable.

It was nearly four o'clock in the afternoon before he reached Berkeley Square.

After the fight he and his friends had lunched together at the local Inn, he had paid his bruiser and seen that his wounds were attended to—all of which had taken time—before eventually he left.

He entered the Hall and found to his surprise that Mrs. Denvers and Abbey, his Head Coachman, were waiting there for him.

"Oh, M'Lord, thank God you have returned!" Mrs. Denvers exclaimed in an agitated voice.

"What is amiss?" the Marquis enquired, handing his hat and gloves to one of the footmen.

"It is Miss Fortuna," Mrs. Denvers answered.

"Miss Fortuna?" the Marquis asked sharply. "Where is she, I wish to see her."

198

"That is something you cannot do, M'Lord, and why we're here to tell you what has occurred," Mrs. Denvers replied.

Her voice broke on the words. She lifted a handkerchief to her eyes.

"Miss Fortuna has been abducted, M'Lord."

"Abducted!"

The Marquis heard his own voice echo round the Hall like an explosion.

"What the devil do you mean by that?" he enquired. "What happened, Abbey?"

His old Coachman lifted his hand respectfully to his forehead.

"It's true, M'Lord. Abducted she were under our very eyes. I've never seen anything like it, never in my whole born days."

"What happened?" the Marquis insisted.

Then he was suddenly conscious of the round eyes and open mouths of the footmen listening to the conversation.

"Come into the Morning-room," he said abruptly.

He entered the room, crossing it to stand with his back to the hearth; Mrs. Denvers and Abbey waited respectfully just inside the door.

"What do you mean by saying Miss Fortuna has been abducted?" the Marquis asked, and there was a concern in his voice which seemed to override both his surprise and his anger.

Mrs. Denvers explained how they had driven to Madame Yvette's shop and Fortuna had stepped out first onto the pavement.

"A footman in livery spoke to her, M'Lord," she explained. "I couldn't hear what he was saying, he appeared to be asking Miss Fortuna something. Then as I reached her side wondering what was his business, she turned, asked me to wait for her and followed the footman up the street."

"In whose employment was he?" the Marquis asked.

Mrs. Denvers glanced at Abbey.

"They were wearing a plain blue livery, M'Lord, which I didn't recognise," the Coachman said, "but I'd have known the horses which were adrawing the carriage anywhere. Sold at Tattersalls they were last year, the property of Lord Mansell. As fine a pair as ever came up in a sale-room. I asked Your Lordship to buy them but you said as that you weren't interested."

"Who did purchase them?" the Marquis asked.

Just for a second the Coachman looked uncomfortable, then he said:

"They were bought, M'Lord, by His Grace the Duke of Accrington."

"Accrington!"

The Marquis seemed almost to shout the name.

"So it is His Grace who has abducted Miss Fortuna," he said more quietly. "You are sure of that, Abbey?"

"Unless he's sold that pair of horses, M'Lord, which I know full well he hasn't, then it was His Grace who carried off Miss Fortuna in a closed carriage."

"Why the hell did you not go after him?" the Marquis asked.

"You see, M'Lord, the carriage was facing towards us. As soon as they'd bundled Miss Fortuna inside they drove off, passing us, into Bond Street. By the time I'd turned m' own carriage they was out of sight, there weren't a sign o' them. I drove the whole length of Bond Street, but they might have turned off into Grosvernor or Bruton Street. I did m' best, M'Lord."

"Yes, Abbey, I am sure did you," the Marquis said.

"We must get her back, M'Lord, we must! We must!" Mrs. Denvers cried. "We can't let her stay with that wicked man. Gentleman he may be by birth, but Your

200

Lordship knows as well as I do what he's called. And not without reason, from all I hears."

"His Grace will not harm Miss Fortuna in the way in which you mean," the Marquis said quietly. "But we are going to find it difficult to find out where he has taken her, for I know one thing and that is he means to keep her hidden."

Neither Mrs. Denvers nor the coachman spoke, and after a moment the Marquis said:

"Send Jim to me."

"Jim, M'Lord?"

"Yes. He is the man for this job, I am sure of it. At the same time, Abbey, keep your ears open. What I want to know is where His Grace has taken Miss Fortuna, and that means we have to discover in what direction his carriages have travelled."

"I understands, M'Lord, I'll send Jim to you right away."

As the Coachman left the room, Mrs. Denvers lingered.

"Miss Fortuna wasn't herself this morning, M'Lord," she said.

The Marquis raised his head to look at her. Mrs. Denvers continued:

"By her appearance she'd been crying most of the night, and she seemed very low in her spirits. I just thought I should mention this, M'Lord."

"Thank you, Mrs. Denvers," the Marquis replied.

"If I'd only gone with her," Mrs. Denvers said, "if I'd not let her go up the pavement alone . . . I know she told me to wait, but it was wrong, M'Lord, I should have accompanied her."

"You must not blame yourself, Mrs. Denvers," the Marquis said. "If she had not been abducted at that moment, it would have happened sooner or later. You can be sure of that."

"I'll never forgive myself," Mrs. Denvers said in a strangled voice.

Her handkerchief to her eyes she went from the room as if she could bear no more.

The Marquis sat waiting. It was some time before Jim came siddling in through the heavy mahogany door.

He was a small, under-sized stable-boy whom the Marquis had seen hanging about the racing-stables at Newmarket and taken into his employment because he had realised he had an extraordinary knack of handling the most unruly horses.

Jim had been kicked in the side of the face when he was a child, and the rough life he had led had not added to his looks. But his hands were as gentle as a woman's and the Marquis would have trusted him to ride any horse in his stable, and even preferred him to any of his more conventional grooms."

"Ye wants me, M'Lord?" Jim asked.

"I suspicion they will have already told you what I require," the Marquis answered.

"I'll hang about 'is Grace's stables right away, M'Lord," Jim replied, "and if I can't find out where they've ataken the fancy mort, then no un can."

"You will speak respectfully of Miss Fortuna," the Marquis admonished him.

"Yes, M'Lord, I means to, M'Lord."

"And do not waste time," the Marquis said sharply. "Find out where the carriage has gone. Damn it all, they cannot abduct a young woman without someone being in on the secret."

"No, M'Lord."

Jim seemed to linger.

"What is it?" the Marquis asked.

"I'll want a bit o' blunt, M'Lord. If I've got to make someun talk they talks best with th' booze inside 'em."

"Yes, of course," the Marquis answered.

He took a sovereign from his pocket and threw it across the room. Jim caught it neatly.

"Keep yer pecker up, M'Lord," he said, "I shan't let ye down."

He was gone before the Marquis could reprove him for his familiarity. He was used to it from Jim, for Jim was a law unto himself. No one could make him speak respectfully, no one could make him choose his words with care.

It seemed to the Marquis that never had the hours passed more slowly. It was the greatest frustration he had ever known not to be able to go out and enquire for himself where Fortuna might be.

He would have liked to get his fingers round the Duke's neck and throttle him into telling the truth, but he knew that he would learn nothing and Fortuna would only be hidden away even more completely.

He cursed himself for not having anticipated that the Duke would make a move of this sort. It was always cork-brained to underestimate one's opponent, and the Duke was an extremely formidable adversary and always had been. He would have made his plans carefully.

Wherever he arranged to hide Fortuna it would be difficult to find her. There was one consolation. If he had her carried to the Isle of Man, then Alistair Merrill would know of it when he reached the island.

But the Marquis had the feeling that the Duke would not push his luck in the same place twice. He had hidden the Grimwoods; it would be overbidding his hand to hide Fortuna in the same place.

No, he would think of something more subtle. It could be anywhere in Scotland or Wales or Ireland where he would transport her.

It seemed to the Marquis that in this instance possession was nine points of the law. The Duke had

Fortuna, he had nothing; and for the moment not a single clue could suggest to him where she might be.

"Damn and blast, how am I to find her?"

He said the words out loud, and as he said them realised it was already three hours since Jim had left him. The door opened and he looked up eagerly. But it was only Clements, the butler.

"Will you be changing before dinner, M'Lord? Chef would be grateful if Your Lordship would say at what time you would eat."

The Marquis was about to reply that he never wanted to see food again, but he told himself that was foolish. He might have to ride a great distance, he might have to set off in the middle of the night.

It would help no one if he felt weak, and already he was tired after having been awake most of the night before. His pride forced him to behave in a normal fashion.

"I will change immediately, Clements," he said. "Inform Chef that I shall be ready for dinner in just over half an hour."

"Very good, M'Lord."

The Marquis went upstairs; as he went he could remember himself leaving behind the small, forlorn figure standing in the centre of the Hall looking after him.

A sudden thought went through his mind that the Duke might destroy Fortuna. Obviously the easiest way out of his difficulties was that she should die.

"God, save her!"

He said the words aloud.

"Did you speak, M'Lord?" Clements asked.

"Only to myself," the Marquis answered and knew that was untrue.

It had been a prayer, the first prayer that he had said for years—a prayer for Fortuna's safety.

9

"Inaction is the most intolerable and frustrating of all human circumstances," the Marquis quoted to himself for the nine hundred and ninety-ninth time as he strode up and down the Library unable to sit still.

"If only I could do something positive," he thought.

He wanted to confront the Duke, search personally for Fortuna, ride, drive, walk in an effort to find her!

Anything would have been better than to wait as he was waiting now, without even a positive hope of obtaining the answer to the question which repeated and repeated itself in his brain:

"Where is she?"

That the Duke had outwitted him was something he could hardly bear to admit even to himself, but it was a fact and he knew that somehow he had to find Fortuna, although the question of how to do it was the most difficult problem with which he had ever been presented.

It had been a stroke of genius, he admitted, for the Duke to have captured Fortuna in such a manner that it was impossible for him publicly to say that she had been compelled by force to enter the coach.

Even if he had gone to some legal authority, he knew that in the position in which he placed Fortuna it would be difficult to affirm convincingly that she had not found

205

a protector she preferred to himself and had left him of her own free will.

No, the Duke had won, a victory that had somehow to be turned into a defeat—but how?

"What shall I do? What can I do?"

The Marquis asked himself the questions and wished despairingly that Colonel Alistair Merrill was in London and not on his way to the Isle of Man. He at least would have understood the dilemma in which the Marquis found himself.

There was no one else to whom he could even admit that Fortuna had gone, save his personal servants, and they were deeply involved in striving to find out where she might be hidden.

The Duke had either covered his tracks well or inspired so much fear in his retainers that Jim had so far elicited only one fact—that the Duke's Private Secretary had left on some unexplained journey, accompanied by the Assistant Cellarman at Merrill House and another man whose identity was not known.

The Duke's Private Secretary was, the Marquis knew, a man who could neither be bribed nor bullied, and who would be loyal to his master.

He learnt from his own Secretary that Masterman had been with the Duke for over twenty years and with his wife and family was resident on the Duke's property. There was not the slightest chance that any of them would talk.

The unknown man might have been an attorney of some sort of perhaps just a man hired for the occasion, but being unidentifiable was of little consequence.

The Assistant Cellarman therefore remained their only hope.

The Coachmen would know what had happened, but there again they were old family servants who had been in the Duke's employ since they were stable-boys and, as Abbey said:

"A Coachman, M'Lord, if he be worth his salt, neither sees nor hears anything that might be detrimental to his Master's interests."

The Marquis acknowledged this was true. He had always trusted his own Coachman and he knew full well that many vital secrets of the fashionable world were theirs and they could, if they wished, make trouble both for him and for many other distinguished people if they had ever repeated where he had been or at what time he visited other persons of quality.

"I know I have always been able to rely on your discretion, Abbey," he said to his Coachman, "do you believe that His Grace can trust his retainers in the same manner?"

"I'm sure of it, M'Lord," Abbey said positively.

The Marquis knew that it was a point of honour that he should support those of his own calling and attribute to them the same loyalty that existed within himself.

"Very well," the Marquis said with a sigh. "If Jim can find out nothing more from the stable-boys and you are convinced, Abbey, that the Coachmen will not talk, then there only remains this young man. His name is Jarvis, I believe."

"That's right, M'Lord."

The Marquis said little more, but when his Coachman had left the Library he had wondered despairingly if Fortuna was lost for ever.

"Why," he asked himself, "should the Duke command such loyalty when by all accounts his staff dislike him even as his tenants do?"

His Grace was harsh, he was impatient, he was at times unjust, and yet he was served well. There was no rhyme or reason for it, the Marquis thought savagely; then wondered if the same could be said of himself.

It was the fourth day after Fortuna had been abducted, and the Marquis, as he walked up and down the Library, looked out at the sunshine playing on the small fountains and thought how Fortuna had played with his dog in the garden the first day of her arrival.

The sun had illumined the strange paleness of her hair and seemed to become imprisoned in the grey loveliness of her eyes. The Colonel had been spellbound by her beauty. Then the Marquis's memories were interrupted as the door of the Library was flung open.

The Marquis turned round and saw Mrs. Denvers standing there, and realised immediately that something untoward had happened because she was still wearing her bonnet and black mantle.

"I've discovered where Miss Fortuna has been taken, M'Lord," she said in a voice which was triumphant and yet at the same time had a hint of tears in it.

"You have found her?" the Marquis exclaimed. "Where is she?"

"I'll tell you everything, M'Lord," Mrs. Denvers said in a voice that suddenly sounded weak and faint. "I've come here so quickly to bring you the news that I'm indeed a trifle breathless."

With an effort the Marquis controlled his impatience.

"Come and sit down," he said kindly, "and I will get you a glass of brandy."

"No, M'Lord, nothing to drink!" Mrs. Denvers protested.

"I insist," the Marquis said. "A glass of madeira if you prefer it."

He walked to the grog tray while Mrs. Denvers stood holding onto the back of a chair, her breath coming fitfully between her lips, one hand clasped to her breast as if the beating of her heart was paining her.

"Sit down, Mrs. Denvers," the Marquis said, and it was a command.

She did as he requested, sitting on the very edge of a chair. When he brought her the glass of madeira she took two quick sips, then said:

"They've taken her to France, M'Lord."

"To France!" the Marquis exclaimed. "But where?" He checked himself.

"Tell me the story from the very beginning."

"When I heard yesterday evening," Mrs. Denvers began, "from young Jim that it was Ted Jarvis, the Assistant Cellarman to His Grace, that had left Accrington House, I suddenly remembered that my sister's daughter-in-law's cousin had married a man called Jarvis in His Grace's employ. I'd been annoyed about it at the time, M'Lord, thinking that considering the friction between the two houses, 'twas best that there should be no connection, even one as slight as that of the cousin of my sister's daughter-in-law."

"As you say," the Marquis remarked, "the connection was very slight."

"Nevertheless, since the trouble, M'Lord," Mrs. Denvers said reprovingly, "those on the Thane Estate and in London have kept themselves to themselves."

"I am grateful for your loyalty," the Marquis said, "but go on."

"I therefore went out this afternoon, M'Lord," Mrs. Denvers began, "to call on my sister."

She went on to tell how her sister had given her the address of her daughter-in-law, who in her turn had directed Mrs. Denvers to young Mrs. Jarvis, who lived in two of the rooms over the stables situated in the Mews behind Accrington House.

"I feared I might be recognised, M'Lord," Mrs.

Denvers continued, "so I wore a veil; but indeed there seemed few people about in the part of the Mews where Mrs. Jarvis lived."

"You had met her before?" the Marquis enquired.

Mrs. Denvers nodded.

"On but one occasion, M'Lord, when she was much younger. But I would have known her again. She recognised me."

"Was she suspicious as to why you had called?" the Marquis enquired.

"I think if I speak frankly, M'Lord, that Lucy Jarvis is a somewhat simple girl save in one particular thing."

"What is that?" the Marquis asked more because it was expected of him than because he was interested.

"She's greedy for money, M'Lord, and so's her husband."

The Marquis bent forward in his chair in which he had seated himself. He began to see where Mrs. Denvers' discourse was leading.

"We talked of many things," Mrs. Denvers said, "and then I asked about Ted Jarvis, his position and what were his chances of promotion."

" 'He finds it dull enough,' Mrs. Jarvis had replied. 'He's clever, is my Ted. He's had a good education, and what's more he can speak French and German.'

" 'He can!' I exclaimed in surprise.

" 'Yes,' she answered. 'It's wasted he is at Accrington House. He has hopes for the future, but as I says to him, it don't cost anything to dream.' "

Mrs. Denvers explained how she had asked what Ted Jarvis's ambitions were, and had learnt that the one thing he longed to have above everything else was a wine shop of his own.

There was nothing, in fact, he did not know about the wines according to his wife. But the Head Cellarman to His Grace was not yet fifty, and there was no reason to suppose Ted Jarvis would step into his shoes for at least another fifteen years.

" 'And is that what you would like,' I asked, 'a wine shop of your own?'

" 'If we had one I'd serve in it,' Lucy Jarvis replied. 'You don't think I enjoy sitting about here all day with nought to do but clean these two stuffy little rooms. If we'd a wine shop with Gentlemen calling I could talk to them. And there'd be other persons too. I gets fair fed up with me own company, I can tell you.'

"I was wondering what I should say next, when there was the sound of heavy footsteps on the stairs and a moment later Ted Jarvis opened the door. His wife jumped up and threw her arms about him.

" 'You're back, thank the Lord for that,' she exclaimed. 'I couldn't have stood another night here alone wondering what had happened to you.'

" 'I'd have been back sooner,' he answered, 'but the sea was rough.'

"He saw me and stopped suddenly, and I knew by the expression on his face that he wished the words unsaid. I went forward holding out my hand and introduced myself.

" 'I was visiting my daughter-in-law,' I explained, 'and she told me that this was where you were living, so I thought as I was passing I would call in and see how you both were.'

" 'We're well enough,' Ted Jarvis said, and I saw the suspicion in his eyes and knew he guessed why I had come.

" 'Have you brought me a present?' Lucy asked excitedly. 'You always bring me a present when you've been away. Don't tell me you've forgotten this time.'

" 'I'm not likely to do that,' Ted Jarvis answered, 'with you reminding me a dozen times before I left.'

"He pulled out a package from the deep pocket of his coat. She snatched it from his hand and tore open the paper while he watched her with a grin on his face. It was only a cheap bit of china, but while Lucy Jarvis unpacked it and held it up like an excited child, I saw one word written on it which I recognised.

"It was Calais, M'Lord," she said to the Marquis, "Calais written clearly with some other words which I couldn't understand. I suppose they must have been French."

"That was clever of you," the Marquis said approvingly.

"But just as I saw them Ted Jarvis realised too what he'd done. He snatched the ornament away from his wife but it was too late. She gave a cry and started to argue with him.

" 'I want to talk to you, young Jarvis,' I said. 'What if Lucy made me a cup of chocolate?'

"He hesitated and I thought for a moment he was going to turn me out, but while he was deciding what he should do his wife snatched back the ornament from him and ran into the kitchen.

" 'Shut the door,' I said to him, and to my surprise he obeyed me. 'Now, Ted, I've a proposition to make to you.'

" 'I don't want to hear it,' he said. 'You've seen and heard too much already, and if you say one word you know as well as I do Lucy and I'll be turned into the street. Will you keep your mouth shut?'

"It was quite plucky the way he spoke, but I just looked at him and he added more quietly:

" 'I knows full well why you've come here, and I can

only ask for Lucy's sake to leave us alone. It's not easy to get employment these days.'

" 'But surely,' I said softly, 'you'd rather be your own master?"

Mrs. Denvers went on to explain how at first Ted Jarvis would not listen to her, then finally she said:

" 'How much do you need to set yourself up in a wine shop of your own?'

" 'You're crazed!' Ted Jarvis answered. 'It'd cost a thousand pounds at least for me to buy the wine I wanted from abroad, import it and find the right sort of shop in a decent area.'

" 'Then that's what I'll promise you,' I answered quietly.

" 'You will?'

"The expression on his face was almost comical—he was so astonished.

' "A thousand pounds if you'll tell me where you've taken that young lady,' I said. 'Don't be a fool, Ted Jarvis, I know it's in Calais. It won't be difficult for His Lordship to find someone in Calais who has seen you and the Gentleman with you. There's nothing them Frenchies won't do for money, and it seems a pity that good English gold should go into their pockets rather than yours.' "

Mrs. Denvers drew a deep breath.

"I hope I did right, M'Lord, 'tis a lot of money."

"You did absolutely right," the Marquis approved. "Now tell me where she is."

"At 'The Convent of Our Lady' on the outskirts of Calais," Mrs. Denver answered. "I got Ted to write down the name of the road."

She drew from her reticule a small piece of paper and passed it to the Marquis.

"Mrs. Denvers, you are a genius!" the Marquis cried.

"I could not have believed it possible that anyone could be as skilful as you have been."

"Thank you, M'Lord, but I only did my duty to that poor child," Mrs. Denvers replied, "and, of course, to Your Lordship."

"I shall leave at once," the Marquis said, "but first, see that young Jarvis is given the money so that it is not traced directly to me—not at present at any rate. And advise him not to give in his notice for at least a fortnight. Is that understood?"

"It will be as you wish, M'Lord."

Mrs. Denvers rose to her feet and carried the madeira glass across the room to set it down on the grog tray.

"I thank Your Lordship," she said respectfully, "and I hope you'll forgive me for appearing before you in my walking clothes. I couldn't wait to impart to Your Lordship the news."

"And I cannot wait to find Miss Fortuna," the Marquis said with a note of elation in his voice.

He went from the room as he spoke and Mrs. Denvers stood looking after him. He was looking slimmer than he had been four days ago, she thought, indeed the Chef had remarked over and over again that the food from the Dining-room had come back almost untouched. And for four days His Lordship had hardly left the house.

"Perhaps," Mrs. Denvers murmured to herself, "things are really agoing to change for the better."

The Marquis's yacht sailing into Calais harbour caused little interest.

A few seamen helped it berth and there was a ragged collection of beggars who clustered around the gangway as the Marquis came striding ashore almost before the ship was moored to the quay. He was followed by old Abbey, two younger Coachmen and two footmen.

The Marquis, in passable French, asked the way to the nearest livery-stable, and in a surprisingly short time he had hired a well-sprung carriage with fast horses and they were leaving the town.

The Marquis's servants had on their best livery, and people in the streets turned to look at the coach with admiration as it flashed past them into the bright sunshine.

The coach was pulled by four horses, and the Marquis seated inside lay back against the soft cushions with an air of indifference which was, however, belied by the alertness in his eyes and the fact that he bent forward every few seconds to see where they were.

The Convent was, in fact, situated some three miles outside the town, and by the time they reached it the Marquis was wondering somewhat anxiously if they were indeed on the right road.

Suddenly they saw it in front of them, with a big, barred gate topped by a statue of the Madonna. It appeared to be the only entrance. The grey roofs of the buildings could only be vaguely seen over an enormously high wall surrounding the entire Convent, being nearly a mile in circumference.

The horses circled the Convent twice before the Marquis gave an order to Abbey, and then they proceeded for the third time round, moving very slowly while the second Coachman on the box blew loudly upon a hunting-horn.

The sound seemed to ring out in the still air of the countryside.

The second Coachman, who, as the Marquis had known when he commanded his attendance, was an enthusiastic rider to hounds, played his horn almost like an artist.

He varied the notes, he gave even an artistic touch to the sound, and yet always the music of it could be heard ringing out—the call to the field when a fox has been sighted.

"Tally-ho! Tally-ho!"

The Marquis almost repeated the words to himself as all the time with the window down he scanned the wall along which they were passing.

They went down the whole length of one side, the road turned at the far end, but still the wall on their left was strong, grey and impregnable.

"It must be nearly ten foot high," the Marquis thought.

The Coachman paused for a moment as if to wet his lips, then he blew again.

"Tally-ho! Gone away!"

Then just ahead of them, high on the wall, there appeared the head and shoulders of a small figure.

The Marquis must have seen it simultaneously as old Abbey pulled the horses to a standstill, and while the coach was still moving he sprang out and ran to the wall.

For a moment he felt it could not be Fortuna who was looking down at him for she was wearing a black habit and a black veil over a white wimple. There was no sign of her hair, only her small pointed face and large frightened eyes were unmistakable.

Then without words, knowing what she must do, she scrambled over the wall and hung by her hands from the top of it, even as the Marquis stopped below to hold out his arms.

"It is all right," he called, "drop, I will catch you."

Just for a moment she seemed to hesitate, then she fell into his arms; and light though she was, she made him stagger. Her veil fell off and he saw the white wimple encased her head and covered her throat.

"You . . . have . . . come," she said in a breathless voice, "you . . . have come . . . for . . . me."

He held her close against his breast and it seemed for a moment as if he was unable to answer her.

Then behind them there was the sound of a bell ringing.

"Quickly . . . quickly . . . take me . . . away," Fortuna begged. "That means . . . they will . . . search for . . . me."

The Marquis wasted no more time. Still carrying Fortuna in his arms he strode quickly to the coach and lifted her inside.

The footman slammed the door and almost before he could jump on behind Abbey had turned the horses and they were speeding back towards Calais, the dust from the dry road billowing out behind them in a great cloud.

Inside the coach Fortuna had not moved from the circle of the Marquis's arms but had hidden her face against his shoulder.

Very gently he untied the wimple from round her throat, pulled it over her head and threw it on the floor as her hair, released from the confines of the white linen, fell in glorious profusion over her shoulders.

Then he realised she was crying. Putting his fingers under her chin he turned her little face up to him.

"Tears?" he asked. "And I imagined you would be glad to see me."

"I thought . . . you had . . . forgotten . . . me," she whispered.

"Forgotten you!"

For a moment his voice was raw, then he said more gently:

"If I was a long time in calling it was because you had omitted to leave an address behind."

217

She gave a little choke which was half laughter and half a sob.

"I was sure you . . . would never . . . find me," she said. "And I imagined that as . . . you were . . . weary of me . . . you would not . . . trouble."

"Who said I was weary of you?" the Marquis asked, and with a softness in his voice she had never heard before.

"Have you not forgiven me," he added, "for my bad temper the night we left Thane?"

"You were angry with . . . me," she murmured, "and I wondered . . . and wondered . . . what I had done to . . . incense you."

"I was not angry with you," he said, "but with myself."

Her eyes searched his face as if for confirmation that that was the truth. Then she gave a little cry of happiness and hid her face once again against his shoulder.

"I thought I would . . . never be . . . free again," she murmured, "I have been so . . . frightened."

He could feel she was crying but he knew they were tears of relief and happiness. For a moment he said nothing but just held her close.

Finally she raised her face to his. There were tears on her cheeks and tears glistening on her dark eyelashes, but her eyes were like stars.

"I . . . have no . . . handkerchief," she confessed.

He took his own and wiped her tears away.

"You look very thin," he said accusingly. "What have they been doing to you?"

"I was ill," she answered simply. "It was the stuff with which they drugged me, it made me so terribly sick."

"You must tell me what happened," the Marquis said. "But in a few minutes we shall be in Calais.

When we reach the quayside cover yourself with the cloak I have brought you and walk quickly aboard. I do not wish to be imprisoned for abducting a nun. It would indeed seem somehow at variance with my previous reputation."

She laughed a little unsteadily but her eyes were looking into his.

"You are . . . here," she said, "I can hardly believe . . . it. I have thought of you all the time . . . dreamt of you until I feel this is just a story I have imagined in which you have rescued me . . . that I am with . . . you . . . again."

There was something almost ecstatic in the wonder of her voice.

Just for a moment it seemed to her that the Marquis's arm tightened around her; then the horses drew to a standstill at the quay and the Marquis seized the cloak of which he had spoken and draped it round her shoulders.

"Pull the hood low over your face," he commanded, "and hurry, there is no time to be lost."

It seemed to Fortuna as though it was only a very short while before the Marquis had paid his dues, the grooms from the livery-stable had taken possession of the horses, old Abbey and the other servants had come aboard and the yacht was moving out of the harbour.

She had gone down to the cabin and was looking around her at the comfort of the armchairs, the cushioned seats fastened to the walls, the thick carpet covering the floor and the inevitable grog tray with its crystal glasses set in a small alcove from which it could not be dislodged by a heavy sea.

She had discarded the cloak that the Marquis had given her as being too heavy, and as he entered the cabin he stood for a moment staring at the dark black habit she wore, its very austerity seeming to throw into contrast the pale wonder of her hair as it fell over her shoulders down to her waist.

She stood looking at him for a moment until like a child that seeks security she ran to him and put her arms round him and hid her face against his breast.

"It is true! It is true!" she murmured. "I really am . . . here. We are going back to . . . England and I am . . . safe."

"You are safe for the moment," the Marquis answered. "Tell me how you could have been so foolish as to enter the carriage. Did you know who wished to speak to you?"

"It was stupid of me, I see that," Fortuna said in a low voice, her face still hidden. "The footman said it was the Duke of Accrington who desired to speak with me and that it would be to your advantage."

"To mine?" the Marquis asked in surprise.

"I should not have believed him, of course I should not," Fortuna said, "but I thought perhaps he really meant to help you in some way, perhaps to return some of the lands that were rightfully yours."

The yacht gave a little lurch as it reached the open sea.

"Let us sit down," the Marquis said, "or we may find ourselves falling on the floor."

The matter-of-factness of his tone made Fortuna relinquish her hold on him and they sat down in the comfortable chairs which were fixed to the floor, facing each other across a small table on which a few moments later luncheon was served.

"If you are not hungry," the Marquis remarked, "I am."

"Now I come to think of it, I am hungry too," Fortuna answered.

"It does not appear as though they have given you much to eat in that holy place," the Marquis said.

He noted the dark lines under her eyes and the faint hollow in her cheeks which had not been there before.

"For three days I was ill," she answered, "and after that the food was so horrible that I did not wish to eat."

"And now you must make up for it," the Marquis said. "In the meantime tell me exactly what happened."

Fortuna told him how the drugged liquid had been forced down her throat in the carriage.

"After that I knew nothing," she went on, "except that I vaguely remember having to drink it again. But everything was dark until I awoke in a small room almost like a cell. I was being very sick and there was a nun sitting beside me who kept saying *'Pauve petite, ma pauvre petite'*, and I realised I must be in France."

"They were kind to you?" the Marquis asked.

"Very kind in their own way," Fortuna answered. "When I was well enough to get up I was taken to the Mother Superior. She told me that my Guardian had brought me to the Convent, that I was to stay there and take the vows."

" 'If you are speaking of the Duke of Accrington,' I said, 'he is not my Guardian, he has no jurisdiction over me.'

" 'You must leave such matters in our hands, my child,' she answered. 'Everything is arranged for your future. You will find in time that you will be happy here. Sister Marie tells me you have been ill, but tomorrow you should be well enough to have your first religious instruction.'

" 'I am a Protestant, Reverend Mother,' I replied, 'I do not wish to be instructed as a Catholic.'

" 'It is your Guardian's wish,' the Mother Superior replied, 'and God's.' "

Fortuna paused a moment, then she said:

"That was the answer to everything I said. When I talked to the Priest, he said the same thing and added:

" 'It may take time, my child, but gradually you will find that God knows what is best for you.'

"There was something in the way he said it that made me feel terrified because time meant nothing. They were prepared to be endlessly, uncomplainingly patient to get the result they wanted."

Fórtuna gave what was almost a little sob.

"I thought . . . you had forgotten . . . me," she said, "and I knew that eventually . . . they would wear . . . me down."

"But I have rescued you," the Marquis said with a smile.

"It is wonderful, more wonderful than I can begin to tell you," Fortuna cried. "I was walking in the garden with another postulant who shared my cell. We were never allowed to be alone, we did everything in pairs. She was a nice girl, a bourgeoisie from Boulogne who has a real call for the Church. Everywhere I went she came with me."

"I guessed," the Marquis said, "that you would be allowed to exercise either just before noon or immediately after it."

"That was intuitive of you," she said. "We had a service at eleven o'clock, the third service of the day. Afterwards if the weather was fine we walked in the garden. It was then I heard the horn."

"I thought it was the one thing you might recognise," the Marquis said.

"Of course I remember meeting your hounds when we were at the Castle," Fortuna replied, her eyes shining. "It was so clever of you to know that I should be thinking of our ride together and how your Huntsman had blown the horn for the hounds to follow him."

She looked at the Marquis and instinctively put out her hand.

"I thought of how . . . after that . . we rode . . . together through the pine-woods," she said in a low voice.

The Marquis covered her hand with his for a moment and then as her fingers clung he took his hand away and said abruptly:

"Go on with your story."

"I had already thought that the only way to escape would be to scale the wall," Fortuna said. "I knew that the great gate into the Convent was always guarded by a nun whose duty it is to unlock it for visitors. So I walked round the whole length of the garden pretending to examine the shrubs and flowers, but really seeing if there was any way the wall could be scaled from the inside. There was only one possibility, an old pear-tree whose branches reached right to the top of the wall."

"It is a good thing you can climb," the Marquis smiled.

"Gilly used to be annoyed at me because at one time I was always climbing trees," Fortuna answered. "I used to have an urge to be high above the world or perhaps it was just fate training me in an activity which would one day be useful."

"It certainly seems providential that you were something of a tomboy," the Marquis smiled.

"I have told you before that I shall never be able to behave like a Lady," Fortuna said. "I read the wrong books, and, as you know, no society Miss would scramble up a pear-tree, especially wearing a nun's habit."

The Marquis's eyes twinkled.

"I wonder what your companion did?" he asked.

"I heard her screaming at me," Fortuna replied. "She was horrified, and I am quite certain that when I disappeared over the wall and into your arms she ran hastily into the Convent to report my reprehensible behaviour."

"And if they had caught you, would you have been punished?" the Marquis asked.

"They have a series of punishments," Fortuna replied, "bread and water in a solitary cell, spending the night on the marble floor of the Chapel on one's knees, repeating a series of prayers over and over again. But it was not that which stopped me running away."

"Did you want to do that?" the Marquis asked.

"I wanted to, but I had no money and no clothes except my habit, so I knew I would soon be caught and taken back. But it was not those things which prevented me from trying."

"Then what was your reason for not attempting it?" the Marquis enquired.

"I just hoped almost . . . against . . . hope," Fortuna answered in a low voice, "that you would . . . perhaps come in search of . . . me, and then . . . I might not be . . . there waiting for . . . you."

"You know who you have to thank for your rescue?" the Marquis said. "Not me, but Mrs. Denvers."

He told her how Mrs. Denvers had discovered where she was.

"Oh, that was clever!" Fortuna cried, clapping her hands together. "I must thank her, indeed we must give her a present for her cleverness. Could we . . . would you . . . mind if we bought her something special when we reach Dover?"

"You can give her anything you wish," the Marquis answered, "but I think personally it will be enough of a reward for her to see you again. My 'most considerate staff', Fortuna, were considerably upset at your disappearance."

"They were?" Fortuna asked.

"Mrs. Denvers was in tears," the Marquis answered,

224

"and judging by the doleful faces of the housemaids I encountered in the passages, they too must have wept into their pillows at night. As for old Abbey, his hands were almost too shaky to tool the reins, and Chambers has been so disagreeable with his rheumatics that two of the footmen gave in their notice."

"I do not believe it," Fortuna laughed, "you are telling me this to make me feel of import. Tell me what . . . you have done while I have been away. Have you been very . . . gay?"

"Not very," the Marquis said quietly.

"I thought of you gaming at White's, going to mills, dining with your friends, and, of course"—her voice dropped—"being amused by lots of . . . lovely and intelligent . . . L . . . Ladies."

She did not look at the Marquis as she spoke and her eyelashes were dark against the pale transparency of her cheeks.

For a moment it seemed as if he would say something to her, then he changed his mind.

"I suggest," he said, "we no longer trouble our heads with what has passed, but think about the future. To-day, Fortuna, is the 2nd of June, the day after tomorrow I have something very special for you to do."

She raised her head to look at him.

"What is that?" she asked apprehensively.

"It is a part I want you to play," the Marquis said, then added quickly: "And before you ask, it is nothing as difficult as what happened at the Palace of Fortune, nor, indeed, are there likely to be any unsavoury and unpleasant results such as happened on that occasion."

"I am glad of that," Fortuna said.

"It is just something that requires a little play-acting," the Marquis said.

There was a note in his voice which made her uneasy.

"Must I do it?" she asked.

"If you want to help me," he said drily, "and, incidentally, yourself."

"How will it help me?" Fortuna enquired.

"That is my secret," the Marquis answered. "You must let me have some secrets, Fortuna, but I promise you that this should be the very last thing I will ask you to do which you do not understand and which I cannot yet explain. Will you trust me?"

He put out his hand across the table and she laid her own in it.

"You know I trust you," she said simply. "I will do anything you ask, anything, especially if it will help . . . you."

"Then I will tell you exactly what I require," the Marquis said, "and this time you must promise to obey me."

"I promise," Fortuna said quickly.

His fingers for a moment tightened on hers, then her hand was free. She felt in some way that he was relieved that she had not argued or protested, and she wondered what he had in store for her.

She remembered that before they had been to the Palace of Fortune he had been slightly nervous. She had the feeling that once again he was tense, and because of it she felt apprehensive of what lay ahead.

Then because she realised that to question the Marquis would only annoy him, she set out to amuse him and try to make him laugh.

He would never know, she thought, what it had meant when she had looked down from the height of the wall and seen first the Thane livery on the Coachman driving the horses and had then seen the Marquis himself jump from the carriage and run across the rough grass to stand below her.

226

It had been a thrill beyond words to fall into his arms, to feel him holding her closely against him!

Now looking at him across the table she thought that even her memories of him when he had not been there were surpassed by reality.

He was even more handsome than she remembered him and she knew that he only had to speak kindly to her or to have that note of gentleness in his voice to make her heart turn over in her breast and for her to know that she was wax in his hands and he could do with her anything he wished.

"I love you," she whispered to herself, "I love you . . . I love you."

But she knew that despite finding her again, even though it had apparently brought him some pleasure, the old problem still remained.

He was still fighting the Duke, still struggling for the return of his lands, still possessed by the poisonous hatred of the man who had deceived and tricked his father . . .

It was late in the afternoon when they reached the English coast and Fortuna stood on the deck of the yacht, the Marquis beside her, to see the white cliffs ahead and to know that she was nearly home.

"It will not be long now," the Marquis said, "my horses will be waiting for us and though we shall arrive late, we can sleep tonight in Berkeley Square."

Instinctively Fortuna drew a little nearer to him.

"I wish in a way," she said, "we did not have to return. If only we could go on sailing over the sea until we reach the edge of the world. Perhaps by the time we returned all your problems would have disappeared and you would not wish to go back."

"Are you indeed so enamoured of the sea?" the Marquis asked.

"It gives me a feeling of being separated from all the difficulties and toils that are waiting for our return," Fortuna said. "Also, it is wonderful to be alone with you and know that no one can disturb us."

She was thinking as she spoke of the dark, passionate beauty of Lady Charlotte and of the vivacious prettiness of Odette.

The Marquis would never know, she thought, how she had tortured herself those nights at the Convent thinking of him beside them, touching them, perhaps kissing them, quite unaware that she was crying out for him with all her heart and soul.

"Do you not think," she heard the Marquis say, "that such isolation might become a little monotonous?"

"For you perhaps," she answered, "but I know that I would like it above . . . all things."

She spoke very softly and she thought perhaps he had not heard her, for a moment later he crossed the deck to give an order to a seaman and left her alone.

They drove to London from Dover in the Marquis's travelling carriage which was extremely comfortable, and a fur rug covered Fortuna, keeping her warm despite a chill wind blowing in from the sea.

At first she talked, and then gradually she found her eyes drooping and sleepiness overcoming her.

She had slept little enough in the last few nights; and the Convent rose very early, the bell tolling for prayers at five o'clock. Soon, despite every resolution to keep awake, her eyes closed completely and her soft breathing told the Marquis she was asleep.

He could see her quite clearly in the light from the lantern.

There had been no hairpins on the yacht with which she could dress her hair, so she had swept it back with a bow or ribbon into the nape of her neck and it

228

framed her tired little face which seemed in the light of the candle almost as white as the wimple she had been wearing when he had found her.

A bump in the road caused her to stir from her sleep and she put out her hands as if she searched for someone. Still with her eyes closed he heard her murmur:

"Apollo . . . Apollo . . . come and . . . find me . . . come . . . for . . . me."

Then as if even in her dreams she sensed that he was really there she turned towards him and her hands went out to clutch the lapel of his coat.

She laid her head against his breast and with a little sigh of utter contentment she snuggled against him with a confiding gesture of a child who finds security when it has been afraid of the dark.

There was only the sound of the horses' hooves on the road and the soft whirl of the wheels.

But the Marquis, his arm round Fortuna, was wide awake as he stared with unseeing eyes into the darkness which lay ahead.

10

"Will you be sorry to be leaving Eton at the end of the summer?" the Duchess of Accrington enquired.

"No."

The Viscount Merr's reply was positive.

"I expect you are feeling too old for school," the Duchess said lightly. "After all, you will be eighteen in August and I am sure you will enjoy Oxford."

There was a moment's pause and then the Viscount in a sullen tone answered:

"I have no wish to go to a University."

"Why not?" the Duchess asked in surprise. "You know His Grace has set his heart on your going to Magdalen College, where he went and his father before him."

There was a silence. The Viscount stared ahead, a brooding expression on his face. His hand lying on the carriage rug, the Duchess noticed, had ink on the thick fingers and his nails were none too clean.

She felt, as she had felt so often before, not only a slight repugnance but also an impatience with his slowness, the manner in which an answer appeared always to be dragged between his lips, the sullenness which seemed a habitual characteristic however much she tried to interest him or enthuse him with new ideas or fresh plans.

"What would you wish to do if you had the choice?" she asked.

Her voice was deliberately gentle as if she would coax him into a better humour.

"I would like to be in the Army."

The Duchess gave a little cry.

"But that is impossible! You know His Grace would dislike it above all things. Besides, the Army is never a career for the eldest of a family, and even more so in your case where you are the only son."

Even as she spoke the Duchess thought that her voice sounded false. "The only son!" The words seemed to be questioning her, and she knew as she had known, she thought, since the very first that they were untrue.

They were driving along the bank of the river Thames in the company of a large number of open carriages, all conveying distinguished personages accompanied by their sons.

This was the most fashionable day of the year at Eton, when on the 4th of June they celebrated King George the Third's birthday with a procession of boats on the river, ending with a great display of fireworks.

There were not only carriages accompanying the boats; masters and boys galloped along the tow-path on horses, there was a variety of vehicles from elegant open landaus and dashing High Perch Phaetons to rickety gigs which had been hired for the occasion.

There was also a large crowd of boys cheering their friends rowing down the silver river with the grey majesty of Windsor Castle looming behind them. They all made their way to Fellows Eyot, from where they would watch the fireworks bursting brilliant and golden against the darkening sky.

The Duchess either did not see or ignored the bows of her friends and acquaintances.

She was looking back into the past, hearing dis-

231

tinctly the whispering voices of the Midwife and a woman who had assisted her as they stood at the end of her bed.

"Poor lady," she heard the woman say, " 'tis been too much for her. Her be over-old to be bearing children."

"She is indeed," the Midwife agreed, "and eight's more than enough for any woman, be she Duchess or pauper."

" 'Twas a bad time her's had," the other woman said in a sympathetic tone. "Do ye think Her Grace'll be all right?"

"She'll be right enough," the Midwife answered cheerily. "She's unconscious now from the pain and the long hours of labour. Maybe 'tis a good thing."

"Maybe," the assistant agreed. " 'T'll be a terrible blow to find 'tis another girl. Her had, I guess, high hopes 'twould be a son."

The Midwife gave a deep sigh.

" 'Tis what His Grace will be asaying as worries me. He always speaks as though I were to blame."

"He be a hard man to please," the woman answered. "But then men always blame everyone save themselves."

Their voices had come to her, the Duchess thought, like waves. One moment they would seem near, the next far away. She remembered all too well her feeling of disappointment which was so sharp that it was almost worse than the physical pains she had just endured.

Another girl! She closed her eyes deliberately and sought oblivion. There was even the faint hope that she was dying. Yet when she opened her eyes again it was to find the Duke smiling at her.

"Congratulations, my dear, a son at last."

They brought the baby and put it in her arms, a

large, dark child which in her weakness she had felt was almost too heavy to hold.

She felt also strangely and unnaturally an instant revulsion against it. She did not wish to touch it, she did not want to feel it against her. She had been thankful when they had taken it away.

She had known the truth—of course she had known then—even though she had tried to convince herself that the conversation she had heard was part of her delirium, just a nightmare which had no substance in reality.

And yet now, sitting in her carriage with this dark, surly boy beside her, she could not forget the descriptions which Alistair Merrill and Sir Hugo Harrington had given her of the girl who they said bore a strange resemblance to herself.

With an effort she forced herself to watch the boats moving down the river, the crews wearing straw hats bearing the name of their boats and the coxes in Admiral's uniform with a three-cornered hat and a sword.

"How pretty they look," she said. "Are you friends with any of the oarsmen?"

Even as she waited for the reply which was, as usual, a long time in coming, she saw her—saw the girl of whom she was thinking.

There was no mistaking the Marquis's landau, black and yellow, drawn by a superbly matched pair of horses, their silver bridles and the livery of his servants completing a smarter turn-out than any others moving over the rough grass.

The Marquis himself, leaning back indolently with his top-hat at an angle on his dark hair, seemed only to accentuate the elegance of his vehicle and in some way to provide a background for the girl who sat beside him.

All in pink, the colour of a rose in bud, she kept jumping up in the carriage to watch the boats, asking questions about them in a clear excited voice.

It seemed as if the Marquis's carriage was attempting to pass the Ducal landau. For a moment the two were side by side and the Duchess, staring with an undisguised curiosity, saw quite clearly under the flower-trimmed bonnet two large grey eyes fringed with dark lashes in a tiny heart-shaped face.

It was so familiar that she drew in her breath sharply to prevent herself crying out loud.

It was her own face she saw, an exact replica of the reflection that had stared back at her forty years before when she had come to London and first realised how unusual and entrancing the O'Keary beauty could seem to the fashionable world.

The Duke's coachman flicked his horses into action as if annoyed at being passed. The Marquis's landau fell back and the Duchess no longer had a sight of Fortuna.

A strange numbness seemed to seep over her. It was only with an effort that she forced herself not to turn round, not to go on staring at that small animated face.

"We are there," the Viscount said beside her, and she heard her own voice ask almost stupidly:

"Where are we?"

"At Fellows Eyot, Mama, and see, the fireworks are already starting."

The last glimmer of the sun had disappeared, but the sky was still light, although the first evening star twinkled above the Castle.

"You must get out, Mama, it is no use the horses being too near the bank or they might be frightened."

"Yes, of course," the Duchess agreed.

It seemed as if her voice came from a very long

distance. It was a warm night and there was not a breath of wind, but she knew that she was shivering.

The Duchess descended, noting almost absent-mindedly that the Viscount Merr made no effort to assist her as he should have done.

Only as she stood on the dry grass and the carriage moved away did she look round to see the Marquis's landau had drawn up almost beside them and the girl in pink was being assisted to alight.

"How exciting this is," the Duchess heard her say, "and what fun it must be for the boys. Do you not wish you were at school again?"

The Duchess did not hear the Marquis's reply; for at that moment a rocket set off on the island in the centre of the river shot into the sky with a trememdous shriek. A shower of gold and red stars came floating down over the spectators.

There was another rocket and another, and then fireworks were lighted on the ground—a cascade of silver and blue, a wheel which twirled in a kaleidoscope of colour faster and faster until finally it disintegrated with a bang.

The Marquis and Fortuna were standing near the Duchess and the Viscount Merr. It was impossible for the older woman to think of anything but the small figure in pink; she could listen only to the young, excited voice, watch her little hands clapping enthusiastically as each new firework seemed more elaborate and impressive than the last.

There were more rockets, until suddenly there was a tremendous explosion which seemed somehow nearer than the others and which emitted a cloud of dark smoke.

Twilight had almost come and it was difficult to see what had happened, but as the smoke cleared the Duchess gave a sudden cry.

Lying on the ground almost beside her was a still figure in pink whose bonnet had fallen back from her pale hair. There was a babble of voices.

"A piece of the rocket must have hit the poor girl!" . . . "I have always said it was dangerous here, the fireworks are too near." . . . "You can get a nasty burn if you are not careful." . . .

Without hurry, his face expressionless, the Marquis bent down to lift Fortuna in his arms.

"It has knocked her unconscious," a Gentleman exclaimed. "Is there anything I can do?"

The Marquis did not reply, but made his way through the crowd towards his carriage which was drawn up with the others a short distance from the river bank. He walked slowly, and Fortuna with her eyes closed, her small face turned up towards the sky, did not move.

Then just as he reached his carriage and the footman sprang down to open the door, the Marquis heard a voice behind him.

"Wait—Lord Thane . . . please wait!"

He stopped, and still with Fortuna in his arms turned round to face the Duchess.

"Your Grace!" he ejaculated, as if in surprise.

"Is she hurt? I must know if she is hurt," the Duchess asked.

"Your Grace is most kind," the Marquis answered, "but I assure you the matter is of no consequence."

"But it is!" the Duchess contradicted. "I mean . . . Your Lordship will take her at once to a physician, will you not?"

It seemed to the Duchess as if the Marquis looked down at Fortuna with an expression of utter indifference.

"I am convinced," he said slowly, "that the girl has come to no harm. She is indeed, Your Grace, stronger

236

than she looks, for she comes of good farming stock. A mere firework should, in fact, do little damage."

"But you will make sure?" the Duchess begged insistently.

The Marquis looked at her and his eyes were hard.

"I regret, Your Grace," he said at length, "that I find sick women, like sick horses, a vast inconvenience."

He moved towards his carriage as he spoke, and stepping into it set Fortuna down on the back seat.

Then sweeping his tall hat from his head he bowed to the Duchess, who stood looking up at him with her hands clasped together.

"I bid Your Grace good-day," the Marquis said, "and I am, I can assure you, most appreciative of your gracious consideration for someone who should, in fact, be beneath your notice."

The Duchess did not reply. With what appeared to be an air of resentful impatience the Marquis sat down on the back seat beside the still unconscious Fortuna. The Coachman whipped up the horses and they drove away, the first carriage to leave Fellows Eyot.

No one noticed that following them at a respectful distance was a small, under-sized little groom with a deeply scarred face which had once been kicked by a horse. He carried under his arm a box which could easily have contained a firework.

The Marquis was at breakfast the following morning when a message was presented to him on a silver salver.

"When did this come, Clements?" he enquired, deliberately helping himself to another lamb cutlet before taking the note from the salver.

"It's just been delivered, M'Lord, by one of His Grace's grooms," the butler answered.

There was a faint glint in the Marquis's eyes, but he

delayed opening the note until he had finished his cutlet.

"The man is waiting, M'Lord," Clements said respectfully.

Unhurriedly the Marquis opened the parchment. The expression on his face did not change, but again he could not entirely control the sudden sparkle in his eyes.

> His Grace the Duke of Accrington proffers his compliments to the Most Noble Marquis of Thane, and would be obliged if His Lordship could meet him in White's Club at his earliest convenience.

The Marquis read the note and set it down beside him on the table.

"Ask the groom to inform His Grace," he said, "that I shall be at White's within the hour."

"Very good, M'Lord."

The Marquis turned back to his breakfast as if the interruption was of no import.

Anyone watching the Marquis tooling his horses to St. James's Street forty-five minutes later would not have believed that this was anything but a casual visit to his club, such as he made almost every day of the week.

He handed over the reins to his groom, walked slowly and deliberately up the steps and into the Hall where he gave his hat and gloves to a waiting servant.

The only thing that was unusual about the visit was that it was so early in the morning. The fires had been laid, but the grates were still being polished, the brasses rubbed, the leather armchairs dusted and trays of dirty glasses and used dishes left from the night before were being carried through to the kitchens.

"His Grace is in the Card Room, M'Lord."

The Marquis nodded his head and climbed the staircase with an air which seemed to be almost one of boredom.

The Card Room was empty save for the Duke, who was standing by the fireplace staring into the flames of the newly lit fire.

The Marquis approached him, bowed and waited for the older man to speak.

The Duke was looking tired as if he had not slept. He never looked well, but it seemed this morning as if the lines on his face were more pronounced than usual and there was a lack-lustre look in his eyes which made the puffy pouches of debauchery more obvious.

For a moment the two men stared at each other, then the Duke in a voice which was strangely like the croak of a crow said:

"Very well, Thane, you have won! What do you want of me?"

In answer the Marquis drew from the inside pocket of his coat two documents. He set them down on the nearest card-table.

"You have but to sign these, Your Grace."

The Duke's lips tightened, then as if he felt there could be no agreement he walked to the table and seated himself in a chair.

"This," the Marquis explained, pointing to the document on the top, "acknowledges the girl now known as Fortuna Grimwood to be your legitimate daughter born on 27th August, 1801, and for whom you caused to be substituted a male infant, being, in fact, the offspring of a farmer and his wife named Grimwood living in a farm on your Estate."

The Duke stared down at the document without speaking. The Marquis gave a flick of his fingers and a steward who had been out of view until this moment came into the room, set down on the table an ink-pot and a quill pen, and withdrew.

The Marquis, dipping the pen in the ink, handed it to the Duke. He inscribed his signature and the Marquis, lifting the document, revealed one that lay beneath.

"Another?" the Duke questioned.

"This one," the Marquis replied, "acknowledges Alistair Merrill, Colonel in the King's Dragoon Guards, as your heir presumptive. It also empowers him to claim from the Merrill Estate such moneys as should have been his for the last seventeen years since the time when his place was taken by a usurper known as the Viscount Merr."

The Duke muttered an oath beneath his breath as he signed.

"I thought it best," the Marquis continued, "so that there should be no scandal which will affect your daughter, Lady Fortuna, that the boy Grimwood should leave the country almost immediately."

He paused as if expecting the Duke to speak. He then continued: .

"I have therefore spoken to the Colonel of the 5th Huzzars, who informs me that a detachment of the regiment will be leaving for Canada in two days' time. He has agreed to take with them a young man called Grimwood who will purchase his commission."

The Marquis's voice was stern as he went on:

"I suggest that in all fairness documents should be drawn up immediately whereby Your Grace will provide this young man with the sum of three thousand pounds a year so long as he shall live. Furthermore, should he wish to settle in Canada a further ten thousand pounds shall be forthcoming to purchase him a farm in any part of the country he chooses."

"You have thought of everything, have you not?" the Duke asked sarcastically.

"A scandal would not, I imagine, be to Your Grace's liking," the Marquis replied. "In fact, once young Grimwood is at sea and out of this country, it will be easy for Your Grace to announce that your son and heir, the Viscount Merr, while on holiday, has met with a most unfortunate accident. If he has been drowned at sea there will be no questions of a family funeral and, we hope, no questions asked."

The Duke pressed his lips together and for a moment his old fingers clenched slowly. Then harshly, so that his voice seemed to echo round the room, he asked:

"Now we get to the real question, do we not? What do you want for yourself? All the lands I took from your father, or will you be content with a portion of them?"

The Marquis picked up the signed documents and put them in his coat pocket. He straightened his back.

"I want nothing," he said. "I do not traffic in people."

There was a moment's silence, and then as it seemed the Marquis would walk away he was arrested by the Duke giving a cry of sheer uncontrolled fury.

"Curse and blast you to hell!" he stormed. "How dare you proffer me your charity! Do you think I will accept favours from you? You do not 'traffic in people' indeed! Is that not typical of the way your father would talk, of the damnable way in which he invariably put me at a disadvantage, or case me down for behaving in a manner to which he would not stoop. I endured for long enough this cursed virtue in your father. I warn you, Thane, I will not take it from you!"

The Duke brought his clenched fist down on the card-table so that the ink-pot rattled and the pen fell

241

from its holder. The Marquis stared at him in sheer astonishment.

"I mean what I say," the Duke roared. "You will take back your blasted lands in exchange for this girl whom I will now acknowledge. I refuse to be beholden to you!"

"As I have already informed Your Grace, I will not bargain over your daughter."

"God! You are your father over again!" the Duke exclaimed. "It was that which made me long to cheat him, to humble him, to bring him down. I know everybody believed I was taking my revenge simply because he stole my bride. That was hurtful enough at the time; but at least it showed he was human, at least he did one act which was not entirely honourable, entirely virtuous. But after that . . ."

"You mean," the Marquis said slowly as if he could not prevent himself asking the question, "that the reason Your Grace tricked my father was not that you desired your revenge at his having taken my mother from you?"

"I hated him for that," the Duke replied, "but I hated him much more afterwards. Can you imagine what it was like to live always in his shadow, to hear men say day after day, year after year, how charming, how brilliant, how honourable Thane was? In the county I was never consulted on anything of consequence, even though I was of higher rank. No, it was Thane to whom they went, Thane who would give them the right answers, Thane who was so wise, so sympathetic, so influential, Thane who was appointed Lord Lieutenant."

His voice rose.

"I tell you, everything I did, everything I said, everything I thought was cast into the shade by the intolerable superiority of your father. 'The most beloved man in England', someone once said of him; and at times I thought the only way I could be free of him was to murder him."

"I had no idea of this," the Marquis murmured.

"Nor did anybody else," the Duke said. "Do you think I wanted to parade my feelings, to let them see how belittled and humiliated your father made me feel? But I beat him in the end. I only hope that in Heaven—where doubtless he enjoys the highest esteem—he learnt that I had tricked him on his deathbed and taken his lands from his heir."

He paused, then said in a quieter voice:

"But my revenge has not been successful and I suppose you will say it is poetic justice that I have now been outwitted by your father's son."

The Marquis's lips twisted in a faint smile.

"As my father's son, Your Grace, you will understand that having reinstated Fortuna as your daughter and Alistair Merrill as your rightful heir, I require no payment for these services."

"And as I have already told you, Thane, I will not accept your charity," the Duke said.

He glared at the Marquis, then continued:

"You may think I am speaking idly. But I assure you, either you accept back your lands, which have been a headache to me ever since I have had them, or else I will go downstairs and give them to the first waster I find swilling port in the Morning Room."

"Does Your Grace mean that?" the Marquis asked in a low voice.

"I swear that is what I will do," the Duke replied. "Perhaps that will·be a revenge in itself. It will amuse me to watch you squirm over the lands which I have offered you in exchange for my eighth daughter, but which through some nonsensical quirk you have let pass to an outsider."

The Duke sneered as he spoke, but the Marquis knew that he was not speaking idly.

It was indeed the kind of irresponsible, senseless thing he would do to give away in a moment of spite the lands which had been so hotly contested.

The Marquis hesitated and then he said:

"I will not accept the lands as a gift, Your Grace, but I will game with you for the last time. I will wager everything I have against all the Estates which were once in my father's possession, and which you now hold."

"You will wager what?" the Duke asked incredulously.

"The Castle, my house in London, and the whole of my fortune," the Marquis replied.

"Are you crazed?" the Duke enquired.

"No, the Marquis answered. "The stakes are about equal, but shall I say I believe in my luck?"

"It has not stood you in particularly good stead until this last month," the Duke said sourly.

"I have a feeling that it has changed," the Marquis answered.

The Duke's hooded lids came down over his eyes. For a moment his tiredness seemed to vanish. The gambling instinct had ascendency over everything and it seemed almost as if his hands twitched for the cards.

"There is one condition under which we play," the Marquis said quietly.

"What is that?" the Duke asked.

"I have told you that I believe in my luck," the Marquis answered. "There will be no skill in this game, Your Grace, it will indeed be just a question of fortune. I will cut you through the pack, the first ace wins."

244

"You should be in Bedlam," the Duke retorted. "What will you do if you lose?"

"I will leave the country," the Marquis replied. "As it is, I have few interests left in England."

The Duke raised his eyebrows, the Marquis pulled a chair from the table and seated himself. Immediately a steward appeared with a pack of cards. A glass of wine, as was usual, was set down beside the Duke.

"We will neither of us touch the cards," the Marquis said. "May I suggest Your Grace draws first."

"I will accept that small concession," the Duke answered and turned up a ten.

The Marquis followed with a two, the Duke drew a King, the Marquis a nine. The Duke drew a Queen, the Marquis an eight.

A faint smile creased the Duke's face. It was a smile cynical and almost triumphant, a smile of a gambler who believes his luck is in. His next card was a nine, the Marquis drew a five.

Another card and yet another, twenty in all, and now both men were drawing more slowly. It was as if each willed the card before they touched it to be the one they sought.

The Duke drew another King, and then as the Marquis put out his hand it seemed to him he heard a soft voice say:

"I know I shall bring you luck . . . I am sure of it."

He heard it so clearly that for a moment he thought that by some strange magic Fortuna was beside him. Then he turned the card. It was the Ace of Hearts! He stood staring at it as if he could not believe it true.

The Duke made no movement whatsoever, but the

familiar ritual took place. The steward brought in the great pile of deeds which had been shuffled backwards and forwards for five years between the two men and had changed hands half a dozen times, together with deeds which had still not been contested.

Slowly the Duke signed each one, fifteen deeds in all, totalling thousands of acres of land and affecting the lives of thousands of people who lived on them.

As the last deed was signed the Marquis rose to his feet.

"I will bring Lady Fortuna to Merrill House this afternoon, Your Grace, at two o'clock," he said.

Without another word he turned and walked from the Card Room and down the stairs to the Hall.

As he waited for his hat and gloves to be brought to him, through the door into the street came Colonel Alistair Merrill.

"I have just arrived, Sylvanus," he cried. "I heard you were here. I have the confession! It was exactly as you thought!"

He spoke excitedly, but the Marquis's face did not change.

In reply he drew from his pocket the second document which the Duke had signed and put it into his friend's hand.

"You are too late, Alistair," he said, "the matter is already settled."

Then without another word, so that the Colonel was left staring after him in surprise, he went from the club, and climbing into his Phaeton drove his horses back to Berkeley Square.

Fortuna, when she came downstairs, had been told that the Marquis had left the house, and she wondered somewhat disconsolately how long he would be and if she would be alone for the rest of the day.

She was in the Library when she heard him return: the dogs barking a welcome was a signal which was unmistakable. But even as she put down the book she was reading and rose to run towards the door, the Marquis came into the room.

"You are back!" she exclaimed in delight. "I was so hoping you would not be long."

Then she saw by his face that something had occurred.

She was not certain what it was, but there was something grim and foreboding about him that she had not known since she returned from France.

"What has happened?" she asked involuntarily.

In answer the Marquis walked slowly across the room to help himself to a glass of brandy from the grog tray.

"Is something wrong?" Fortuna asked with a note of fear in her voice.

The Marquis drank the brandy. She had the feeling, though she could not explain why, that he was choosing his words with care. Finally he said:

"I have the honour to inform you that you are no longer Miss Nobody. You are, in fact, Lady Fortuna Merrill, by which name you will be known in future."

There was a silence. The Marquis did not look at Fortuna, but her eyes, wide and frightened, were on his face.

Finally, in a voice so low that he could hardly hear it, she said:

"Then . . . the lady who spoke to us . . . yesterday, whom you called . . . Her Grace, was . . ."

"Your mother," the Marquis said.

"And my . . . father?"

247

"The Duke of Accrington."

"Oh no," Fortuna cried, "it cannot be! I hate him for what he has done to you!"

"He is still your father," the Marquis said.

"So Gilly was right . . . I was exchanged for the Grimwood's son," Fortuna whispered, "and by the Duke . . ."

"You were his eighth daughter," the Marquis explained, "and he wanted an heir."

"And if Gilly had not looked after me I would have . . . died," Fortuna continued still in a very low voice. "The Duke did not worry about . . . that, nor did the . . . Duchess."

"I think when the truth comes to be told," the Marquis replied, "you will find your mother was not aware of the exchange, not, at any rate, until it was too late for her to do anything about it."

"She could have searched for me," Fortuna replied, "but she accepted the Grimwood baby as her . . . own. That was the boy who was with her yesterday . . . was it not?"

The Marquis nodded his head. There was a long silence.

"Must . . . I call . . . myself by their . . . name?" Fortuna enquired hesitatingly.

"You will take your proper place in society," the Marquis said. "The Duke has accepted you and acknowledged that you are his legitimate daughter. Young Grimwood is to be sent abroad. Colonel Alistair Merrill is again recognised as heir presumptive to the Dukedom."

"But I would . . . rather remain . . . as I . . . am."

"That is impossible. I am taking you to your parents this afternoon, you will be ready at two o'clock."

"You are taking me to the . . . Duke and to . . . the Duchess?" Fortuna cried incredulously.

"They are your parents," the Marquis replied. "You will meet your sisters and become a member of the family. As I have already said, you will take your place in society."

"But what . . . if . . . I do not . . . wish . . . that?" Fortuna asked.

"There is no alternative. You are a Lady of Quality, Fortuna."

"I have no desire for such . . . a position."

"I do not intend to argue," the Marquis said.

Fortuna fought back the tears which were misting her eyes.

"How did you make the Duke accept me?" she asked. "But of course, I know how you did it! You gave me to him in exchange for your lands. That is the truth, is it not?"

"It is not the truth," the Marquis retorted, and his voice was loud. "I accepted nothing in exchange for you, Fortuna."

"In which case I need not go to them," Fortuna said quickly. "If it had been a debt of honour, I could understand that I must not refuse to pay your dues. But if there has been no bargain, then I can stay here with . . . you."

"It is impossible," the Marquis said, "quite impossible. You have your chance now, at last, to lead a proper life, Fortuna, the life into which you were born."

"But I do not want it, do you not understand? I do not want it!" Fortuna cried. "I will not go to these people whom I do not know, who have no interest in me, who were prepared to abandon me as soon as I was born. Oh, Apollo, let me stay with you. I will do anything you say. I will obey you . . . I will be no trouble . . . if only I can remain here where I am . . . happy . . . where I am . . . safe. Please . . . please . . . let me . . . stay."

The Marquis set down his glass with a bang on the table.

"I have told you, Fortuna," he said harshly, "I will not argue on this matter. You will be ready at two o'clock when I will convey you to Merrill House."

He walked from the room as he spoke and slammed the door behind him.

Fortuna stood listening to his footsteps crossing the Hall and knew he was leaving the house. When she could hear no more she very, very slowly sank down beside the Marquis's favourite chair and laid her cheek against it.

11

Three hours later the Marquis returning to Berkeley Square saw his town landau standing outside Thane House.

His coat of arms was emblazoned on the painted panels of the doors, the lamps, handles and accoutrements were all of polished silver and the coachmen in their bright liveries with crested buttons made a spendid picture as they waited for their owner.

The pair of chestnuts drawing the carriage had cost the Marquis over a thousand guineas at Tattersalls three months earlier. Their superb blood was almost excelled by the horses ridden by the outriders, who, with their white wigs and peaked velvet caps, were waiting behind the coach.

It was obvious the Marquis intended to carry Fortuna to Merrill House in style, but his face was grim and his eyes were hard as he dismounted from his Phaeton.

Making no acknowledgment of the respectful salutes of his retainers, he passed through the front door and into the marble Hall.

He did not hand his hat and gloves to the attendant footman, but said instead in an impatient tone:

"Inform Her Ladyship I am awaiting her."

There was a moment's pause before Clements, stepping nearer to the Marquis, said in a low voice:

"Her Ladyship is not here, M'Lord."

"Not here?" the Marquis enquired. "It is after two o'clock."

He glanced at the grandfather clock as he spoke as if to confirm the time.

"Mrs. Denvers would speak with Your Lordship upstairs," Clements said apologetically.

For a moment it seemed as if the Marquis would refuse. Then with a dark expression his face he climbed the staircase to where on the landing of the second floor Mrs. Denvers was waiting.

She said nothing as the Marquis approached, but he felt that she was tense and her hands were clasped together over her black apron.

"What is this nonsense, Mrs. Denvers?" the Marquis asked harshly. "I told Her Ladyship to be ready for me at two o'clock. Inform her that I am waiting and that we leave immediately."

"You don't understand, M'Lord," Mrs. Denvers replied. "Her Ladyship has gone."

"Gone!" the Marquis ejaculated, and the word sounded like a pistol shot.

"Yes, gone, M'Lord, and 'tis sore troubled I am."

"She cannot have gone," the Marquis said almost as though he spoke to himself, his face curiously pale. "It is impossible."

"There's something I don't understand, M'Lord," Mrs. Denvers said. If Your Lordship will permit me to show you."

She led the way without waiting for the Marquis to reply into Fortuna's bedroom. The room was bright with sunshine and there were flowers on the table.

"Look, M'Lord, there's the gown Her Ladyship was wearing today," Mrs. Denvers said pointing to a chair. "But if she's left here, as indeed she must, I can't conceive in what clothes Her Ladyship was garbed, because all her gowns, every one of them, are in here."

She opened the door of the wardrobe as she spoke and the movement made the dresses hanging there flutter in a kaleidoscope of colour and fashion as if they came alive.

"You do not think . . ." the Marquis began, and the words were hesitant.

"No, M'Lord, there's no treachery this time, of that I'm sure. No one could have broken into the house. But Miss For . . . I mean Her Ladyship could have let herself out."

The Marquis said nothing but there was a white look about his mouth. After a moment Mrs. Denvers continued:

"But it puzzles me in which she could have robed herself. I swear to you, M'Lord, there is nothing missing. I've been through the closet a hundred times already."

Then Mrs. Denvers gave an exclamation.

"M'Lord, I've just thought of it!"

She crossed the room quickly, pulled open the drawer of the chest standing in a corner and looked inside.

"Yes, yes it's gone! That's what Her Ladyship's awearing!"

"What is that?" the Marquis asked, even though he knew the answer.

"The black habit in which she returned with Your Lordship from France. I placed it here with the veil and wimple."

Her eyes met the Marquis's and there was an appeal in them which was unmistakable.

"Do not be afraid, Mrs. Denvers," the Marquis

253

said in a low voice, and the colour returned to his face. "I will fetch her back. What time do the stage-coaches leave the White Bull in Piccadilly for Dover?"

"There's one early in the morning, M'Lord, and another which leaves half of the hour after noon."

"That is the one on which she will be travelling," the Marquis said. "Pack Her Ladyship's clothes, it was something I omitted to tell you to do this morning, for they were to have been conveyed to Merrill House. Pack what Her Ladyship will need and send them immediately in my fastest chaise to the Castle."

"You will stop her, M'Lord, you will not let her go back," Mrs. Denvers pleaded. "It wouldn't be right, it would be a crime against nature itself for someone so sweet and young to be shut in such a place for the rest of her life."

"I swear it will not happen," the Marquis promised, then he added in a hard voice: "I will collect Her Ladyship—and take her where she belongs."

He turned from the room and proceeded down the stairs.

"Send away the landau," he said to Clements, "and order the Phaeton and my fastest horses. When I have left convey a message to His Grace the Duke of Accrington at Merrill House."

He paused, his brows knit.

"And the message, M'Lord?" Clements prompted.

"Inform His Grace," the Marquis said slowly as if he were picking his words, "that owing to unforeseen circumstances I am unable to fulfil the engagement I had with His Grace this afternoon. Tell him that instead I am leaving for the country and I will call at Merrill Park later this evening. Is that clear?"

"Absolutely clear, M'Lord," Clements said.

"Inform me when the Phaeton is here," the Marquis said, and walked away into the Library.

254

He stood staring at the fountain in the garden until he was told that the Phaeton was at the door.

Then he swung himself into the driver's seat, picked up the rein and set off round the Square at a pace which made old Abbey, who was watching him go, purse his lips.

Fortuna, crushed between a large, fat farmer's wife and a thin, tight-lipped apothecary, thought miserably that the hours which they had been travelling seemed like a century of time.

The darkness and despair within her made it impossible for her to take the slightest interest in the country through which they were passing or to touch the refreshments that were offered to the passengers at the posting-houses where they changed horses.

She felt almost as if she had died, that her old life was left behind and there was nothing in front of her but a desert of loneliness in which she could only pray she would not linger long.

She wondered if anyone had ever really died of a broken heart; if it were so it must be because they really had no longer any wish to live.

She knew that without the Marquis she herself was to all intents and purposes dead. She could not contemplate the years ahead without him, she could not imagine what her existence would be without the expectation of seeing him, hearing his voice, watching his handsome face, knowing he was near.

Even if he was incensed with her, she thought, it was better than being with anyone else who was kind and good-humoured. Even if he hated her, it was better to arouse some emotion within him rather than the utter indifference with which he could cast her away and send her into a world where she knew he would never encroach.

She had not cried since the Marquis had left her in the Library, but now she felt the tears prick her eyelids and bent her head lower so that her fellow passengers should not see her misery.

They had indeed made no effort to speak to her. She knew it was the protection of her habit and veil which kept her isolated from them so that they had no desire to intrude upon her solitude.

Only a young commercial traveller in one corner gave her sidelong glances as if, despite her calling, he found her attractive.

"Oh, Lord," Fortuna whispered to herself, "if only I could be old and grey. Then there would not be so many years left for my suffering."

The coach had changed horses for the third time and they had been travelling for over three hours when unexpectedly, on a desolate part of the road where there were no houses in sight, the huge vehicle came grindingly to a halt.

There was a sound of raised voices, an altercation of some sort. Then the door was flung open, the movement waking the passengers who had been snoozing, and drawing an angry exclamation from an elderly gentleman.

"Why are we stopping, Coachman?" he asked. "This delay is intolerable. We're late enough as it is."

"There be a nun here," the Coachman answered. "Kindly step out, M'am, ye be wanted."

All eyes in the coach were turned on Fortuna.

"N . . . no one . . . can . . . be asking for . . . m . . . me," she stammered involuntarily.

"There be no other nun here, M'am, the Coachman replied, "and the Gentleman seems to think it be urgent."

Fortuna sank back and made no effort to rise.

"Go, m' dear," the farmer's wife said, nudging her,

"Maybe 'tis someun ill who wishes th' consolation of yer prayers."

"I'll thank you, Ma'am, to step out sharply," the Coachman insisted. "We be late, and there be still some fifteen miles to Dover."

"Yes . . . yes . . . of course," Fortuna said weakly, sensing an almost hostile atmosphere arising within the coach because she was wasting valuable time.

Feeling suddenly very cold she struggled through the knees which almost touched each other inside the coach and was assisted by the Coachman onto the road.

As soon as she had alighted he slammed the door and climbed with the agility of a monkey back into his place on the box. The horses were whipped into action and the coach rolled on.

Fortuna stood very still.

A short way down the road, she saw a High Perch Phaeton moving from its position where, drawn across the highway, it had forced the coach to a standstill. The loaded vehicle passed and by now she knew that the occupant of the Phaeton was waiting for her.

Afraid, and yet at the same time with an irrepressible lift of her heart because she was to see him again, Fortuna walked down the dusty roadway.

The Marquis was accompanied only by Jim, who gave Fortuna an impudent grin as he assisted her onto the box. Then he jumped up behind and with a flick of his whip the Marquis turned his horses and set off back towards London.

He did not look at Fortuna and she felt her heart sink.

She glanced sideways at him and realised from the set of his chin, the hard line of his lips, that he was enraged with her. She clasped her hands together and tried to prevent a little sob escaping her.

He was angry, and rightly so. She had defied and disobeyed him, and yet there was some consolation—an irrepressible one—in knowing that she had a little while longer in his company, that she was beside him.

Some time later, as he turned off the main road, she knew without being told where they were going.

The Castle was a fair distance away, but in a few miles they were on the ground that had once belonged to his father, ground that was familiar to him, ground which he had striven for so many years of his life to regain.

Because she felt embarrassed by the clothes she was wearing, Fortuna pulled the veil from her head and undid the wimple.

She thought that she had arranged her hair securely, but the wind whipped away the few hairpins with which she had arranged it and it fell in a pale golden cloud over her shoulders.

Her appearance was the same as when the Marquis had brought her back from France, triumphant because he had saved her from being incarcerated in the Convent. They had been so happy, Fortuna thought, when he had held her in his arms on the road to Calais, when they had crossed the Channel in his yacht.

She wondered if he remembered how she had slept with her head against his breast when they had driven back to London in the dark.

She glanced at him again and thought that he had never seemed more unapproachable.

That he should be angry with her suddenly seemed too overwhelming to be borne, and once again it was with difficulty that she prevented herself from sobbing aloud.

The beauty of the Castle in the late afternoon sun

had no power to thrill her as it had thrilled her before. She could only tremble and feel small, insignificant and helpless as Jim assisted her to dismount from the Phaeton and she followed the Marquis up the stone steps and in through the huge iron-hinged front door.

The great Hall with its carved staircase seemed somehow grim and unwelcoming.

"When you are changed and decently attired, Fortuna," the Marquis said in an icy voice, "I wish to speak with you in the Library."

He walked away as he spoke and Fortuna, fighting her tears, climbed the staircase step by step, feeling she had no strength left to reach the top.

Then on the landing, to her surprise, she saw Mrs. Denvers. There was something in the housekeeper's familiar face and the smile on her lips which was a comfort beyond words.

Impulsively Fortuna ran to her and the tears that had been suppressed so long flowed down her cheeks as Mrs. Denvers put her arms about her.

"There, there, Miss—I mean M'Lady," she murmured, "everything'll be all right. Don't cry, my dearie, I'm convinced there's no reason for it."

"But there . . . is," Fortuna sobbed, "His Lordship is . . . incensed with . . . me. But I had to . . . go . . . I had to!"

"Now come along to your bedroom, M'Lady," Mrs. Denvers said soothingly. "I've a hot bath ready for you and I've brought your clothes from London."

"I did not . . . expect to see . . . you here," Fortuna sobbed, the tears still running down her cheeks.

"I know, M'Lady. But when His Lordship told me to send your gowns to the Castle, I thought it best to come myself. I felt you might be needing me."

"Oh, I am so glad . . . you came!" Fortuna cried. "Mrs. Denvers, what am I to do? I will not go to . . . Their Graces . . . I will not . . . I will not!"

"Now don't you be troubling about anything for a moment, M'Lady," Mrs. Denvers replied. "See, there's some nourishing soup for you to drink and something to eat as well. You had no lunch."

"Clements did ask me before I went upstairs if I would like anything to eat," Fortuna said. "You must not think he was . . . neglectful of my . . . comfort, but I felt that food would . . . choke me."

"Well, you'll want something to eat now before you see His Lordship," Mrs. Denvers said practically.

"But I must . . . hurry, he is . . . waiting for . . . me," Fortuna said in a small voice.

"Let His Lordship wait," Mrs. Denvers advised, "maybe it'll cool his temper. And I wouldn't wish His Lordship to see you as you are now, M'Lady, with your hair tangled and wearing that horrible habit. I should have burnt it when you first brought it back from France; but there, just like my old mother, I always was a hoarder."

Fortuna could not help a faint smile coming to her lips, and then because she felt so exhausted she was thankful to surrender herself into Mrs. Denvers' capable and comforting hands.

In the warm bath scented with jasmin she felt herself relax and Mrs. Denvers helped her to dry herself.

To please the elderly Housekeeper clucking over her as if she were a chicken that had got lost in the long grass, Fortuna ate some of the food which had been provided and sipped the soup.

She ate little enough because she could hardly force anything between her lips, but she knew that what she did swallow gave her more strength and she was no longer near the point of collapse, as she had been as she climbed up the stairs.

As Mrs. Denvers dressed her she could think of nothing but the grimness of the Marquis's profile and the coldness of his voice when he had said that he would await her in the Library.

It was only when finally she was ready that she looked in the mirror and saw that Mrs. Denvers had robed her in an evening gown, and glancing towards the clock she realised it was almost dinner-time.

It was a gown she had never worn before. Of lace embroidered with tiny dewdrops of diamanté, it was set over silver lamé so that Fortuna appeared to be dressed in water—the shimmering silver of the lake beyond the Castle, or the broken waves of the sea over which they had sailed in the Marquis's yacht.

"I must go . . . downstairs," Fortuna said almost in a whisper.

They were the first words she had spoken for a long time.

"You're ready now, M'Lady," Mrs. Denvers smiled. "And be not afraid. His Lordship will, I'm convinced, not be enraged with you for long. Besides, he has good news to impart. He's gained back his lands from His Grace, every acre of them! They're his again! And when it's known, there'll be rejoicing on this Estate such as hasn't taken place since the old Marquis brought home his bride."

"His Lordship has his lands back?" Fortuna asked incredulously.

"Yes indeed," Mrs. Denvers replied. "His Lordship hasn't mentioned it yet, but Mr. Clements' nephew is a steward at White's Club, M'Lady, and though he should have kept his mouth shut he couldn't prevent himself from bringing the news to the house just before I was leaving. Oh, Your Ladyship, 'tis a joy for all

261

of us! The uncertainty and maybe the unhappiness of the past years is now over!"

"So the Marquis has his lands again," Fortuna said in a strangled voice.

She turned and went from the room no longer afraid. She carried her little chin high. She crossed the Hall and a footman opened the door of the Library.

The Marquis was standing at the window looking out onto the trees in the Park where the rooks were going to roost. He turned as she entered and for a moment they stood staring at each other. His face was expressionless save for a look in his eyes she could not translate.

Then she said, and her voice was strangely unlike her own:

"Why did you . . . . lie to me?"

She saw the quick frown between his brows as if he felt the accusation was impertinent.

"Lie?" he queried.

"You told me that you had not exchanged me with His Grace for your lands," Fortuna said "I believed you."

"And you can still believe me," the Marquis replied. "I took nothing—do you hear me, Fortuna— nothing in exchange for the Duke's acknowledgment that you were his legitimate daughter."

"Then how," she demanded, "have you come into your own so unexpectedly?"

"I won back my estates from the Duke," the Marquis answered. "If you want the truth, I was forced to game with him. His Grace would not take you unconditionally, in fact he threatened that if I would not receive the lands which he wished to give me because he would not accept my charity, then he would bestow them on the first member of the club he encountered in the Morning Room."

"Then what were your stakes," Fortuna enquired, "if it was not to be me?"

"The stakes for which I played," the Marquis replied, "were the Castle, my house in London and my entire fortune against the lands the Duke held which had once belonged to my father."

Fortuna gave a little gasp.

"Were you crazed to stake so much?"

"That is exactly what the Duke asked me," the Marquis said with a twist of his lips.

"And if you had lost?"

"It would have been of no consequence," the Marquis replied. "I should have gone abroad as I intend to do now."

"As . . . you . . . intend . . . to . . . do . . . now?" Fortuna said, repeating the words one by one as if she could not be hearing him right. "But you have retrieved your lands . . . your people are under your care again. You can start on the plans of which we have talked so often . . . the improving . . . the rebuilding."

"They are of no consequence," the Marquis interrupted, and turned towards the window.

There was a silence, then he was aware that Fortuna had come very near to him.

"How can you say they are of no consequence?" she asked in bewilderment. "What can have occurred? Why have you changed like this? Why are you no longer interested in what you have striven for so long to attain? Tell me . . . please tell . . . me."

"It is not of these things I wish to speak," the Marquis said sharply, "but of yourself, Fortuna. I gave you instructions and you have disobeyed them. Why did you run away?"

He turned round to face her as he spoke. She was looking up at him.

The evening sunshine was on her hair and on the

beauty of her wide, troubled eyes. Her dress seemed to shimmer and made her look as if she was scarcely real, a nymph that had risen from the lake and crept into the room like the mist in the early morning.

"You know . . . why I . . . went," she answered at length.

"How can you be so obstinate?" the Marquis asked, and his voice seemed unnaturally loud. "Do you not understand the difference that has been made in your circumstances? You are the daughter of a Duke, Fortuna, the whole social world is open to you."

"I do not . . . like the . . . social world," Fortuna replied.

"Of which you know nothing!" the Marquis said scornfully. "What experience have you had of any society, save of the degraded dregs to which I have subjected you. It was the only way in which I could reinstate you, but now you have to forget it."

"And have I also . . . to forget . . . y . you?" Fortuna asked.

"That will not be difficult when your mother introduces you to the Beau Ton," the Marquis replied. "You will find some decent, clean-living young man who will offer you marriage, and with him you will find happiness."

Fortuna drew in a deep breath, and there was a glint of anger in her eyes.

"And do you imagine," she asked, "that some decent . . . c . clean-living young man of the Beau Ton will offer marriage to the cast-off . . . d . doxy of the . . . M . Marquis of Thane? I think it most . . . u . unlikely. But . . . if . . . I am in . . . n . need of . . . a man . . . I can, of course, seek the . . . protection of . . S . Sir Roger Crowley, or someone like . . . him."

The Marquis stiffened, then he reached out his hands

and seized Fortuna fiercely by her shoulders. His fingers bit into her soft skin. He shook her backwards and forwards with an anger and a violence which made her as helpless in his hands as a rabbit in the mouth of a terrier.

"How dare you speak in such a way!" he stormed. "How dare you talk as if I had left you anything but pure and innocent! You are saying such things merely to incense me. If Crowley or any other man presumes to touch you I will kill him!"

The Marquis was suddenly still. It was as if his words had thrown a naked sword between himself and Fortuna.

His hands were still on her shoulders, and without moving them he looked down at her—at her eyes wide and frightened, at the colour flooding into her cheeks because of the violence of his shaking, at her pale hair blown around her small face, at her lips trembling yet parted because her breath was coming quickly between them.

For a long, long moment they looked at each other.

"Oh my God!" the Marquis ejaculated.

It was a groan of irrepressible pain as if a dam within him broke its banks. Then he swept Fortuna crushingly into his arms and his mouth was on hers.

He held her so tightly that she could not breathe and for a moment his lips hard and brutal hurt her so that she could only feel the pain of them, until it seemed as if a flame was ignited in them both, a flame leaping higher and higher . . .

His kiss became gentler and yet more demanding, possessive and yet at the same time so tender that she could feel her own lips respond to his.

To Fortuna the whole world was golden with light; there was the song of the birds, a music which came from Heaven itself.

They were alone, man and woman linked together indivisibly so that no one could separate them. They were one—one in a kiss which joined them for all time.

At last the Marquis raised his head and looked down at Fortuna, at her eyes shining as if a thousand candles were lit inside her, at her face transfigured into a beauty such as he had never seen before.

"Oh, my darling—my precious—my little love," he murmured brokenly. "How could you tempt me so, how could you prevent me doing the only good thing I have ever done in my life in giving you up?"

"I cannot . . . leave . . . you, you know I . . . cannot," Fortuna whispered.

"This is madness!" The Marquis replied. "Do you realise what I am like? You know my name is an apt one. I have sought nothing but vice and degradation for the last five years. You have tried to give me a halo, my darling, but it will not fit."

"You have . . . always been . . . Apollo to me," Fortuna murmured, "and when the sun is not . . . there, there is only . . . darkness . . . fear and . . . despair. I cannot live . . . without . . . you."

"I have tried to do what is right," the Marquis said desperately, "but you have made it too hard for me. Now I cannot let you go. I want you, Fortuna."

"Do you . . . l . love . . . me?" she whispered.

"I have loved you from the first moment I saw you," he answered. "But I fought against it! I tried to hate you because I knew whose daughter you were, and yet when I realised your sweetness, the purity and innocence of you, I knew you were not for me."

He tightened his arms around her.

"Do you realise that you have driven me nearly insane? It has been a hell through which no man should go—not to touch you, not to kiss you, not to make you mine."

"Why did . . . you not . . . do so?" Fortuna asked.

"Because I loved you," he answered simply, "because I would not spoil or besmirch what was the most beautiful and perfect thing that any man could ever know. I do not mean only your beauty, my sweet love—that is breath-taking enough—but you yourself. You are everything that any man could want, could yearn for and desire."

His lips sought hers again and it seemed to Fortuna as if no one could experience such a joy and not die of the wonder of it.

When at length he released her she asked very softly:

"You will not . . . send me . . . away? I can stay with . . . you?"

"How soon will you marry me?"

"There is . . . no . . . n. need to . . . m . marry me if . . . y . you would rather . . . n . not," she stammered.

He drew her so violently against him that she gave a little cry.

"You will marry me!" he said fiercely. "I will tie you to me by every law of God and man, by every service, book and ring that exists. I have lost you twice, Fortuna, I will never lose you again. You will be mine—mine for ever, do you understand?"

"That is all I have ever . . . wanted," Fortuna said softly.

"Then let us be married," the Marquis smiled.

Her eyes widened.

"Now?" she enquired. "Can we?"

"I will tell you a secret, my precious," he replied. "When I came to France I was afraid there might be difficulties in carrying away from a Catholic country a novice from a nunnery. And so I took with me a special marriage-lisence. We can be married at any moment, here tonight if you permit it."

"That would be the most perfect . . . the most wonderful thing that ever happened to me," Fortuna said, and the Marquis was almost blinded by the radiance in her face.

"Then I will give my orders," he said, and laid his cheek against hers. "Oh, my darling, is this really happening?"

"I keep feeling . . . I am in a . . . dream," Fortuna replied.

"Let us hope that we never wake," he answered.

Still with his arms around her he drew her across the room to the fireplace and pulled at the bell-rope. As he did so, as if he could not help himself, he sought her lips again.

They heard the door open, but even though the Marquis took his arms from Fortuna they knew that Bateson the butler had seen them, for there was a smile on his old face.

"I am to be married, Bateson," the Marquis said. "Will you send for my Chaplain and inform him that I have the lisence."

"My heart-felt congratulations, M'Lord, and to you, M'Lady," Bateson replied, "and I speak on behalf of all the staff at the Castle, and indeed of everyone on Your Lordship's Estate."

"Thank you, Bateson."

"If Your Lordship will excuse me," Bateson went on, "I anticipated that the Reverend Gentleman might be wanted and asked him to hold himself in readiness. The Chapel is being decorated by the gardeners, M'Lord, at this very moment, it should be finished in a quarter of the hour. And Mrs. Denvers has brought down from London the family lace veil and the flower tiara for Her Ladyship."

Bateson bowed.

" 'Tis good news, 'tis very good news, M'Lord."

He went from the room, leaving the Marquis staring after him open-mouthed.

Then he looked at Fortuna and saw the twinkle in her eyes and heard her laugh.

"I told you they know everything," she said. "Can you not realise that your valet would have seen the special lisence? And perhaps when I had left Berkeley Square you betrayed . . . your affection for . . . me?"

"But I meant to take you to your father and mother at Merrill Park," the Marquis protested.

"I would never have gone to them," Fortuna said. "Even now, if you will not marry me, I would rather journey to the Convent with no hope for the future, than be with people I despise, who will never ever mean anything in my life."

The Marquis caught her in his arms and drew her to him.

"I cannot believe that you will be my wife," he said hoarsely, "that you will belong to me, that you will be mine and that we shall be together. I ought to make you behave sensibly, but all I can think of is that I love you."

His fingers closed over the round softness of her neck, then he said:

"All these years I have fought for the return of my father's Estates, but when at last they were mine I realised that I did not want them if I could not have you too. The triumph of gaining them was just dust and ashes. They meant nothing—nothing because I thought I had lost you."

"Is that why you were going abroad?" Fortuna asked.

"I could not bear to remain in the country and not see you," he replied.

"But you risked so much on the turn of a card," Fortuna said. "How could you have done it?"

"I knew when I held you in my arms when I brought you back from France that life without you was completely and absolutely empty," the Marquis answered. "It was you who showed me that hatred and greed can only destroy a man. You were right when you told me that the Duke was not only taking from me my lands but my soul! What is left of it, Fortuna, you have given back to me."

"Oh, I am glad! So glad!" she cried. "And now it is all over, you have won!"

"I have won you and your love," the Marquis said. "Nothing else is of the least import."

"We are together and there is so much for us to do," Fortuna cried. "All those plans we dreamt about, we can start on them right away. Can you imagine how happy we can make your people in Waterless, the people in Lambeth. Oh, Apollo, I swear you will never be bored when your days are so fully occupied!"

"Do you imagine that I could ever be bored with you?" the Marquis asked.

"That is the only . . . thing which makes me . . . afraid," she answered.

"You need never be afraid," he said gently, and his voice held a tenderness which no woman had ever heard before. "As long as you are with me, that is everything I ask to bring me happiness and contentment. And please God I shall make you happy too."

"I am happy," Fortuna answered, "but I am apprehensive in case you find me a trifle . . . dull after all those . . . lovely and . . . intelligent . . . Hataira."

The Marquis swept her into his arms.

"You are never to mention them again," he commanded her masterfully. "They belong to a past—a past of which I am utterly and bitterly ashamed. Do you understand me, Fortuna, you are never to think of such women, of whom indeed you should know nothing."

He kissed her, but when he released her lips she dimpled at him.

"You are very autocratic," she said softly.

"I intend to be," he said. "But, my precious love, we are really starting our new life in the wrong way from a social point of view. We should have a grand wedding with the Archbishop to marry us at St. George's, Hanover Square, with the Regent and the Beau Ton watching us being joined together in holy matrimony. Am I depriving you of all this, of the sort of wedding every woman enjoys?"

Fortuna gave a little laugh.

"And who would be my bridesmaids," she asked, "the Corps de Ballet?"

Just for a moment the Marquis frowned, then he laughed as if he could not help himself.

"You are deliberately provoking me!" he said. "I see I shall have to beat you, my sweet, into behaving with the propriety of a Marchioness. But at the moment I only want to kiss you."

He drew in his breath, then continued.

"Yet there is indeed one thing I want to beg of you, one thing I would ask before you set me the formidable task you have planned so carefully to restore prosperity and comfort to all the people on my Estates."

"What can it be?" Fortuna enquired in puzzled tones.

"Could we not have a honeymoon together first where we could be—alone," the Marquis said.

There was something in his voice and the look in his eyes which made Fortuna feel suddenly shy and the colour rose in her cheeks.

"You see, my innocent little love," the Marquis went

on, "you have taught me many things, but there is something I want to teach you."

"What is that?" Fortuna asked.

"You described it to me as 'ecstatic delight'," he answered. "But it is, in fact, love—the true perfect love of a man for a woman when they really belong to each other, when they are one."

Fortuna gave a little murmur and hid her face against his shoulder. He put his fingers under her chin and turned her face up to his.

"Could we not go away together," he asked, "alone in my yacht to the very edge of the world?"

"Could we do that?" Fortuna asked breathlessly.

"We can and we will," the Marquis said firmly. "Before you slave-drive me, Fortuna, I must have you alone. Give me your answer?"

His arms tightened about her and she turned her lips to his, whispering as she did so:

"I love you . . . oh, Apollo . . . I love you . . . and all I want . . . is to be with . . . you . . . for ever."